D1330030

A FEATHER FOR A FAN

A FEATHER FOR A FAN

A WASHINGTON TERRITORY STORY

KARLA STOVER

FIVE STAR
A part of Gale, Cengage Learning

GALE
CENGAGE Learning®

Farmington Hills, Mich • San Francisco • New York • Waterville, Maine
Meriden, Conn • Mason, Ohio • Chicago

GALE
CENGAGE Learning

LIBRARY OF CONGRESS CATALOGING-IN-PUBLICATION DATA

Stover, Karla Wakefield.
    A feather for a fan : a Washington territory story / Karla Stover. — First edition.
      pages ; cm
      ISBN 978-1-4328-2915-5 (hardcover) — ISBN 1-4328-2915-7 (hardcover) — ISBN 978-1-4328-2922-3 (ebook) — ISBN 1-4328-2922-X (ebook)
      1. Girls—Fiction. 2. Frontier and pioneer life—Washington (State)—Tacoma—Fiction. 3. United States—History—19th century—Fiction. I. Title.
    PS3619.T699F43 2014
    813'.6—dc23   2014026879

First Edition. First Printing: December 2014
Find us on Facebook– https://www.facebook.com/FiveStarCengage
Visit our website– http://www.gale.cengage.com/fivestar/
Contact Five Star™ Publishing at FiveStar@cengage.com

Printed in the United States of America
1 2 3 4 5 6 7 18 17 16 15 14

Dedicated to my husband, Ed, and my parents,
Ted and Virginia Wakefield,
storytellers and history lovers.

INTRODUCTION

During the year I spent writing *A Feather for a Fan*, I read every issue of the *Tacoma Herald* from its beginning in 1877 until its demise in 1880. What a pleasure. The editor, Francis Cook, had a column called "Local Intelligence" in which he wrote of the many small events happening not only in New Tacoma but also Old Tacoma and the surrounding settlements. With the exception of the skunk story and the bear at the picnic (it was a cougar), the happenings in which Hildy and her family and friends find themselves involved did take place. The little songs the girls sing were well-known at the time.

Wikipedia says New Tacoma and Old Tacoma merged on January 7, 1884, and HistoryLink.org says December 1883.

A FEATHER FOR A FAN CAST

ACTUAL SETTLERS IN NEW TACOMA

Mr. & Mrs. William (Alice) Blackwell did run the Northern Pacific Hotel on the wharf.

General John Sprague was a surveyor for the railroad and ran their offices in New Tacoma.

Mr. & Mrs. M. V. Money did run a store on the wharf as described, and Mrs. Money did raise and sell birds.

Mr. Fife did have a store and was the postmaster. I relocated the store from the wharf to town.

Mr. Cosper was a traveling salesman with a new wife in the 1870s.

The Potato Brook story happened as described.

Louis Levin did have a saloon on Pacific Avenue.

The Tacoma Invincibles was an early baseball team.

Mr. Guild did give a phonograph demonstration.

Sheriff Davidson was the sheriff and did spend a lot of time in Old Tacoma.

Mr. Doherty was a cobbler in Tacoma, and he did have a three-foot space with a roof over it. His shop was believed to be on the wharf. I relocated it for convenience.

The following individuals were important in New Tacoma's development. The incidents in which they were involved did take place: Father Blanchet, Dr. & Mrs. Bostwick, Mr. Chilberg, Mr. & Mrs. Clark, Mr. Cogswell, Francis Cook, Col. Ferry, Mr. Graham, Abe Gross, Mrs. Halstead, Mr. Henderson,

Mr. & Mrs. Hosmer, Father Hylebos, Mr. Kelly, Mira Kincaid, Mr. Longpray, Delmar Manches, Charlie Newcomb, Mr. Quade, Caroline Richings, Frank Ross, Mr. Scott, Mr. Shoudy, Edward S. "Skookum" Smith, Dr. Spinning, Mr. & Mrs. Spooner, Mr. & Mrs. Stair, Mrs. Steele, Mr. & Mrs. Wilkeson, Mr. Witt, and Mr. Wren.

Tabitha Tickletooth did write a cookbook in 1860 but "her" name was actually Charles Selby, who wrote under a *nom de plume*.

Alverson's pain medicine was a real product.

The animals mentioned as roaming the streets did.

FICTIONAL CHARACTERS

Hildy Bacom: twelve-years-old when the book starts, nearly fourteen when it ends.

Verdita Bacom

Ira Bacom

Reuben Bacom

Dovie Bacom

Uncle Edgar: mentioned briefly, he is Verdita's brother who lost an arm in the Civil War at the Battle of Dry Wood Creek.

Aunt Glady: Ira's sister, she is married to Uncle Stayton.

Cousin Elsie: their daughter.

Nell Tanquist: Hildy's best friend.

Ike: one of Nell's brothers.

Freida Faye: his girlfriend.

Josie and Indiana: Nell's sisters.

Kezzie, Ellen, Fern, Sarah: school friends.

Samuel Adams Andrews

Isabeau Andrews

Dyson Andrews

Chong: a character representative of the Chinese in New Tacoma; his interactions with the community did happen.

Cast

Miss Rose, Violet, and Lily: characters representative of the local prostitutes.

Miss Sparkle

Mr. Rogers and Mr. Peak: railroad men.

Mr. Boyer: a man who operates a pile driver

All three characters are representative of the single men in New Tacoma.

MISCELLANEOUS

"I Dad" was a Western-American expression of exclamation.

"Mansion of Happiness" was a nineteenth-century board game.

Teetotem was an actual device.

CHAPTER 1

Fog rolled down from Canada and pressed against the smoke a Northern Pacific engine emitted, obliterating the view outside the train's windows of old-growth timber on one side of the tracks and Commencement Bay on the other. Inside the stuffy passenger car, twelve-year-old Hildy Bacom leaned against the cold glass and closed her eyes. She and her family had left Kalama early in the morning and, with the exception of one stop, traveled slowly through seemingly unchanging scenery. The stop had been out in the middle of nowhere. Conductor Tom Hewitt appeared in the doorway of the lone passenger car.

"I have to walk the track to New Tacoma to make sure it's clear. You can stretch your legs if you like. I'll be gone a couple of hours."

Now, though, they were on the last leg of the trip. Reuben squeezed between Hildy and the grimy window and pressed his nose against the glass trying to penetrate the murky haze. Across the aisle, Hildy's father, Ira, gave a deep hacking cough and immediately covered his mouth with his handkerchief. At his wife's sideways glance, he said, "Don't worry so much, Verdita, it's just a cough."

Farther back in the passenger car where the group of miners and loggers sat, one said, "It's sure and certain he won't make old bones."

Hildy heard the remark and looked at her mother, who stiffened in her seat. Hildy knew they hadn't left family and friends in Johnstown, Pennsylvania, and come this far just for Papa to die. Away from the coal mines Ira would get well. He had to.

"How much longer, Papa?" Reuben asked.

Ira pulled a gold watch out of his vest pocket and looked at it. "Not long now."

"Where will we go when we get there?"

"Why, this train is going to stop right next to a great big old hotel and we'll just walk in and demand their best room." Ira coughed again, though not so deeply.

"Why don't you look at your book?" Verdita handed it to Reuben. "We'll be there before you know it."

"I've already read it," Reuben began, but Verdita held up a hand and said, "Hush, or you'll wake Dovie."

The baby, Dovie, slept on the seat snuggled down between her parents, oblivious to the dimming light, the smells, and the nauseous motion of the train. Hildy sighed and wished she could sleep to make the time pass faster. She wondered how she could be tired when all they'd done since before dawn that morning was sit. She had a dozen questions about Washington Territory: where, exactly, it was, would there be a school, a library, and some girls her age to play with. But she knew better than to ask right now. Mama had that pinched look she got if she was tired and getting a sick headache.

When they left home, Mama said that Hildy was going to have to grow up quick and be a help. Mama looked sad when she said that, and Hildy hugged her and said she could already bake bread and change Dovie. But sometimes she wanted to be a little girl again and sit on her mother's lap and feel her breath as she read fairy stories. Next to her, Reuben fell asleep, his head drooping on Hildy's shoulder. Verdita smiled at her daughter, making the girl feel grown-up. Then she, too, dozed off.

The train chugged on. Some of the men slept and snored; darkness fell. Dovie woke hungry and Verdita put the baby to her breast. Hildy felt a change in the train's rhythm and shook her brother. "I think we're about there."

He woke slowly. "Where are we?"

"You know. We're at the Blackwell Hotel, or almost. I expect we'll have to get off the train and walk inside it."

Verdita pulled the laces of her corset cover and quickly tied them. Hildy took the baby, giving her mother time to gather up their things. *Oh, I'm so tired and my stomach is all churned up. I wish we were home. I hate changes and everything will be strange.* She looked at Reuben, who was wide awake and anxious to be outside. *Reuben's like Papa. He'll make friends and think everything is . . .* She stopped for a word and remembered a song in her Uncle Edgar's music book, *Essence of Old Kentucky. Hunky-dory. He'll think everything's hunky-dory. And Dovie's too young to know anything about Johnstown.*

The train gradually slowed to a stop. The loggers and miners grunted and stretched as they stood and crowded the aisle. Ira helped Verdita up and they started down the aisle to where a man was opening a door and pulling down a set of steps. Reuben jumped off first and Hildy handed Dovie to him before she took Mr. Hewitt's hand and stepped down. Her mother and father followed and her mother took the baby while Reuben ran a few yards ahead.

"Where's the water?"

A tall, well-built, and well-dressed man standing nearby laughed. "A few more feet there, young fellow, and you'll know where it is."

"It smells," Reuben wrinkled his nose.

"Why, that's just good saltwater and the low tide. Take a deep breath and tap your chest." The man followed his own instructions and breathed out with a large gust. Reuben did the same and laughed.

"I can feel it all the way to my stomach."

"Well now, I bet that's just because it's empty and we can take care of that in a jiffy." The man turned to Ira. "You folks must be the Bacom family. We got your telegram. Ma'am," he took off his hat and addressed Verdita. "William Blackwell at your service. I'm here to escort you to the finest hotel in New Tacoma, Washington Territory."

"And the only one, I'll bet." Reuben piped up.

"Reuben. Mind your manners." Ira stepped forward and extended his hand. "Ira Bacom, Mr. Blackwell, my wife, Verdita, Reuben, you've already met, and this is Hildy and the baby is Dovie."

"It's a pleasure, and if you'd like to come this way, we'll get you all settled."

Mr. Blackwell offered his arm to Verdita and as they turned toward a large building several hundred yards away, Dovie woke up and began to cry.

"I'll hold her, Mama." Hildy took the crying baby back. "Sometimes she gets quiet for me."

"Thank you, dear." Mr. Blackwell offered his arm again and, with Ira restraining Reuben, they followed the bobbing lanterns of the engineer and brakeman.

Hildy jiggled the baby and lagged slightly behind. In the water to her right the bulky outlines of ships barely penetrated the fog. She heard them pull and protest against their rope restraints. Water slapped against wooden pilings, interrupting men's voices. On her left, under a high embankment were corrals with a few cattle and horses. Somewhere, too, was a chicken coop. Hildy smelled it. A large bird swooped out of the darkness and grabbed something off the ground. It screeched in pain as the bird lifted and disappeared. Hildy's startled cry was lost in Reuben's excited exclamation.

"Jehoshaphat! What was that?"

"An owl after a wharf rat, most likely," said Mr. Blackwell. "We have a lot of them."

"Owls or rats?" asked Ira, and Mr. Blackwell gave a great laugh.

"Both Mr. Bacom, both. Now," he gestured toward a lighted door, "there's Alice come to greet you. She'll be mighty glad to have a nice young family here. New Tacoma's a little short on them, right now."

A woman stood in front of the doorway of the Northern Pacific Hotel, which Hildy later learned was known up and down the coast as the Blackwell Hotel. As Hildy got closer, she saw the woman watching them. Then, Dovie cried and Hildy saw the woman's hand go to her throat and a funny expression appear on her face. It disappeared by the time they reached the door, replaced by a professional and warm greeting. However, Hildy knew she'd seen pain a moment before.

"This is my wife, Mrs. Blackwell."

"Welcome." She shook hands with Ira and Verdita. "Welcome to the Northern Pacific Hotel. I've made the trip up from Kalama myself, and I know firsthand how exhausting it is." She turned and gestured them inside. "I have a nice room with a good size bed that will be just right. It's at the opposite end of the corridor from where the railroad men sleep, and I'll have one of the boys put a pallet on the floor for the children."

As she spoke, Dovie let out a wail. "Your poor baby's not very happy."

Hildy looked at her defiantly, "She's wet, that's all. She's a good baby."

"Hildy," said Verdita with a warning tone in voice.

"I'm sure she is," Alice smiled. "We don't get many babies here. Most of the lodgers are unmarried."

William invited Ira to share a drink and they left the ladies.

17

Mrs. Blackwell picked up an oil lamp and Hildy glared at the woman's back as she led them across a large room and up a flight of stairs to the second floor. At the landing, Alice opened a door. "This is one of the necessaries." She held up the light. "We have two. The other is at the end of the hall."

Verdita nodded but Reuben, having stuck his head inside, said, "It's full of long johns."

"Yes." Alice closed the door and resumed walking. "The men hang them up here so the ammonia smells will kill any vermin they're carrying." She opened another door that led into a small room holding a hipbath. "This is one of the bathrooms. We have two of them, also. I will send one of the boys up to your room with some buckets of hot water. If you want a full bath, it's extra."

"The buckets will do for tonight," said Verdita.

Alice shut the door and continued down the corridor. "How many boys do you have?" asked Reuben.

"Twelve." At Verdita's startled expression, she laughed. "They're the Chinese men we employ."

Three-quarters of the way further on, she opened a third door. "This is your room." Alice set the light on the dresser and lit one on a nightstand. "The bed is comfortable. We imported Dahong pula from Hawaii for the mattress's stuffing." At Verdita's look, she added, "Pula comes from tropical grasses. The sheets are clean and these are feather pillows."

The room contained little else except a table and chair, and a rope attached to the wall and curled up on the floor near a window. Hildy wondered if fires were a problem.

"We'll be having dinner in about fifteen minutes," Alice moved toward the door. "Go back the way you came and down the stairs. You'll see the dining room."

"Thank you." Verdita untied the ribbons to her hat and put it on the table. From somewhere out of sight came the faint sound of pots and pans clattering, cooking smells, and excited chatter.

Before she shut the bedroom door, Alice looked hesitantly at Verdita. "I wonder if I might help you out and take the baby." To Hildy's horrified look she added, "I have some clean flour sacks and I can mind her while you settle in. William will keep your husband talking until I ring the dinner bell."

"I can take care of her," Hildy said when her mother looked at a loss for words.

Alice addressed her next words to the girl. "I know you can. I can see that you're a big help, but perhaps you could help your mother get settled. You see, I don't have any little girls and it would be a pleasure for me."

Verdita dropped into a chair and rubbed her forehead. "Hildy, I would love for you to bathe my forehead and, if Mrs. Black-well is kind enough to help us out, let's do it just this once." She smiled at the expression on her daughter's face. "You know, sometimes I need you just as much as Dovie does."

Torn between her mother's words and her desire not to give an inch to this unknown woman, Hildy hesitated. Then, when her mother leaned back in the chair and closed her eyes, she stepped forward and handed Dovie to Alice. "I'll send Kai up with your water." Alice took the baby and held her against her shoulder. "He speaks English fairly well if you need something else." Then she looked at Hildy and said a quiet thank you.

After the door closed behind Alice, Hildy said, "I'll look for one of your headache wafers, Mama." She began rooting in the carpet bag Reuben had carried from the train and dropped on the bed. A few minutes later, there was a knock at the door. When Reuben opened it, a short man wearing white trousers, a white jacket, and a white cap, came in carrying two buckets. When he turned to set them down, Hildy saw a long braid of black hair hanging down his back

"Wanchee water?" the man asked.

Reuben's mouth fell opened and Verdita stood and smiled. "You must be Kai. Just set the buckets down, please."

Kai put them near the washstand, gave a little bow, and left.

"Jehoshaphat," said Reuben. "A Chinee."

Verdita poured a glass of water and swallowed the headache wafer. Then she filled the washbasin and said, "Quit staring at the door and come and wash, dinner will be ready soon." As she spoke a bell sounded. "See. Come on now, chop chop."

Hildy looked at her and laughed. "Mama," she said, "you made a joke."

A few minutes later, the three left their room and joined a throng of men all looking for seats at the long tables in the dining room. Ira came through the crowd and steered them toward a corner table. "The Blackwells have invited us to eat with them."

Looking around, Hildy saw Mrs. Blackwell enter the room carrying Dovie. The baby was wearing a hastily basted nightgown and clean diaper. She clutched a sock stuffed with something that rattled. Alice sat her down on a chair piled with pillows and used rag strips to fasten her to the back. Hildy scowled while Dovie alternately waved the sock or chewed it, and seemed perfectly content.

When they were all seated, several men began carrying bowls and platters to the tables. Verdita turned to Alice. "How do you find time to cook and care for the hotel?"

"I have a Chinese boy to help me with the hotel and Chinese men to do the cooking but the guests prefer white men to serve."

Mr. Blackwell spread his napkin on his lap and said to Verdita, "I was telling Ira that I might be able to get him a position with the railroad."

"William says the railroad is looking to lay tracks up into the foothills of Mount Tacoma to the coalfields up there and I told him about my experiences at the Caddy mine back home."

"The foothills . . . ?"

"Don't worry, Mrs. Bacom." William stopped speaking as Alice began ladling stew into bowls and passing them around. Applesauce and warm rolls followed. When everyone had been served, he continued, "I wouldn't think of expecting you to move up there. There aren't even any towns yet. No, what I have in mind is working in the office here with occasional trips up to check on the quality of the fields and to oversee the labor. Most of the work, though, would be downstairs in the Northern Pacific offices."

A rattling cough stopped Ira from responding. Verdita's eyes met those of William and they shared an understanding.

While the grownups talked, Hildy looked around the room. Except for their table, all the others had men sitting at them, tall men and short men, mostly white but a few black, and at a separate table, several Indians, loggers, and railroad workers. There was little conversation among them as they ate. The servers seemed able to anticipate their needs. Stoves puffed out heat and oil lights flickered, making strange shadows on the rough wooden walls. The air was hot and heavy with smoke. It clashed with the smells of food and unwashed bodies, but no one else seemed to notice. When everyone had eaten their fill, the waiters cleared the tables and carried in apple pies.

"Is it hard to get produce here?" Verdita asked as Alice cut and served large, sweet-smelling slices.

"At this time of the year, we have to have things shipped up from Portland," she said as she passed the plate. "But the Chinese raise wonderful produce. Some of them have even created their own irrigation systems using water from the local springs."

"I've . . ." Verdita hesitated a moment. "I've never dealt with Celestials before."

"You'll get used to them soon enough. They're hard working

and clean in their ways. They do just about every job that no one else wants to."

"In addition to working here at the hotel, Alice hired a Chinese boy to help her on a piece of land she bought on the hill above the hotel," William said. "She raises chickens, hogs, and roses."

"Do most of them speak English?" Verdita said.

"Well enough."

They finished their pie and behind her hand, Hildy tried to hide a yawn. "Time for bed for you three." Verdita stood. She untied Dovie and smiled at Alice. "We thank you for your welcome and your kindness."

"If you're not too tired and want to talk, I'll be here for a while."

"All right."

Back in their room, Verdita emptied the washbowl into a slop bucket and refilled it. Hildy peeled off her shoes and dress and made quick use of the lukewarm water, while Verdita helped a squirming Reuben. Someone had brought up the pallet, but she pulled back the bed covers and put Dovie in the middle. "Get in, now, quick."

"But what about the pallet?"

"You go to sleep here where it's soft and warm and we'll move you later." Verdita smoothed back a wispy lock of her daughter's dark hair and wrapped her arms around the girl. "I don't know what I'd do without you, Hildy," she whispered, "but don't grow up too fast. Leave Dovie to others sometimes."

"Dovie needs me."

Verdita hesitated. "Or is it that you need Dovie?" She knelt down on a small piece of carpet. "Someday you'll be all grown up and will get married and Dovie has to be able to get along without you. Besides, dear, you're entitled to have the best childhood your father and I can provide." She kissed her daughter and stood up. "Now, go to sleep and tomorrow maybe we can go shopping for a house. Mr. Blackwell says the weather is changing and the fog will be all gone."

Hildy turned over and snuggled down. "I love you, Mama."

"And I you, my darling."

After Verdita turned the oil light off and left the room, Reuben yawned and echoed Hildy's earlier thought. "How can I be tired when I sat in that train all day?"

"I guess," said Hildy, giving his words careful consideration, "the part of you that was sittin' isn't used to it so it got wore out."

Reuben mulled over her words and then said, "You're awful good at explaining things, Hildy." He turned over and was instantly asleep. Hildy heard his breathing while she listened to the sounds of snoring that came from the bedroom next to them, easily penetrating the thin walls. Her mother was rarely physically demonstrative. The unexpected kiss made Hildy both happy and sad. After a few minutes, a fat tear rolled down her cheek and she rubbed her nose on her sleeve. She fell asleep hoping she'd wake up and find that this was all a dream.

CHAPTER 2

Though the first train out of New Tacoma left the Blackwell Hotel at five thirty, breakfast was served as late as nine o'clock. The Bacoms were finishing when William crossed the floor to their table with a Chinese boy behind him. Ira wiped his mouth with his napkin and immediately stood up.

"Good morning, Ira, Mrs. Bacom," William said. "Did you sleep well?"

"Yes, indeed." Verdita smiled at him and put her napkin next to her plate.

Reuben, who had been forking in huge bites of flapjacks and had syrup on his face, said, through a mouthful of food, "There was a lot of snoring, though."

"Reuben!" hissed Hildy.

Thoroughly embarrassed Verdita said, "What have I told you about talking with your mouth full? And Mr. Blackwell was not addressing you."

While Reuben looked suitably chastised, William pulled up a chair, saying, "Now, if you don't mind, I'm going to join you for a minute." He gestured toward the Chinese boy. "This here is Chong. Chong, say hello to these nice folks."

Chong gave a little bow and muttered something that sounded like, "herro." Reuben snickered and Hildy kicked him under the table. The previous night she had been too tired to pay much attention to the various Orientals the hotel employed. Now she took a close look at Chong. The boy looked to be about twelve. He had a long braid of black hair, and skin the color of light honey. His white clothes were made out of heavy osnaburg cloth, and he wore some sort of sandals. As he straightened up and saw Hildy staring, Chong smiled. Hildy had been prepared to be wary but she found herself smiling back. He looked both wary and hopeful. And William, who had been covertly watching the exchange, smiled to himself.

"Now, folks, I wanted you to meet Chong because I have a little proposition I thought you might find helpful." He turned to Ira. "I've arranged for you to meet General John Sprague, who's in charge of the railroad office, at eleven o'clock. He'll want to show you around and extend the meeting through lunch. And I know you," he smiled at Verdita, "want to go up to town and look for a place to rent. So, here's my idea. Chong will be spending the morning cleaning oil lamps and he can watch little Miss Dovie, here, at the same time." William saw Hildy's perceptible stiffening and ignored it. "I know any decision about a house has to be a family decision but when it comes to making a home, well, we men sort of go along with what our woman folk decide on." Ira chuckled and William continued. "Mrs. Bacom, with Miss Hildy's help, I figure you can find what you want, and while you're up in town, Reuben can stand in for his father as the man of the family and help you if anything needs seeing to. That will leave Ira free to talk as long as the General wants."

Before either Verdita or Ira could respond, Hildy said, "Does Chong speak English?"

"Not much, Miss Hildy, but then I don't suppose Miss Dovie does, either." William smiled at the little girl and unexpectedly she smiled back. Hildy had made up her mind that she liked the middle-aged gentleman with his salt and pepper hair and chevron-style mustache.

"That's kind of you, Mr. Blackwell," said Verdita. "But I

certainly don't want to inconvenience either you or your wife. I'm sure that between the three of us, we can manage Dovie."

"Under ordinary circumstances, I'd say 'yes,' but it's shank's mare up the hill to town, I'm afraid, and the trail is plenty muddy this time of year. Come summer the city is going to lay planks but it's too wet now. You'll have all you can do just to keep your footing. It's no trouble at all to Alice and me. We want to do everything we can to help you. New Tacoma needs up and coming young families. Now," he stood up. "Ira, I'll expect you after you've freshened up and you, Mrs. Bacom, can leave Miss Dovie here, with Chong, and have no worries."

While William walked away, Ira turned to Verdita.

"I call that mighty nice," he said. "William's a real standup fellow."

Verdita, who was wiping Dovie's hands and face, hesitated. "I—I don't know if I can do that, Ira. Look for a house? Without you? I wouldn't know what to look for."

Ira laughed. "That's rich." He caught hold of one of Verdita's hands and held it in both of his own. "Anytime I've been stumped over something, you've been able to talk me right through it. You have a good head and I'd trust you with my life." He stopped and took a deep breath, trying to smother a threatening cough. Seeing it, and Hildy's frightened expression, Verdita straightened her shoulders. "Well, if you think I can do this—but, if we find something, you will have to give final approval."

The cough successfully suppressed, Ira leaned forward and gave his wife a quick kiss. "Good," he said, "now let's skedaddle."

"Ira," Verdita laughed as she untied Dovie from her chair. "If you keep on using slang, how will Reuben ever learn not to?"

Forty-five minutes later, while William and Ira left for the Northern Pacific offices, and Dovie sat on a blanket near

Chong, Alice Blackwell led the other three out a door and down the wharf. As William had predicted the previous night, the weather had changed. The fog was gone, and they saw enormous fir trees reaching up to pierce a clear blue sky. Boats bobbed on frisky wavelets in the bay, and voices carried clearly in the morning air, which smelled of fir and sawdust.

"Mrs. Blackwell," said Reuben, who had been so busy looking around that he'd had to hurry to catch up to them, "what's a Chinook? Mr. Blackwell said the Chinook would change the weather and he did."

"It's not a he, it's a what." Alice smiled at the eager face. "A Chinook is a warm wind that comes in from the ocean in February or March and makes the weather feel like spring, even in winter."

"Well, I like it."

Alice laughed. "I do, too, but don't get too attached. It's a fickle friend."

Reuben ran ahead and didn't hear the words, but Hildy did. "What do you mean that it's a fickle friend?"

"In the case of a Chinook, it means that you can't rely on it. The winds disappear as quickly as they arrive and the weather forgets it was ever warm." She stopped at a place where a wide track was easily discernible. "This is the path to town." She picked a stick up off a small pile and handed it to Verdita. "Take it slowly. Even in the best weather it's tricky and when it's been raining it will be very slippery." While Hildy and Reuben found their own walking sticks, Alice added in a low voice, "Stay away from D Street, the houses up there aren't homes in the sense of being family establishments."

Verdita's pale complexion took on a rosy glow as the meaning of Alice's words registered. "Gracious me," she said, shocked that Alice would voice something like that. "I most surely will."

Alice turned away and Reuben started toward the path. Verdita caught his arm. "I'll go first, young man, and Hildy will follow me." When Reuben began to protest, she added, "no argument."

The path was wide and gave evidence of having been well traveled. Two side-by-side planks up the middle either rested on the mud or were supported by trestles. Verdita picked her way slowly, thankful for the walking stick.

The trail they followed was nearly three-quarters of a mile long. Partway up, Reuben called their attention to the view. "Jehoshaphat. Look at all the boats, and you can see Mount Tacoma, too."

None of them had ever seen anything like the expanse of bay filled with every kind of vessel from three- and four-masted schooners to steamers to bateaus, watched over by Mount Tacoma's snow-covered peaks. They heard the sounds of mill saws and pile drivers, and the grinding noises of chains unwinding to drop anchors into the water. A horse whinnied; seagulls swooped and soared; and on a tree branch high above the trail, a crow called out a message. The hillside was covered with lichen-covered brush, ferns, and vines that crowded the trees. While the countryside around their old Pennsylvania home was full of hardwoods and was easily walkable, this was an impenetrable thicket. And where Johnstown was located down in a valley, New Tacoma was out in the open. The sight frightened Verdita for a moment, but Hildy felt curiously exhilarated. Birds chirped in the budding underbrush and their movements made rustling sounds. A slight salty tang overlaid the other smells. She took a deep breath and smiled. The sight dulled Verdita's trepidation and the day seemed brighter.

When the three crested the hill, they were struck dumb with amazement. The area had been cleared recently, but burned and logged-off stumps remained. They were at the north end of the main street. One- and two-story wooden buildings lined each side with the occasional vacant lot between them. Some of the buildings had a wooden sidewalk in front but most did not. Horse-drawn wagons splashed through the mud; chickens roamed freely; and men were everywhere, loading or unloading wagons, going in or out of the buildings, waving and shouting and crossing the road by jumping from one piece of wood to the next in order to keep off the sloppy wetness.

Bisecting the main road were shorter ones that went either uphill or toward the bluff. The dwelling places—none of them could think of them as houses—were mostly combinations of shacks, tents, and in some instances the remains of cedar trees that had been hollowed out and roofed. As they looked around in dismay, a large rat ran across the road and disappeared near a building.

"Good God," breathed Verdita.

"There's people living in tree trunks," said Reuben. "No one in Johnstown lives in a tree trunk. I never even saw one that big."

"Where are the houses?" Hildy looked around.

"I don't know."

They might have stood there indefinitely had not a dark-haired boy about thirteen years old appeared.

"Pardon me," said Verdita. "Can you please tell me what's on the other streets?"

The boy gave her a puzzled look. "More of the same."

"I'm looking for the residential area."

"Residential area?"

"We're looking for a house," Reuben explained.

"Whose house?"

"A house for us. Are you short in the upper story or something?"

"Reuben!" snapped Verdita. "Be quiet." She turned to the boy and said slowly, "We're looking for a house to buy or rent.

We're moving to New Tacoma, we're setting down roots here."

The boy laughed and his gray eyes filled with fun. "I never heard that one before. Seems like folks hereabouts are mostly grubbing out roots."

"Papa is going to work for General John Sprague," said Reuben proudly. "And we have to find a house to live in."

"Well, I reckon I can show you around, but there ain't much to see."

"Why aren't you in school?" asked Hildy.

"School's out right now, teacher's sick. I reckon she's gonna die."

"Goodness." Verdita was taken aback at his blunt words. "Why do you think that?"

"I hear things." The boy looked around. "We can do without. Don't need a lot of schooling to get on in New Tacoma. Just a little savvy."

"I like school." Hildy's brown eyes turned almost black. "Books teach you things."

The boy gave her a considered gaze and said, "It makes no never mind to me if you do or don't. You're just a little girl."

Hildy's face went red and then white as it always did when she was upset. "I think you're nothing but a mudsill."

"Hildy!" Verdita snapped before the boy could respond. She'd seen a look of surprise and then pain come and go in his eyes. "You and Reuben, both, apologize at once. That is no way to talk to people."

"But . . ."

"You heard me." She turned to the boy. "What's your name?"

"Samuel Adams Andrews."

"Reuben, Hildy, say you're sorry to Samuel."

Reuben grinned and stuck out a hand but Hildy narrowed her eyes and stared. "I apologize," they said almost in unison.

Sam grinned and a dimple near his mouth gave him a roguish look. "Ah, that's okay. You're just little, still stuck between hay and grass."

As he spoke, Reuben began hopping from the sidewalk to a piece of wood in the road and back. But Hildy sputtered in outrage and turned her back on Samuel. *Little girl, indeed!* "Mama, what about a house?"

"You're right. Samuel," she smiled at the boy, "in spite of my rude children, does your offer to show us around still stand?"

"There ain't much." Sam looked off in the distance for a moment. "So many folks comin' to town, they move in on the shirttail of someone else movin' out. This here is Pacific Avenue and there's no houses on it but you come with me. I know a place on A Street no one's found yet."

Sam stepped into the muddy road so Verdita could walk on the mired-down rounds of wood. If she had thoughts about putting her gloved hand on his unexpectedly offered arm, she didn't show it. Reuben followed them closely, watching Sam, who had clearly become his hero. Hildy picked her way carefully at a safe distance behind.

They continued down the road, crossed at an intersection of sorts, and turned left toward a street running parallel to Pacific Avenue and the bluff. It was slippery going; the road was a mire, and there were no sidewalks. The sound of axes on wood and men shouting reached them. A Street had a scattering of houses. A cow tethered near one of them mooed, and a dog ran out to sniff. When Sam gave it a pat, the dog joined them as they approached the last house on the road.

At first glance, it was an uninspiring sight: two stories built of well-weathered wood and a shake roof with some of the shakes missing. A single step led to the front door. The glass was gone from all the windows. The building was close to the bluff and half-hidden among alder and big-leaf maple trees.

"Folks who lived here lit out for Seattle a while back," Sam said.

"Who owns it now?"

"Mr. Money. He has the shop down yonder." He gestured toward the wharf. "Sells pencils and writin' paper, and Mrs. Money raises canary birds." Unexpectedly, Sam grinned. "Wait until you see Mrs. Money."

"Canaries," said Hildy, not hearing his last words. "I surely would like a canary. Can we go to the shop, Mama?"

"Perhaps. We'll see. But, let's take a look inside first, shall we?"

If the front door had been locked before, it wasn't now. Sam opened it and let Verdita precede him inside. Again, his good manners surprised her. They stepped into a minuscule entryway. On the left, a parlor led directly into a dining room. On the right was a steep flight of stairs. A narrow hall divided the two. A long kitchen ran across the back. They climbed the stairs and found four rooms of equal size.

"I like this room, Mama." Hildy stood in one of them. "I can look right into the trees from this window and at the water from that one." She leaned out of one of the empty spaces. "You can hear the birds. I bet there are nests."

"That's a cottonwood with all the birds in it," said Sam. "Yonder, there is a dogwood and down on the bluff, that peeling pink tree is a madrona. Come spring the dogwood and those bushes, over there, will blossom out real pretty."

"You seem to know a lot about the local flora," said Verdita.

"That's plants and trees," said Hildy, trying to be helpful.

Sam looked at her. "Pa taught me." He turned and started down the stairs. The others followed him.

"This will suit us nicely," said Verdita. "I think we'll ask Mr. Bacom, that's my husband, to see Mr. Money right away."

They left the way they had come. Hildy looked at the trees

Sam had pointed out and tried to think of a way to make amends. The dog disappeared and, at the top of the path leading back to the wharf, Sam stopped. "I'll be going home now."

"Thank you so much, Samuel," Verdita smiled into his suddenly serious-looking face. "After we're settled, I'd like to call on your mother, if I may. Do you think she would object?"

"She mostly works." Sam's expression darkened.

"Oh." Verdeita was at a loss. "Well then." She looked at his retreating back. "You'll come and visit, won't you, when we're settled?"

If the boy heard, he didn't respond.

"Goodbye, Sam," Reuben shouted but Sam kept on walking.

It was well after noon when the three arrived back at the hotel. Dinner was over but Alice seated them anyway, and had one of the cooks bring some venison and potatoes. Verdita was tired; Hildy was quiet; and Reuben wouldn't stop talking. When Chong brought Dovie to their table, he interrupted the flow of words no one was really listening to.

"Missy Dovie velly good."

Verdita fished in her reticule, pulled out a coin, and pressed it in Chong's hand as she took the baby. "Thank you, Chong. Mr. Blackwell was right. We wouldn't have been able to cope with a baby."

Unexpectedly the boy returned her coin. "I wok fa Mista Blackwell. He pay."

"But this is my thank you."

"Baby good, not need."

Chong bowed and walked away as Ira came in from outside and hurried to the table.

"Did you have any luck?" He rubbed Reuben's head and yanked at a piece of Hildy's hair.

"Yes, there is a house on A Street along the edge of the bluff.

I'm not sure of the address. Samuel said a Mr. Money owns it and that houses are scarce. Can you see him today?"

"Samuel?" The leather seat of the wooden chair squeaked as Ira sat down.

"No, Mr. Money. Samuel was a boy we met uptown. An urchin, really, but he knew of this place that was empty and took us there. I was really grateful."

"Well, then," Ira stopped as a deep cough overtook him. Recovery took a long time and left him momentarily exhausted. Verdita and Hildy waited, sick with worry. Reuben was as yet unaware of his father's illness. Jacob Mann, the hotel's bartender, appeared with a small glass of whiskey.

"Takes the chill off the chest," he said, putting the glass down.

Ira took it gratefully and after a few sips felt more comfortable. Color returned to his face and he took a deep, careful breath. "Well, now," he began again, "maybe I ought to bend the elbow more often." When no one responded, he tugged at Hildy's hair again. "Want to go with me while I hunt up Mr. Money?"

"Oh, yes, Papa, I surely do. Samuel says there are canary birds."

Ira smiled. "This Samuel seems to have made quite an impression on my girl."

"Ugh, no, he's just a mudsill and I told him so."

"Hildy!" Ira was shocked. "That was very wrong."

"But it's true. He wore raggedy clothes and doesn't like books and school. What else is he?"

"That's not for you to say. Every person on God's green earth has value. We take them as they are and give thanks where we can. You might have hurt his feelings."

"But he called me a little girl and said I was no account."

"Hildy," Ira lifted her chin. "Listen to me; you, too, Reuben. You're going to meet a lot of different kinds of folks out here.

Not like the ones we knew at home. So you had best be prepared to take them as they are and not pass judgments. Do you understand?"

"Yes, Papa." Hildy was ashamed that she'd upset her father but Reuben had to have the last word.

"I liked him, Papa. He says savvy is better than book learning. Maybe he can teach me some savvy and I won't have to go to school."

Verdita and Ira laughed, and Verdita got up with Dovie. "Why don't you all go and see Mr. Money. I'm going to put Dovie down."

Ira rose and kissed her softly. "I value you, Mrs. Bacom. I surely do."

While Verdita took the baby upstairs, Ira, Hildy, and Reuben went out and turned toward a long line of buildings that stretched south down the wharf. Ships' sails snapped in the breeze. Ducks bobbed for food, and once they saw a muskrat swimming through a mass of seaweed. A wagon came toward them, the horse shying nervously when the wharf shifted on its pilings. A train pulled in and men scurried to unload its cars. There was so much to see, to smell, even to feel every time the pilings shifted that the Bacoms almost missed the Moneys' shop. Ira pushed open the door and a plump woman sorting paper on a makeshift table looked up.

"Good morning," she said.

"Good morning," repeated the parrot, which was perched on her head. It squawked and went into a loud shrill laugh, and she reached up and ran her hand down its back.

While Hildy and Reuben stared at the brightly colored bird, Ira took off his hat, saying, "I'm looking for Mr. Money. I'm here about a house he owns uptown."

"Well, now," Mrs. Money said, "that house just come up empty. Family living there packed their plunder and lit out in the middle of the night."

Ira took a few steps forward. "I'm interested in renting it."

At his words, Mrs. Money opened a back door. "Money!" she shouted. "Get on in here; there's a dude wants to dicker."

Reuben's mouth dropped open and Hildy giggled. Mr. Money came in and he and Ira went to the back of the little store to talk. Hildy went to look at the cage of yellow birds, but Reuben stared at the parrot.

"Doesn't he hurt your head? He looks awful heavy."

Mrs. Money smiled, revealing large yellow teeth. "I guess I'm used to him," she said. "My uncle the sailor gave him to me when I was not much older than you and he's been hitching a ride up there ever since. Of course," she added, "There are accidents sometimes."

When her words penetrated, Reuben's eyes opened wide and he put his hands over his mouth, and Mrs. Money turned toward Hildy.

"Do you like my canary birds?" Mrs. Money asked while she straightened some pencils.

"Oh, yes." Hildy clasped her hands together and raised her large dark eyes to Mrs. Money. "I think they're really nice." She leaned closer and whispered, "I think they sound like angels singing."

"Well, now." If Mrs. Money was taken aback, she didn't show it. "Perhaps your father will buy you one."

"I don't think so, ma'am. You see, we have to have a house first. And Papa has been really sick. We might not be able to feed even a little bird. I'm that worried."

"Goodness." This time she was taken aback. "He looks fit to me."

"It's his chest, you see, Mrs. Money. It doesn't always show."

Plainly, this called for a change of subject. "Well, dearie, how would you like one of Jack Tar's feathers?" She reached up again to stroke the parrot.

"Truly? To keep?"

"Of course." Mrs. Money found a box of feathers, selected several, and handed them to Hildy

"I'll treasure them always, Mrs. Money. I surely will."

Hildy stood looking at the feathers and Ira turned to join her. He bade Mrs. Money a quiet goodbye and they collected Reuben, who had lost interest in the birds and left the store. He stood outside watching a man drive a flock of sheep into a pen near the hillside. As they walked back toward the hotel, Ira whistled until neither Reuben nor Hildy could stand the suspense any longer.

"Papa, quit teasing us." Hildy said. "Did you get the house?"

"Don't you want to live in the hotel anymore?" Ira asked.

Reuben answered for both of them. "No, it's noisy at night and there are rats underneath. I saw one."

"But don't you think I should tell your mother first?"

"Please, Papa," Hildy said. "If you tell us now, we'll act surprised when you tell Mama, won't we, Reuben?"

"Hah!" Ira laughed. "You're as transparent as creek water." He stopped and pretended to consider the situation. "Well, if you promise, then, yes, we have a house."

CHAPTER 3

"We have a surprise," Ira said when they returned from seeing Mr. and Mrs. Money.

"We bought a house," Reuben shouted before Ira could continue.

"Bought?" Verdita's hand went to the brooch at her throat. "I thought we were going to rent."

Ira sat on the bed, careful not to disturb Dovie. "Mr. Money doesn't know if they'll stay in New Tacoma or not. General Sprague is threatening to take the railroad's business to another printer. If he does, they'll have to move. Not enough work to keep them here. Mrs. Money wants to go to Portland, and they decided that owning a house would slow them up."

"But, bought? Can we afford it?"

"We can."

Ira smiled and Verdita's face lit up. "Well, just wait until Glady hears. Her last letter said she and Stayton would have to rent for another year because the cost of houses was so dear."

"We can't live there, though, until the roof is repaired and the walls chinked up," Ira continued.

"Bats might come in through the holes." Reuben screwed up his face. "I saw one." He held his arms out and pretended to fly around the room. Reaching Hildy, he rubbed his hands in her hair crying, "bats, bats in your hair."

Hildy laughed and obligingly squealed. Ira and Verdita exchanged looks as the dinner bell sounded.

The five weeks after that day were hectic. The house needed many repairs, most of which Verdita had to find workers for while Ira settled into his new job. But as it turned out, Reuben was responsible for finding shakes to fix the roof.

"We can get 'em from Skookum's mill," he said.

"Skookum?" Ira had asked.

"Skookum Smith. He just opened a mill."

"Reuben, if he does have such a peculiar name, he is Mr. Smith to you."

"But everyone calls him that."

Verdita sighed. "The sooner you get into school the better."

Reuben started to protest but a look from his father kept him quiet. And Ira did buy the roofing material from Smith's mill, hiring a laid-off mill worker to do the repairs.

Now, sitting in her little bedroom, close to an oil lamp with her journal on her lap, Hildy savored the peace after the hectic weeks of work. Reuben and Dovie were in bed, Chong had gone to his lean-to, and her father was at a meeting. Ira, Mr. Blackwell, and General Sprague were starting a local chapter of the Grand Army of the Republic. As Hildy looked at what she'd written, the house was quiet except for the rustling sounds her canary, Jenny Lind, made in her cage.

While we worked getting the house ready, Hildy wrote, her pen flying across the page, *spring came and went. One day the sun beamed down and the next it rained, and Reuben has taken to our new life like a seal to the Sound. With nothing else to do until we moved, he roamed up and down the wharf every day making friends and having adventures.*

Remembering her mother's comment about Aunty Glady, Hildy looked at the dress hanging on a hook on the back of the door. As soon as they arrived in New Tacoma, her father's sister, Aunt Glady, sent them a package of her children's old clothes. "Mama says Aunt Glady is a good, churchgoing woman, but she wears every mile out of the clothing before she passes it on," Hildy told the canary. "That's why we have so many quilts. Some of the clothes are fit for nothing else."

Nevertheless, Hildy was always excited when a box of items arrived. "Hope springs eternal, I guess."

The most recent package contained a suit Reuben could grow into, and the dress hanging on the hook that her mother had altered to fit her. Half the gathers had been detached from the waistband, and there was a large, right-angle tear near the hem. But its bright colors hadn't faded. Verdita easily reattached the gathers and then trimmed off a piece of the sash. She fashioned it into a flower and stitched it over the rip.

"Reuben and I start school tomorrow," Hildy continued. She drew her knees up and rested her arms on them. "Reuben will love it. I hope there are some nice girls my age."

After the purchase of their home, the Chinook weather came again and stayed long enough for Ira to arrange to have their belongings shipped up from Portland where they had been stored. Hildy and Verdita caulked the spaces where the wall boards didn't meet and whitewashed the rooms—coat after coat, the last one tinted with pig's blood in some of the rooms to give them a rosy hue. It was barely dry before their furnishings arrived. While Verdita and Hildy unpacked, and Ira worked for General Sprague, Chong and Reuben cleared the property of underbrush, and began digging a vegetable garden. Chong's presence in their lives was something Hildy enjoyed writing about to Cousin Elsie. *It was all thanks to Alice Blackwell.*

The evening of the home purchase, Hildy shyly told William Blackwell all about it. William, of course, knew the Moneys and knew the house. He had a word with his wife and Alice sat down with Verdita after dinner to talk. Hildy played with Dovie but remained within ear range of the conversation.

"Chong is young and he has no family here. He would make you a good houseboy." Alice's fingers flew in and out of the sheets she was mending.

"How did he get here?"

"The Chinese speak their own language and keep to themselves. The community may know but we don't."

"Community?"

"The Chinese one. Walk to the far south end of the wharf or the other way toward Old Tacoma and you'll see their houses. They don't live like us or even eat the same foods. Some folks around here don't like that—don't approve."

"I'm not sure." Verdita carefully unraveled yarn from an old sweater and wound it into a ball. "I've never been around Celestials. Are you sure they're—well—clean?"

"Exceptionally. I've had nothing but Chinese helpers ever since we left Utah and moved. Before we came here, we lived in Portland and then Kalama and we've had Chinese help at every hotel with never a problem." Alice put down the finished sheet and picked up another. As she did, her corset creaked and Hildy ducked her head to hide her smile. How in the world, she wondered, could Alice work as hard as she did running the hotel and still be so plump?

Threading her needle, Alice added, "They're quiet and work hard. They don't question our ways the way a white servant girl does; besides, there aren't any white girls to hire."

"But he barely speaks English," Verdita protested. "How will we communicate?"

"He understands well enough and will learn from you. The Chinese seem to pick up our ways quickly."

"Maybe he won't want to come."

Alice stopped what she was doing and looked at Verdita. "He loved taking care of Dovie." She let her hands rest in her lap. "I think he must have left siblings behind. He's probably sending

41

his earnings home to them. He's younger than most of the other Chinese men here, and I think he's very lonely."

"Well if Ira agrees." Later on, Verdita told Ira that William Blackwell might be the businessman in the family but his wife knew how to line up and deliver her arguments.

Remembering the conversation, Hildy smiled. She heard her mother add a piece of wood to the fire downstairs and move the fire screen back in place while she waited for Ira to return. The room was getting cold. They couldn't afford to order glass from Portland so Verdita had covered the windows with opaque, oiled cloth, and Ira hired a man to make shutters that they pulled over the windows at night. But on an evening like this, when the wind was ushering in the rain, drafts crept around the edges and made themselves felt. The front door opened and Ira's footsteps sounded. He and Verdita started up the stairs to their room and Hildy heard their soft-spoken words.

"I missed you," Ira said.

"How was the meeting?"

"These are good men, Verdita. They're a different breed from back home, not that folks there don't work hard, but back east a person is born into his place in life. Why, in New Tacoma, with hard work and a little luck, we can become leading citizens." There was a pause and then he added, "Wallpaper and glass instead of whitewash and oiled paper, for you, and real silk dresses."

"And for you?"

"A lifetime of years together."

Snuggled under heavy quilts in her corner bedroom, Hildy listened and hoped she'd have a marriage like her parents' someday.

Their voices faded and she relished the quiet. Hildy liked being awake at night, and counted it a loss when she slept the night through. She loved the late hours when everyone else slept and she could be alone with her memories and dreams. Now she thought that she would never again have five weeks of sheer happiness such as those behind her. Everything about her new life, from her friend, Mrs. Money, to her pink bedroom, was perfect.

Several afternoons, while Papa was at work, Verdita rested with Dovie, and Reuben explored and made friends with the merchants, Hildy walked down the muddy trail to see Mrs. Money.

"Good morning, dearie," the lady said the first time Hildy walked in the shop alone. "Are you here to buy a canary?"

"Oh, Mrs. Money," Hildy's large, dark eyes glowed with intensity. "I wish ever so much that I could, but you see I have hardly any money of my own and I can't ask Papa. He's so busy right now just providing for a roof over our heads."

Mrs. Money hid a smile. "Well, then, perhaps you would like to help me. The warblers have a big new cage and I have to move them into it."

"Yes, please, Mrs. Money. I would dearly love to help you."

The birds' new home was on the opposite side of the store. A partition separated the domestic birds from the robins, owls and various other wild birds. While Mrs. Money moved the wild ones, she let Hildy move the canaries and parakeets. She showed Hildy how to hold out her finger and wait until a bird landed on it. Then slowly and gently wrap the bird in a scrap of cloth and carry it to the new aviary. While they worked, Mrs. Money hummed and sang "Listen to the Mockingbird."

"That's a very sad song," Hildy said

"Yes it is. It's about a mockingbird singing over the grave of a young man's sweetheart. It was one of President Lincoln's favorites."

After a chorus or two, Hildy joined her. Customers came and went. One parakeet escaped and led them on a merry chase around the store. Mr. Money finally caught it in his hat and Hildy laughed and clapped, and praised his prowess. When all the birds were moved and it was time for Hildy to leave, Mrs. Money gave her two red feathers. Later in the evening, while at the supper table, she spread them out for the others to see.

"I'm going to make a fan when I have enough."

Reuben was also full of news.

"Mr. Scott's building a scow," he said, dipping a biscuit into his gravy.

"Don't do that, Reuben," Verdita said.

And Ira asked why a dairy man would want a scow.

"He says he can use it to tote hay when he's not delivering milk with his wagon uptown. Last week a loose horse ran down the road and scared his mare. The mare upset the milk wagon and all the milk pails."

"Spilled milk. No wonder the streets smell so bad." Hildy giggled.

"That's not why." Reuben parked a half-chewed biscuit in his cheek.

"Don't talk with your mouthful, dear," Verdita said.

"Then what does make them smell the way they do?"

"There's pigs living under the wooden sidewalks and a lot of cats. Mr. Scott says there's too darn many cats for his liking."

"Reuben! You know better than to use that word. I think you had best spend more time helping Chong dig the garden and less time in town."

Ira had news, too. "Dr. Bostwick is building a big new house two blocks up the hill from town and is going to include a croquet court, and there's talk that an Episcopal church is going to be built."

"It seems to me," Verdita said, "that you all are having all the fun while I work." But she smiled as she said it.

Snuggling under the quilts and remembering her mother's

words, Hildy smiled, too. She shifted the bottle full of hot water tucked under her blankets and listened to Jenny Lind. The room was really too cold for the bird. Hildy never minded the cold but Verdita said that canary birds did.

"They come from far away where it's very warm," she explained, adding, "and you'll be going to school and Jenny Lind needs company." So the following morning Jenny Lind was going to the kitchen where Chong's stove kept the room warm, and Hildy didn't argue. Chong had made Jenny Lind's presence possible.

"I'm going to town," Verdita said a few days after they moved in the new house and were still getting settled.

"Okay, Mama." Hildy took two loaves of bread out of the oven and set them aside while she removed a third. Hildy loved making bread. "Look at the yeast bubble," she said in awe the first time she made it. "It's alive just because of me." No sooner had they moved from the hotel to the house than Hildy mixed flour, sugar, salt, and water and set it aside to ferment. Since then, she'd been making three loaves of bread every other day.

Verdita left the house and Hildy put loaves on a box outside to cool. She was playing with Dovie when someone knocked at the door. Chong opened it.

"Who is it, Chong?"

"You wait," Chong said to the stranger. He shut the door and got Hildy.

With Chong scowling and standing beside her, Hildy opened the door to a middle-aged man. He immediately pulled off his hat and kneaded the brim nervously. "I smelled your bread, miss."

"Are you hungry?"

"It smells like what my ma used to bake."

Hildy knew how her mother felt about people being hungry.

"I can bake more. You take a loaf, sir, and welcome to it."

"Well now." He smiled broadly and Hildy almost laughed aloud. No wonder he wanted bread. He didn't have enough teeth left to chew meat. Before he took his loaf, the fellow reached in his pocket, pulled out a miscellany of string, tokens, and coins, and fished among it. After a minute he picked out a few brass discs and handed them over. "Much obliged."

Hildy looked at the coins and then at Chong, who nodded. "I can make you bread anytime," she said.

"Is that a fact?"

"I make bread every other day. You come on by the day after tomorrow and I'll have more."

"For sure and certain I'll do that, miss. Thank you very much, miss."

After the man left, Chong looked at the strange flat pieces of metal. "Man pay good. You buy bud now."

Hildy grinned. She knew he meant bird. "I need a cage, though."

"I make."

And he did, a beautiful tall slender cage made from thin pieces of planed wood and containing a number of little perches.

When Verdita returned that day and heard about the strange man at the door, she didn't know what to think. "That was a kind thing to do," she said, untying her bonnet and hanging it over a nail. "But Hildy, it was also a dangerous thing to do. A strange man. He could have hurt you. You must never do that again."

"Chong was here, and he had a knife. I felt it. Didn't you, Chong?"

Chong grinned. "Missy get bud now. Sing nice."

Verdita sighed. "We won't mention this to your father." She looked at the coins and slugs Hildy handed her. "What are these?" she asked, fingering some flat pieces of metal.

"Mill money," Chong said.

"Mill money?"

"No money at mill so make own. Have stoo and sell food."

When hunger sent Reuben home, he shed light on the brass discs. "New Tacoma doesn't have any money. There isn't a bank. Mr. Hanson and Mr. Ackerson had their blacksmith make these and the men use them at the company store."

"How do you know all this?" Verdita asked.

"Samuel told me."

"Samuel?"

Reuben took an enormous bite of bread and butter and Verdita held up her hand. "Swallow first."

After a minute of vigorous chewing, Reuben said, "Samuel won't come here so I meet him down the road. Samuel knows everything about New Tacoma and he's teaching me."

Verdita let the issue of Reuben's gallivanting go for a moment. "Why won't he come here?"

"I don't know. Can I have some of those dried apples, please?"

Remembering the conversation as she turned in bed to plump her pillow, Hildy giggled. Much to his chagrin, Reuben had been put to work with Chong digging a vegetable garden. He still got out and about, but only for an hour or two in the afternoon.

Not long after that, while walking down the road one day, Hildy saw Samuel standing on a corner shivering in the wind that swept up the hill. "Reuben has to work," she told him. "He's helping Chong dig a garden. But he can come out in the afternoon."

Samuel nodded, hunched his shoulders, and started walking

"Why won't you come and visit us?" she called after him. But the boy was already too far away.

Hildy's last thought before falling asleep was, I'll ask him at school, tomorrow.

CHAPTER 4

When Hildy and Reuben left for school the next morning, a brisk wind pushed tangled clouds across the sky. And near town the smell of sap from recently cut trees competed with fireplace smoke and the odors of low tide to fill the air.

Reuben took a deep breath and sighed with satisfaction. "Do you like New Tacoma, Hildy?"

Hildy looked at the tents, and rough-board buildings, at the burned stumps and piles of newly cut wood, at the mucky, rutted roads and at an eagle soaring overhead. Around them, birds hopped in and out of newly budded trees and bushes. "Yes, I do."

"Me, too," Reuben said. They looked at each other and smiled. "I wish we didn't have to go to school, though. Why can't a person just go to school when it rains?"

Hildy gave the question careful consideration. "I think," she said slowly, "it's because if you lived somewhere where it rains all the time, you'd have to go to school practically every day and if you lived where it never rains, like in a desert, you'd never go to school, so they figured out what was fair for everyone."

Satisfied with the explanation, Reuben hopped from one piece of wood to another and then stopped to watch a dozen or so seagulls taking shelter. "We're going to have a storm."

"But the sky is mostly blue."

"Yes, but when the seagulls come in from the water it means

a storm is brewing."

"How do you know that?"

"Samuel told me."

"Samuel." Hildy ran to catch up with her brother. "How does Samuel know that?"

"I don't know, but he does."

On the nearby streets, men went in and out of buildings, Monday morning laundry strung over rope lines whipped about in the breeze, and a cow mooed in protest of something. Away from the townsite, skunk cabbages poked through the mud, their budding yellow flowers filling the air with a pungent scent. Hildy thought about what Reuben said. "Well, maybe it's not true."

"If Samuel says it, it's true. Anyway, where is this school? We've been walking an awful long time."

"It's two more blocks." Hildy shifted her slate from one hand to the other. "Reuben, why doesn't Samuel ever come around? Doesn't he like us?"

"I think it's because he's poor."

"But I head Papa says we're as poor as Job's turkey."

"Well, maybe it's something else. He likes me, though. Say, Hildy, I'll tell you a secret if you promise not to tell."

"I promise." Hildy crossed her heart. "What?"

Reuben looked around, waited until a horse and wagon went by, and lowered his voice. "Mr. Geiger has a new teetotum pin-pool table."

Hildy's eyes widened. "How do you know? Did you see it?"

"No. I heard him talking about it at Cogswell's livery stable."

"Oh, I've wondered about those ever since I read *Through the Looking-Glass and What Alice Found There*. Remember, when the sheep asks, 'Are you a child or a teetotum?' You are lucky to be a boy, Reuben, and get to go anywhere you want. Girls can't do anything." Hildy sighed. "Don't let Mama hear you mention it.

You know how she feels about gambling."

By this time, Hildy and Reuben had reached a small L-shaped building built from weathered, rough-hewn wood. Light showed through glass windows on either side of a door accessed by a plank-covered path. Smoke came out of a short chimney and was whipped about by the frisky breeze. They stopped, uncomfortably aware of being strangers in a strange town. But at that moment, the door opened and a woman's voice said, "You must be Reuben and Hildy. Come along. I'm not heating the outdoors. Of course," she laughed, "it'd take a lot more than my woodpile to do that." She stood aside to let them in.

The room in which Hildy and Reuben found themselves was almost completely filled by chairs surrounding a table made of side-by-side planks resting on sawhorses. A curtain separated the schoolroom from the living quarters. Nine children sat around the table with the boys at one end and the girls at the other. Hildy and Reuben were gestured to seats in the middle, across from each other.

"I'm Miss Sparkle," the woman said. She took the slates Hildy carried and stuck them out of sight saying, "You won't need these."

Hildy wondered what they would write on and the question was soon answered. "We've plenty of chalk; you can just write on the table."

The morning began with a prayer and a hymn. Then Miss Sparkle began going through multiplication tables and Hildy followed along. She soon found out why their slates were unnecessary. When one lesson was done, Miss Sparkle had them wipe off the table planks they'd used with a wet cloth and turn them over. While the underneath sides dried, they wrote on the top sides.

Miss Sparkle was so plump her skirt brushed the walls when she moved around the table. However, she had to spend most of her time at the boy's end of the table where the boys nudged, poked, and made faces at each other. Hildy worked industriously, with her head ducked until someone kicked her under the table. When she looked up, a curly haired blonde with a turned-up nose and dark brown eyes winked at her. Hildy stared, mouth slightly opened, and the girl grinned and crossed her eyes. Hildy giggled, caught herself, and turned it into a cough.

"Are you all right, dear?" Miss Sparkle looked.

"Yes, ma'am." She smiled back at the girl and suddenly, the room seemed less chilly.

After the math lesson, Miss Sparkle led the group through spelling and reading. The school had one *McGuffey's Reader,* and each student took it in turn, reading a paragraph aloud. At eleven, the class broke for recess. Miss Sparkle gave everyone a slice of bread and dripping and sent them outside. While the boys began a game that involved a lot of shouting and running around, the girls found a corner out of the wind and hunkered down on a dry spot with the building wall to their backs. Hildy was uncomfortably aware of their scrutiny.

After a few moments, when the blonde girl was done with her bread and had licked her fingers clean, she said, "Miss Sparkle said 'welcome Reuben and Hildy' so you must be Hildy. My name is Nell. This is Kezzie," she gestured toward a roly-poly little girl with black braids. "And that's Lucy and Ellen." Lucy smiled, showing a space where she'd lost a tooth, and Ellen nodded her head.

"How old are you?" Nell asked.

"Twelve, almost thirteen."

"Me, too." They smiled at having something in common.

"I'm theven and a half," said Lucy. "Mith Thparkle thays I'm the baby. She liketh me betht."

"That's true," said Kezzie. "Lucy always gets to choose first

51

if Miss Sparkle has sweets to be passed around."

While she spoke, a blast of wind blew around the corner of the building carrying rain. Miss Sparkle came to the schoolroom door and rang a bell.

For the next hour she taught geography by drawing maps on the planks, but after a particularly strong gust shook the building, she began bundling the children up, giving them strict instructions to run straight home. Hildy found Reuben; he told her that he was going to go home with the Scott twins, who lived a few blocks south. So Hildy started down the street on her own, pushing against the wet gusts.

Hildy was familiar with thunder and lightning, but she'd never seen anything like the storm in which she soon found herself. With few trees to block the assault, rain blew sideways, lashing at her legs. Her hat blew off, and barely touched ground before disappearing. Without the hat, Hildy's hair blew in her mouth and eyes. At home in Johnstown, she could have pounded on a door and found shelter, but there were no doors to be seen, no lights, and no other people on the roads. Then the wind took a turn and blew against her back propelling her forward and the rain turned to hail. As it did, she slipped in the mud and fell, knocking her breath out. Unable to cry out, she struggled to breathe and then to get to her knees. As she did, someone took her hand, helped her to her feet, and a male voice said, "Come on, run."

Hildy ran until it seemed as if her feet were leaving the ground. When she slipped, her companion kept her from falling. Hailstones covered her hair and melted and dripped down her neck. Others hit her face, leaving scratches.

"Almost there," the person said. He slowed a bit to turn a corner and Hildy saw a light in a window. A few feet from the door, lightning found its mark and split a tree. In the brief flash, she saw half of it break off. As she was pushed through the open door, the tree crashed down, sending water and mud flying. Someone slammed the door shut behind her and breathless and frightened, Hildy fainted and slid to the floor.

CHAPTER 5

Hildy woke to the scent of *sal volatile* coming from a vial someone waved under her nose, and the sight of three female faces bending over her.

"If this don't cap the climax," one woman said. "Look what the storm blowed in. It's a little girl." She leaned down. "Are you all right?"

"What happened?"

"You fainted." The woman straightened up and looked toward the door where wind was making a desperate effort to join them. "Land sakes, just listen to that squall."

The other two women looked at her and back at Hildy. "You best get up off that floor," one said, adding as Hildy scrambled to her feet, "Lordy, you're soaked through. Come over here and plunk yourself down by the fire."

Hildy did as she was told, peeling her coat off and spreading it out on the floor. She sat next to it, squeezed water out of her hair, and looked around. The room in which she had found refuge was small and sparsely furnished. Rose-colored cloth covered the walls and an upright piano stood against one wall. An oil lamp with a brass base and stand supporting a pink-flowered globe sat on a table near the front window. Other than that the furnishings consisted of a few wooden chairs, and boxes with railroad lanterns on them. A dark hallway led off the room, Hildy guessed toward the kitchen and bedrooms.

While she had been looking around, one of the women had

54

left and now returned with a piece of sacking. "Here, dearie, dry your hair," she said. Then the woman unbuttoned and pulled off Hildy's shoes and socks while Hildy rubbed her head. "I'll just put them close to the fire and they'll dry in no time."

"Thank you, ma'am."

"What's your name?"

"Hildy, Hildy Bacom."

"Well, Hildy Bacom, how did you happen to be out in the storm?"

"I got caught on the way home from school. My brother, Reuben, went with his friends but I didn't know anyone to go home with." Hildy shivered and her face became pale and pinched. "If I could just stay here for a little while . . ."

She jumped when the woman turned toward the hall and shouted.

"Isabeau!"

Footsteps sounded and a woman appeared from the back of the room. *"Oui?"*

"Would you please bring our guest some hot chocolate?"

"Oui, Mez Violet."

"Now, dearie, I'm Violet, as you heard, and Rose is over there by the window. This is Rose's house. Lily's gone to her room. She's feeling peaked."

At that moment, a gust of wind came down the chimney, scattering sparks. Hildy was glad the fire was behind a screen. Still, she looked carefully at a coal scuttle full of wood scraps and fir cones to make sure they were safe. "Mama wouldn't let me call you Violet," she said. "It isn't respectful. Don't you ladies have last names?"

Rose moved to a chair near Hildy. "Well, in Georgia, where I come from, folks set a lot of store about good manners. We call older ladies who are our friends, miss. You can call us Miss Rose and Miss Violet."

55

"And Miss Isabeau?"

The two women looked at each other but before they could answer, Isabeau appeared with a tray containing a pot, three cups, and a plate of buttered bread. She put it on a box and poured the chocolate and passed the food. Hildy took a bite of the bread and was surprised at its crusty outside and soft, porous inside. When she smiled, Isabeau said, "Do you like it?"

"Most assuredly I do. You see, I'm a bread baker."

"Oh, *oui*?"

"Yes, I have a business."

Miss Rose frowned. "That's enough, Isabeau. You may go now."

As Isabeau turned to leave, Hildy said, "Oh, no. Please let her stay and tell me about this bread."

Isabeau glanced at Miss Rose, who nodded with a frosty look. "Well, *ma petite*, I am French and this is the bread we eat at home. It's called a baguette."

Isabeau explained that the starter needed fourteen hours to work, that the bread was punched down and allowed to rise three times, and then baked in a very hot oven. Hildy listened closely and nodded. When Isabeau was done and had returned to the kitchen, Miss Violet said, "Your own business you say. Do tell. Ain't that some pumpkins."

"Well," Hildy said. "You see, I bake all the bread we eat. I set it out at night and finish in the morning. I can do everything before school and every other day I sell loaves to Mr. Rogers and Mr. Peak, who work for the railroad." Her words were interrupted by someone banging on the door. When Miss Rose answered it, she stepped aside and a man entered. "Papa!" cried Hildy, jumping up. "How did you know where I was?"

Ira caught Hildy in a tight hug. "I didn't, daughter, but Reuben came home a while ago and said you'd left school on your own. Your mama and I got worried so I set out to look for you.

I've been knocking on doors. How did you end up here?"

"I don't know for sure. I fell and someone came along and helped me up and brought me here. The ladies have been really kind and I learned all about a bread called a baguette. It's French." Hildy stopped as her father doubled in half with a racking cough. Miss Violet handed him her unfinished cocoa and he drank it gratefully.

"We have to go, Hildy. Your mother is very worried." He turned and nodded stiffly to Miss Rose and then to Miss Violet. "I appreciate the care you gave my daughter."

Miss Rose, however, wasn't about to be dismissed so easily. "I tell you true, sir, when I opened the door and your daughter sort of fell in, I said to myself, 'ain't that the beatinest.' And I like to have a conniption fit because we rarely have an opportunity to be around such a pert little girl. Ain't that right, Violet?"

Miss Violet nodded and Ira continued.

"Thank you, ma'am. I'll be sure to tell her mother. Hildy, put your shoes and stockings on and get your coat. Where's your hat?"

"It blew away."

"Well, never mind. It can't be helped. Come along now."

"If you wait just a moment Mr. uh . . ."

"Bacom. Ira Bacom.

"Well, if you wait just a moment, I have a scarf Hildy can wear."

"I assure you, it won't be necessary."

"But it's still raining."

"Please, Papa. Then Mama and I can return the scarf and Mama can thank Miss Rose and Miss Violet."

As Ira hesitated, Miss Violet left the room, returning with a yellow wool scarf that she wrapped around Hildy's head. "Thank you, Miss Violet. I'll be sure and get it back to you."

Hildy dropped a curtsy. "And thank you, Miss Rose. I'll come back and visit you, if I may."

Rose cleared her throat and half-smiled. "If it's all right with your folks, we'd set store on it, dearie."

By the time the door closed behind Hildy and Ira, the wind had died down and the hail turned to a heavy mist. It was what Verdita called candle-lighting time. Hildy took her father's hand and walked silently beside him. After a while, he said, "You're awfully quiet, little cabbage. Are you sure you're all right?"

"Yes, Papa. I was just thinking."

"What about?"

"Miss Rose, Miss Lily, and Miss Violet. Isn't it nice that they all have flower names and that they live together? And they have a lady named Isabeau who takes care of them, but maybe you didn't notice, they were still in their night clothes, just like invalids. Do you think they're ill, Papa?"

Ira's burst of laughter turned into a coughing fit. He stopped walking until he recovered and said, "No, Hildy, I don't think they're sick. I think they keep different hours than we do."

CHAPTER 6

Spring crept slowly into Puget Sound. Hildy thought the dreary winter would never end. Then, one day, pink clusters of flowering currant sent limbs into the air, and tiny wild violets bloomed in marshy spots. School was out and both she and Reuben split their days between chores and visiting with their friends. Reuben worked in the vegetable garden, stacked firewood, and kept the indoor woodboxes full. Hildy swept the floors, helped hang out and fold laundry, helped with Dovie, and, of course, baked bread. She had yet to return the scarf Miss Violet loaned her, and she wanted to visit Miss Isabeau and learn more about making baguettes. In the meantime, however, she sought diversion with Nell.

Nell lived in a house at the edge of town and had come over so Verdita could help her mend a dress. As they sat in the parlor, she tried to explain which road was which in lieu of their lack of signs.

"The men didn't have much imagination when they named the streets, and we don't even have a Main Street. What will visitors think?"

Verdita smiled to herself, wondering who these visitors would be.

"Anyway," Nell went on, "The most important streets are Seventh, Eighth, Ninth, and Eleventh. They all start at the bluff and go up the hill. Then there's A Street, Pacific Avenue, and C Street. C Street is where the Chinese have that big vegetable garden. Those streets all run in the other direction from the numbered streets. Miss Sparkle says New Tacoma is built on a grid just like ancient Greece. I'm west of Pacific Avenue off Eighth Street and you're east of Pacific on A Street."

"Well, that certainly explains it." Verdita found some yellow thread and gave it and a needle to Nell.

"Yes, all those streets and more are being made all the time. Sure makes things lively." Nell had been born out on Bush Prairie near Olympia and loved New Tacoma.

"And where exactly is your house?" Verdita asked.

"It's that little place sort of up and behind Levin's Barbershop. The barbershop used to be the schoolhouse. Say, Hildy," Nell stopped sewing for a minute and looked up. "Did you know that Miss Sparkle is getting married?"

Hildy put down the sock she was knitting. "Oh, how romantic."

"Not really, she's marrying another teacher and moving to Seattle."

"Death-rattle Seattle? That's dreadful. But, Nell, what about school?"

"The building that's going to be North School is finished. I expect we'll go there and have a new teacher."

Nell was one of seven children, six still at home, whose home was so crowded she sought every opportunity to escape. She was a constant source of everything happening in New Tacoma.

"There's too many of us for the house," she explained to Verdita when they first met, "but babies keep showing up. You'd think they'd have enough sense to find a house with more room."

Verdita was shocked at the blunt words but before she could say anything Hildy said, "Like the Blackwells. Mrs. Blackwell doesn't have any babies and there's plenty of room at the hotel."

Verdita started to laugh at Nell's words, but Hildy's remark reminded her of Alice's sadness at not having children.

The three were quiet for a few moments, then when Nell jabbed her finger with a needle and stopped to suck at the blood, Verdita said, "Enough sewing for today. Why don't you girls go out for a while and enjoy the spring weather."

The best place to enjoy the sun was on the proper set of stairs that Hildy's father put in at the front door to replace the single step. From there out to the street, he laid two-by-fours and filled in the space between them with sawdust to make a walkway. From early afternoon on, the sun beat on the wood of the door. Both Hildy and Nell thought sitting on the step and leaning against the warm wood was a good place to sit.

"What would you be doing in Johnstown on a day like this?" Nell pulled her knees up, and tucked her skirt modestly around them.

Hildy, her legs extended straight out, sniffed the elusive scents of new leaves and freshly turned soil and considered the question. A nearby puddle gleamed brightly with the absorbed light it reflected back, and a woodpecker beat a rat-a-tat on an old snag.

"Well," she said slowly, "Dovie was really little and took a lot of time, I tell you. She cried all the time because Mama said she had colic. The hours I spent walking her around . . ."

"Not that stuff. Babies don't do much else but cry. Other stuff. What about your cousin?"

By this time in their friendship, Nell knew about the packages Aunt Glady sent. She considered their contents a source of how the rich lived.

"Hmmm, in the afternoon Aunt Glady received visitors and Cousin Elsie did fancy work."

"What's that?"

"Oh, crocheting edges on pillowcases or tatting."

"What for?"

"Her hope chest."

Nell looked puzzled so Hildy continued. "She's making things for when she's married. That's what girls back there do. They edge sheets and crochet doilies and make tablecloths and save them for when they're married."

"You mean your cousin will have to do that for maybe five years?"

"Yes, and then spend the next twenty using what she made."

"Oh, I would hate that."

"Which part? Sewing or using what you made?"

"Making things for a hope chest. If I made pretty things I would want to use them right away."

"You're so pretty you probably won't have to have a hope chest." Hildy, who considered her own brown hair and eyes, and the mole near her mouth dull and uninteresting, thought Nell was the prettiest girl she'd ever seen.

"A handsome man will just fall at your feet and offer you the moon and the stars."

She shifted on to one knee, clasped her hands, lifted her head, and said dramatically. "Darling Nell, be mine or I shall wither and waste away."

"Pooh." Nell looked disgusted. "If a fellow said silly things like that he wouldn't be worth a tinker's you know what."

The girls laughed and before Hildy could answer, they heard the clip-clop of horses' hooves. Mr. Scott was making milk deliveries. They jumped up and ran to the road to watch his arrival. "Hello, ladies," he called as he approached them.

"Hello, Mr. Scott. How is Martyr-to-the-Cause today?" Hildy rubbed the horse's nose.

Mr. Scott pulled the reins lightly and the horse tossed her head. "She's feeling like a cow in the clover, now that spring is here, aren't you, old girl."

Hildy pulled a piece of dried apple out of her pocket and fed it to the horse. "How old is Martyr-to-the-Cause, Mr. Scott?"

"She's fifteen. I've had her since I was not much older than you." He dropped the reins, and jumped out of the wagon.

"Why does she have such a funny name?"

"Well, we call her that because she'd rather be dozing in the field or eating grass than working, and she feels very put-upon when she has to earn her keep." Mr. Scott lifted two milk pails from the back. "I expect Reuben is down watching the doings, is he?"

"What doings?" Nell loved anything she hadn't seen before.

"The spring salmon run is in. The Puyallups are netting them and salting them down. They'll be camped down at the bay for three, maybe four days." He started around back of the house and Hildy and Nell stood pulling briars from the horse's mane.

Nell's face lit with excitement. When Mr. Scott was out of earshot she said, "Let's go see."

"Papa says the Indians have fleas."

"We won't get that close. I know a trail along the ridge above the bay. We can hunker down and watch."

Hildy caught her friend's excitement and whispered, "When Mr. Scott leaves I'll tell Mama we're going for a walk. That way it won't be a lie."

After the milkman returned, whistling cheerfully and swinging two empty milk pails, Hildy got permission to go for a walk and the two girls set off.

Pacific Avenue petered out north of Fifth Street and the girls began climbing a hill that led to the top of the bluff. Like all of New Tacoma's roads and paths, it was rough going. They worked their way slowly around protruding roots, downed limbs, berry bushes, and lengthy stretches of marsh. Soon they were huffing and puffing and beginning to rethink the idea. But the fresh briny smell of Commencement Bay was enticing, and the sounds of voices began reaching their ears. When Nell, who was in the lead, broke out of the woods and stopped she had a clear view of the Indian's encampment below.

"Gracious." Hildy reached her friend's side and wiped her forehead.

"Ssh. Someone will hear you. Come on, get down."

They lay on their stomachs and inched forward to peek over the embankment. Even there, high above the beach, the smells of campfire smoke and fish reached them.

The sight was like nothing either Hildy or Nell had ever seen. The tide was out and driftwood, discarded shells, and seaweed covered the shore. Far out in the bay, a clearly defined line of brown water showed where the Puyallup River emptied into the salt water. It was the river the spring run of Chinook salmon headed for. Longboats big enough to hold families packed the mouth of the river. From them, men threw out empty nets and dragged them back in full of fish flailing desperately for release. When a boat could hold no more, it returned to the beach, where the Indian women and children converged and threw the fish up on shore. The women wore faded cotton dresses and leather moccasins, the children shirts but no bottoms. Hildy's jaw dropped when she saw a little boy urinating unconcernedly against a log. In the midst of the floundering fish, the women crouched down and with a flash of their knives cut off the heads and removed the backbones. They scrubbed the scales with moss and tossed them into large hogsheads where a man too old to help with the nets added salt.

"Don't they clean them?" Hildy whispered in a horrified voice.

"I don't know. I've never seen this before," Nell whispered back.

"Ugh!" Hildy made a face. "I don't think I ever want to eat salmon again."

Nell poked her. "Hush. Voices carry really well on the water." Her fear was ungrounded, though. Indian children ran up and down the beach or into the cold water, letting it lap around their knees. Their screams, accompanied by dogs barking and seagulls screeching as they fought over the fish heads, filled the air.

"They aren't very pretty, are they?" Hildy said.

"Some are, some of the young girls, but the old people aren't. They're all wrinkled and brown like old apples."

As the girls continued to watch, several canoes landed on the beach. The men hopped out and pulled them higher up on the shore. Nell poked Hildy again and pointed. "That's a handsome Indian."

Hildy's eyes scanned the beach until they lit on a slender, well-built figure. While the older men wore leather breeches, the young man Nell indicated wore nothing but a loin cloth. "Gracious," she whispered, shocked at the sight of so much naked skin.

Beside her, Nell giggled. "I'll bet he's cold."

Hildy was unable to quit staring. She guessed the man's age to be around fourteen. His skin, much lighter than that of his companions, was streaked with blood. In spite of his youth, his arms and legs were muscular. While she continued watching, a darker-skinned young man swung a fish and whacked him across the shoulders. Then he dropped the fish and ran. Soon the two gripped each other in a mock fight while the children cheered them on. When one of the older men picked up a basket, scooped water out of the bay, and threw it on them, they broke apart laughing. That was when Hildy recognized the fellow in the loin cloth. "Why, that's . . ." she started to say and then closed her mouth.

"Sakes alive! Do you know one of them?" Nell turned wide eyes on her.

For a reason Hildy didn't understand she wanted to protect Reuben's friend, Samuel, from being tagged as merely an

Indian. "No, of course not. But, Nell, how long do you think we've been here? It's getting frightfully cold."

"Can you find your way back?"

"No."

"Drat it all. Come on then." Nell inched backwards and stood up. "I was going to stay and see what goes on later but I can always come back."

"Won't your mother want you home?"

"Yes, but Josie can help her with dinner for once. I'll find someone to tell her I'm at your house and she'll never know."

"But Nell, you can't do that. It's dishonest."

"Pooh. It's the only way I can do anything interesting. Come on."

At the top of the path leading from the wharf to town, the two girls parted ways. Hildy caught sight of her father coming home from work and ran to join him. "What have you been doing, little cabbage?" he asked as Hildy slipped her hand into his.

"Exploring. Nell showed me a place where you can see the bay from the hill."

"Does your mother know where you've been?"

"I told her we were going for a walk."

"And?"

"Well, that's all because I didn't know where we were going."

Ira stopped and turned his daughter to face him. "Hildy, you mustn't run wild. This is a rough-and-ready place and we know very few people. If you want to go somewhere, tell Mama and me. Look how frightened we were the night of the big storm. We didn't know where to look for you."

"I'm sorry, Papa."

"I know you are, daughter. We want you safe, that's all."

Whatever Verdita had planned to say about Hildy's being gone so long disappeared when the girl came in with her father. Hildy rushed around setting the table, getting Dovie into her chair, and carrying food to the table. Verdita had been teaching Chong to cook and this evening he baked a salmon and served it with potatoes and cabbage. Hildy, who hated cabbage, winced when she saw the fish and took as many potatoes as she could.

"Hildy," Verdita said, "Chong will be hurt if you don't eat the salmon."

"Yes, ma'am." Hildy helped herself and was glad that it tasted good.

Ira helped himself to the cabbage and said, "Well, Hildy and Nell went for a walk. Reuben, what did you do with your day?"

"I went to see Mr. Money. His printing press just came up from Kalama."

"Was Samuel with you?" Verdita asked.

"No, he was busy doing something with his pa today." Reuben smashed a generous helping of butter into his potatoes. "Say, Hildy, Mrs. Money wants you to drop by and see her new blue parakeets."

"What's Mr. Money going to do with the printing press?" Ira asked.

"Start a newspaper. May I have some more salmon, please?"

"New Tacoma already has a paper." Verdita put more fish on his plate. "Tom Porsch just started the *Pacific Tribune*."

"Mr. Money says his will be better. Like just today he learned that Mr. John Cade O'Loughlin died all alone in a squalid little shack, that's Mr. Money's words, 'squalid little shack,' at the back of the car shops. Mr. Money says Mr. O'Loughlin was brilliant in spite of years of dissipation. Mr. Money says he'll get out a special edition tomorrow morning and scoop that old Mr. Porsch. Papa, what's dissipation?"

"Mind your manners, Reuben," Verdita said. "Mr. Porsch is a perfectly nice man. And squalid shacks and dissipation are no subjects for the dinner table."

While the conversation went on around her, Hildy thought

about Samuel being with his father. Was Samuel's father an
Indian? She had seen a few of the Puyallups around town. Mrs.
Blackwell bought clams from an elderly Indian woman every
week. Gramma Dayhab was her name and, when she didn't
have clams to sell, she sold baskets that she'd made. Hildy saw
Gramma Dayhab sitting outside of the wharf hotel with piles of
split strips of spruce roots and cedar bark, her nimble fingers
turning the wood into containers of all shapes and sizes. Mrs.
Blackwell had started collecting them. But Samuel didn't look
like her, or like any of the men she'd seen.

"Papa," she asked, "where do the Indians live?"

"On the reservation."

"Yes, but where is it?"

"It's near the Puyallup River. Why?"

"Can we go there sometime?"

"Why would you want to do that?"

"Hmmm, just to see what it looks like. We didn't have reserva-
tions in Pennsylvania."

"No, we can't," Verdita said firmly. "It isn't a place for little
girls to be roaming around and I'm sure the people don't want
you staring at them. Now, if you're finished eating, please carry
your dishes to the kitchen and tell Chong we're ready for dessert."

Hildy sighed. She gathered up hers and Dovie's things and
carried them to where Chong was waiting to wash up before
leaving for his own place. "Mama said we're ready for dessert,
Chong."

"Okay." Chong took a towel off something he'd removed
from the oven and, when he shook his head, Hildy knew it was
rice pudding. Verdita'd had a hard time explaining the concept
of rice with sugar, cinnamon, and a handful of raisins to him.

"That smells delicious." Hildy grinned at him.

"Thunk vely stange."

"Have you ever had rice pudding?"

"Thunk no."

"I'll save you some."

Chong carried the dish to the table and Hildy followed with plates. As she'd promised, Chong had a dish in the kitchen later while Hildy scraped the dinner plates into a slop bucket and stacked them on the dry sink until water heated.

"Chong," she said while she worked. "Do you know Reuben's friend, Samuel?"

"Thunk maybe, yes."

"I thought I saw him on the beach, today, with some Indians."

Chong scowled. "Indians no good."

"Why?"

"Too much go clazy in head with . . ." He stopped to search for the word.

"Alcohol?"

"Thunk, maybe, yes. Fight, faa down. No good."

He hadn't answered her question, Hildy realized. *Probably because he doesn't have the words.* "Chong," she said slowly, "would you like me to teach you proper English. I can do it while school's out. I'm sure Mama would think it's a wonderful idea."

Chong's face lit up. "Thunk maybe, yes, Missy Hida," he said with enthusiasm.

"And did you like the rice pudding?"

At her question, his beaming smile turned to a scowl. "Thunk maybe, no," he said, shaking his head.

69

CHAPTER 7

Verdita agreed that teaching Chong English was a good idea, and Hildy went to bed hoping she'd wake up in the middle of the night so she could think about how to start. She did wake up, several times, but with the beginnings of a stuffy nose. When dawn broke and it was time to punch her bread down and set it to its second rising, she got up with little enthusiasm. Every night, when the kitchen was warm, she set loaves on the back of the stove to rise. However, the house was always cold in the morning and Hildy had to start the stove up and hurry to prepare the dough so it could start rising for the second time. If she didn't work fast enough, the yeast died. Throughout winter, both she and Reuben had learned to pull on robes, step into slippers, and make a dash for the kitchen. With a heavy sigh and trying to breathe through her stuffy nose, she got up before the rest of the family, hoping the kitchen was at least a little warm.

When she reached it, Chong had started the stove and had begun heating the water that Tom Quan delivered daily. However, even the sight of her healthy bread dough didn't lift Hildy's spirits. At least in Johnstown we had a pump, she thought, mulishly, as she ladled water into a bowl to wash her hands and face.

Chong came in while she greased her pans, and began forming the loaves. "When len Engliss?"

"I don't know. I have to check with Mama."

At her tone of voice, Chong said, "You seck?"

"No."

"You no wan teach?"

"No!" Hildy put her pans on the back of the stove and covered them with a clean flour sack. Then she got the milk from the small root cellar and poured a glass. "I'm sorry," she said, as she sat at the table. "I do want to teach you. It will be good practice in case I want to be a teacher someday. Mama has to tell me what time of day, that's all."

Chong nodded but he kept giving her questioning looks. "Wha you do today?" He put the coffee pot on and began frying sausages.

"Hmmm." Hildy had her arms on the table and rested her head on them. She couldn't smell the meat cooking but the room was warming up and it made her sleepy. "Reuben's being punished today for coming home late yesterday. Did you know that? He'll be here all day and has to work in the garden *and* take care of Dovie." Chong muttered something and Hildy grinned. She knew Chong thought having Reuben around to help for a whole day was a mixed blessing. She gave her runny nose a surreptitious swipe and considered the gift of time Reuben's punishment gave her. She had until dinner time at noon to do as she pleased. Her father would be at work and, thanks to a low tide, her mother was going to walk on the beach to Old Tacoma with Mrs. Wilkeson to see the new Episcopal church.

While Hildy traced invisible circles on the table, Chong put a plate of sausages and eggs in front of her. "I'm not really hungry, Chong."

"You eat o I tell motha you seck."

Hildy picked up a fork and cut off a piece of meat. It didn't have much taste and her throat felt funny but she ate it anyway. "I know what I'll do," she said. "I can't believe I forgot. I have to return Miss Violet's scarf."

The scarf loaned to Hildy the night of the storm had long since been cleaned and pressed. Verdita even repaired a small tear by embroidering a violet over it and adding stems and leaves. After that, however, it sat in the sewing basket. Somehow, Verdita found excuses not to return it every time Hildy suggested calling on the ladies. Thinking about the visit made eating easier and Hildy tucked in. She finished breakfast as the rest of the family entered the dining room.

"Have you already eaten?" Verdita asked as Hildy took her dishes to the washbasin and went to check her bread.

"Yes, Chong made me eggs and sausages." She avoided Chong's gaze and slipped the bread into the oven. "I'm going to get dressed." With energy she didn't have, Hildy left the warm room and went upstairs. One of her windows now had glass in it and the sun shone through. However, Hildy was cold and chose a navy blue wool dress that had belonged to Cousin Elsie. Originally, it had ugly brown and yellow trim, but Verdita replaced that with a white collar and cuffs and a bit of lace. *If it weren't for Mama, I'd look awful. Aunt Glady has terrible taste in clothes.*

After she'd dressed, Hildy ran down to the kitchen in time to take out her bread. She now had a third customer, Mr. Boyer, who operated a pile driver. After the first time Mr. Boyer showed up, Papa and Hildy sat down and created a business ledger. Hildy bought her own ingredients and kept track of her profits. Hearing about her enterprise, General Sprague gave her a mechanical bank with Punch and Judy on it. Every time the men paid Hildy, she let Dovie put the coins in the bank and set the figures moving. Of course, not all the money she received fit the slot; the mill money didn't, but Hildy had a cigar box for that.

As per their custom, the men began arriving a little after 9 o'clock. Mr. Peak was always first. He had recently acquired a set of ill-fitting false teeth of which he was very proud. "Good morning, miss," he said with a broad smile when Hildy opened the door.

"Good morning, Mr. Peak." Hildy handed him his loaf and took his coins.

Mr. Peak shuffled his feet awkwardly, looked down, looked around the yard, and finally looked at Hildy. "Miss, can you make pie?"

"Why, yes, I can." Hildy crossed her fingers behind her back. She couldn't but Mama could teach her. "Do you want me to make you one?"

"Yes, ma'am. Come spring Ma always started forcing rhubarb for pies. I surely would like one."

"Well, that's just fine, Mr. Peak. You let me see what I can do."

Mr. Peak left and Misters Rogers and Boyer came and left also. Hildy located her mother's cookbook, *The Dinner Question*, and sat down to read what Tabitha Tickletooth had to say about making pies. In the meantime, Reuben went out to cut wood, her father went to work, and her mother left with Mrs. Wilkeson. Every time a door opened both the canary, Jenny Lind, and Hildy heard birds outside singing, and Jenny Lind responded with trills of her own. Hildy waited for fifteen minutes, put on a red cape-like zouave jacket and straw hat, wrapped the scarf in a piece of paper, and left the house.

Things seemed to be bustling as Hildy walked down A Street. Men's voices and the sounds of hammering filled the air. At Frank Cook's house, near the north end of A Street close to Seventh Street, Mrs. Cook was chasing a stray cow out of her flower beds. At the corner of Pacific and Seventh, Hildy passed two women who were discussing a gold discovery on the Michelle River in the foothills of Mount Tacoma. Almost every business with a hitching rail out front had a horse or two tied up. While Hildy waited for a Cogswell dray full of barrels to pass so she could safely cross the street, she saw several men going into the baths next to Jacob Halstead's hotel. *I'm so glad I don't have to bathe there after them.* Her father bought a hip bath from a family who was leaving town, and Chong boiled water to fill it on Saturday nights.

When the dray was well past, Hildy crossed Pacific Avenue and started up the hill. After Pacific came Railroad Avenue, which was nothing more than an alley, then C Street followed by South D, where Miss Violet lived.

As she walked, Hildy noticed that in the few months since she and her family had been in town, wooden buildings now stood where many of the tents had been. There were few fences, however, and Hildy saw several pigs rooting and wallowing.

At C Street she had to wait for a wagon carrying lumber before crossing. After that, it was a short walk to D Street, where she turned right and continued until she found the correct house. A curtain moved in the window of a house next door as Hildy knocked on the front door. *Perhaps the ladies don't have many visitors.*

This time, Miss Rose opened the door. "Well, look at what the tide brought in. It's Hildy Bacom. We never thought to see you again. Come in, child. Come in."

Hildy entered with a happy smile, glad to see her friends again. Miss Lily, whom she barely remembered, and Miss Violet sat at a table with the remains of breakfast waiting to be cleared away.

"I brought back your scarf, Miss Violet."

"Here, dearie, let me take your coat." Hildy divested herself of the zouave jacket and hat, and Miss Rose put them on a chair. She pulled another chair up to the table and Hildy handed the paper-wrapped parcel to Miss Violet and sat down.

"Isabeau!" Rose shouted while Miss Violet took the parcel.

"We have a visitor. Bring another cup of hot chocolate."

If Hildy was startled at the shouting, or that Miss Rose didn't say "please," she didn't show it. Instead, she watched as Violet unfolded the scarf. "It had a tear and Mama fixed it," she said, as the woman fingered the embroidered flower.

"It's lovely."

Miss Rose looked at the flower. "Well, now, I wonder if your ma could do some fancy stitching for me."

"I don't know. Maybe. Right now she's teaching my friend Nell to mend."

"You must thank her for me." Violet smiled at Hildy.

"Yes, I surely will. She would have come herself but she and Mrs. Wilkeson went to Old Tacoma to see the new church." Hildy turned toward the other side of the table. "How are you feeling, Miss Lily? You were poorly when I was here before."

Before Lily could answer, Miss Rose said, "Mrs. Wilkeson, huh? I met up with her once. 'Good mornin' Mrs. Wilkeson,' I says to her, just as nice as could be and she just puckered up her face and sailed right on by me. Thinks she's a huckleberry above a persimmon, that one. Isabeau!"

This time Hildy jumped at the shout and Isabeau appeared almost immediately with a cup. At the sight of Hildy sitting at the table her eyes widened.

"Good morning, Miss Isabeau. Thank you for the chocolate. How are you today?"

"*Mon dieu.* Does your mama know you're here?"

"Mama was going to come, but she's always so busy and I wanted to return Miss Violet's scarf."

Isabeau muttered something in French and said, "Well, drink your chocolate and then you better go."

"Never mind, Isabeau," Miss Rose said. "I'll see to it."

While Isabeau picked up some of the dirty dishes and left the room, Hildy looked around. The room didn't seem as cozy as it had the night she found shelter there. Daylight showed that the rosy wall coverings were coming loose in areas and that no one had dusted for quite a while. Nevertheless, she smiled at the women.

"Shouldn't you be in school, dear?" Miss Rose tightened the sash around her robe.

Hildy took a deep sniff of her drink and the steam helped open her nose. "School is out." She took a long swallow but the hot chocolate didn't seem to have a taste.

"Do you still have your little business?"

"Yes, ma'am. I now have three gentlemen buying my bread and one asked for a pie. I've never made a pie but I expect I can learn."

"I expect you can. You seem to be a very enterprising sort of girl." Miss Violet smiled.

"Did you ever make a pie?"

"Yes, when I was about your age and before she passed, my ma taught me how to make Chess pie."

"Oh, you're practically an orphan then, aren't you?"

"Yes, dear, I am. I don't even know if my pa is alive or dead."

"That's really sad. I think you're a very romantic figure."

At the words, Miss Violet's eyebrows went up and Miss Rose choked. Miss Lily leaned over and pounded her on the back. Hildy noticed the remains of powder around the neck of Miss Lily's robe.

"I never heard of Chess pie, Miss Violet."

"It's like custard except it has cornmeal in it. When you live on a farm like we did, you have lots of eggs and butter and milk."

"Well." Hildy considered the words carefully. "We don't have lots of anything so I best ask Mama." She finished her cocoa, put the cup on the table, and looked at Miss Rose. "May I ask you a question, please?"

"Well, now you can surely ask. Whether we answer or not depends on what you want to know."

"Do you ladies all live together here without husbands?"

The three exchanged looks and Miss Lily smiled. "Yes, we do, dearie."

"But where does your money come from? Papa says prices in New Tacoma are fearfully high."

"We have friends who help us out." Miss Rose stood up. "Now, dear, if you've finished your cocoa . . ."

"Of course. Mama says a lady's call lasts for only fifteen minutes. I mustn't overstay." Hildy pushed her chair back and stood up. "Thank you for the cocoa. Miss Isabeau makes better cocoa than Chong does. Of course, there isn't any cocoa in China, is there? So how would he know? But I expect he'll learn."

Hildy put on her jacket and hat and the three ladies walked her to the door. Unexpectedly, Miss Violet leaned down and kissed her cheek. "Thank you for the gift, Hildy."

"Oh, but it wasn't a gift, you know. It was *your* scarf."

"It's another kind of gift I'm talking about, dear. Now you be careful walking back, you hear?"

"I will. Goodbye. Thank you for letting me visit."

"You're welcome."

And it was only when Hildy was nearing D Street that she realized she hadn't been asked to come again.

The streets were even busier on Hildy's way home than they had been earlier. Under ordinary circumstances she would have enjoyed watching the activity. However, even walking downhill made her tired and she stopped to look at the big vegetable garden the Chinese had created on Eleventh between D and C Streets. In spite of New Tacoma's rainy weather, the men had created irrigation ditches, filling them with water from the hill's various springs. Tiny green shoots already pierced the surface of the soil. Approaching Pacific Avenue, near Mr. Dobrin's fruit stand, a roaming sheep stole apples. The little town had more unpenned livestock than Hildy had ever seen. She'd gone only a few feet when Mr. Dobrin came running and waving a broom at the animal. Hildy laughed when it ran a few hundred feet, stopped, turned around, and came back.

She was at the corner of Pacific Avenue waiting to cross when she saw a long speckled brown feather in the middle of the road. *Oh, how pretty.* She darted out to get it. Because of her cold, Hildy didn't hear the sound of pounding hooves. An angry bull had apparently escaped from its wharf pen and run up the trail to town. With the feather in her hand, Hildy looked up and saw it charging down the road. The bull's black body gleamed with sweat. When he was only a few yards away, she saw the points on his curved horns, the way he gestured angrily with them, the breath coming from his nostrils, and the fury in his eyes. It flashed through her mind that the bull was in a rage over her red zouave jacket. He dipped his head and changed direction to charge straight at her. Hildy froze. Then someone swept her out of the way, up onto the wooden walk, and smashed her against the building. The animal slowed slightly, undecided whether or not to follow them. Then it gave a bellow and raced by, his hooves pounding the dirt road, sending mud clods flying. For a few seconds, Hildy and her rescuer stayed frozen together. Men ran into the street, shouting in an attempt to corral the animal.

"Are you all right?" Samuel stepped back, letting Hildy see who her rescuer was.

She didn't hear his question. Her face was white and shocked as reaction to the near accident set in. Until Samuel put his arms around her, she felt as if she would faint. Hildy gripped him hard and buried her head in his shoulder, shaking. Eventually, when the trembling stopped, she became embarrassingly aware that Samuel's arms didn't feel like Reuben's, and she wondered if the fast beating heart she felt was his or hers.

"Is she hurt?" shouted a man who had witnessed the bull's near miss.

At his words, Samuel waved at the man to indicate no harm done. Hildy straightened up and pulled away from him. "You saved my life."

"Didn't you hear him? What were you doing?"

"Picking up a feather." Hildy looked at her empty hands and at the road. "I guess it's gone."

"A feather?"

"I've been saving feathers to make a fan."

For a minute Samuel looked at her, then his lips lifted in a smile and the dimple she hadn't noticed before appeared. "You have dirt on your face." He rubbed at the small mole near her mouth and laughed at his mistake.

Hildy became aware that her hat was gone and that her hair had fallen about her face. "Oh, dear." She blushed and looked around. "I've lost another hat. Mama will wonder what I've been doing with them."

At her words, Samuel scanned the area until he saw the hat where it had blown onto a short stretch of wooden sidewalk and rested near the door of George Orchard's grocery store. While Hildy waited, he ran over to get it.

"Thank you, Samuel," she said when he handed it to her.

Samuel stood silently for a minute while she brushed dirt off the brim. "I'll get you some feathers."

"Would you? That would be ever so kind." When she lifted her eyes to his, Samuel flushed. "Samuel," she said, hesitantly, "why won't you come and visit us? Mama wants you to see how we fixed the house you found for us. It's my birthday next week, maybe you can come then. We whitewashed the walls and Mama made curtains and we even have a few glass windows now. Not all of them, of course. Papa has to order them up from Portland and they're very dear, you know." She stopped for breath. "Samuel," she started again, "I saw you yesterday—at the beach."

Samuel's friendly look disappeared. His gray eyes darkened to black and seemed as angry as the bull's had been. Her own eyes widened and she stepped back. "I, I must have been wrong. It must have been someone who looked like you. I . . ."

But Samuel was already walking away.

CHAPTER 8

Walking home after her morning with Mrs. Wilkeson, Verdita thought about how she admired the women in New Tacoma she'd met thus far. Mrs. Money, who was in the thick of things with her husband as they started a newspaper they were calling the *North Pacific Times;* Alice Blackwell, who in her spare time scoured the beach for shells, which she traded with collectors back east; and now Mrs. Wilkeson, who was devoted to horticulture. During their walk to Old Tacoma, Mrs. Wilkeson pointed out native flowers such as Oregon grape with its clusters of bright yellow flowers, trillium with their white, star faces, and the spotted leaves of plants that would result in fawn lilies later on.

"I hear folks over in Steilacoom have a new gorse, something from Scotland called broom," Mrs. Wilkeson said as they walked the high tide line. "It's supposed to bloom bright yellow flowers in spring. I hope to have some in my garden by next year."

There is so little beauty for the women here, Verdita thought as she swung out in a long-legged stride, *but they work so hard to find it where they can and to bring up their children properly.*

She inhaled the salty air and thought that since spring had arrived, New Tacoma had its best possible side on display. Crooked stunted madrona trees with peeling red and yellow bark crowded the conifers. Rhododendrons showed the barest hint of the pink blooms to come, and in the distance lording over it all, was Mount Tacoma, which only recently had been successfully climbed by a former Union officer named Hazard Stevens. As if to agree with her thoughts, a Steller's jay peered down from a dogwood and squawked. When her house came in sight, Verdita's eyes dwelt on it with affection. All of them, working together, had turned the old building into a real home.

At that moment, a mill whistle blasted, letting people know that it was dinner time. Verdita had left a piece of mutton in the oven to slow cook and by now Hildy would have peeled potatoes and set the table. Chong would have the coffee on and soon Ira would be home. She opened the door and called, "hello."

"We're in the kitchen, Mama," Reuben answered.

Verdita entered the room, removing her hat as she did, and saw her son setting the table, Dovie sitting on the floor playing with a strand of potato peel, and Chong poking dubiously at the mutton.

"Where's Hildy?" She tied on an apron and took the peeling away from Dovie.

"I think she's sick, Mama," Reuben said. "She's in bed."

"Sick?" Verdita left the kitchen and hurried upstairs.

The morning's events—the near miss with the bull, Samuel's initial warmth, followed by his abrupt departure, coupled with her cold—had left Hildy feeling decidedly fragile. She'd done her best to fix her hair and hide what she could of it under her hat, walked slowly home, and entered the house with a sigh of relief. In the kitchen, while she'd dipped a glass of water out of the pail, Hildy had heard Chong and Reuben in the yard. Even though they had a clock, Papa had put a noon-mark on one of the windowsills, and she had been surprised to see that the sun's rays creeping up it indicated noon was farther off than she'd thought.

She'd opened the back door and shouted hoarsely, "I'm home."

Outside, Hildy had seen the reason for their loud voices.

Chong had found a length of rope, tied it to a high tree branch, and attached it to a square piece of wood at the bottom. Reuben had been sitting on the seat with Dovie on his lap while Chong pushed them. Chong had grinned at her and Reuben had managed a wave, but Hildy had been too tired to join them. Instead, she'd refilled the glass and had taken it with her as she'd climbed the stairs to her room.

The little corner room was pleasantly warm, but Hildy had been cold. She'd taken her dress off and hung it on a nail and put on her robe. *I'll just rest for a little while.* She'd crawled into bed and fallen asleep, rousing only when her mother appeared.

"Hildy." From the open door Verdita could hear her daughter's raspy breathing. "Darling, what have you been doing? You sound awfully congested."

"I can't breathe very well." Hildy turned her flushed face from the wall. "My head aches."

Verdita put her wrist on Hildy's forehead. "No wonder. You're burning up. I'll get you something for it." She tucked the bed quilts firmly around Hildy, hurried from the room, and returned to the kitchen.

"Chong, I want you to go to town and try to find me some lemons and honey. Hurry, and Reuben, run to meet your father and ask him to bring home some whiskey. Scoot, now, both of you."

Something about her mother's voice upset Dovie and she began to cry. "Oh, dear." Verdita scooped the baby up and cuddled her. Dovie was tired and hungry, and she needed a clean diaper. Verdita changed her and found a piece of cooked bacon for her to gnaw on. After that, she mixed mustard and flour with hot water. Back upstairs, she put a piece of cotton on Hildy's chest, spread the mustard mixture on it, and covered that with another piece of cotton. Hildy turned her head away and gave a deep, bronchial cough, and Verdita ran back to the kitchen to fill jars with hot water. When Hildy was surrounded with the jars, including one on her chest to help loosen the phlegm, Verdita made a list of things for Chong to buy when he returned: chamomile, garlic, and a chicken. Her thoughts stalled as Ira and Reuben returned.

"Reuben says Hildy's sick." Ira handed over the whiskey.

"She's beet red and burning up with fever. Her chest is very congested but she can't seem to cough anything up."

Chong was breathless when he finally returned. Verdita took the lemons and honey and sent him back with the new list. She measured whiskey into hot water, added honey, and carried the drink upstairs. Hildy was dozing but she roused enough to take several sips.

"I'll send Reuben to tell General Sprague that I won't be back this afternoon," Ira said.

Verdita sat on the bed and stroked her daughter's head. "No, there's no need for both of us to be here. We'll just get in each other's way. If you could, please, dish up dinner and eat with Reuben and feed Dovie. It will be better for the other two if you stick to your routine. Hildy will sleep now and I'll be here."

In the kitchen, Ira found that though the mutton was fine, the potatoes had boiled to mush. He salvaged what he could, added butter and meat drippings, and gave Reuben a bowl for Dovie. While Reuben fed the baby, Ira sliced bread and tomatoes and made sandwiches. He poured himself some coffee and Reuben a glass of milk, and made no objection when Reuben dunked. Chong returned while they were finishing and Ira decided to take Reuben down to the wharf. The boy could explore while he worked.

For the next three days, Reuben and Chong took care of the house and Dovie. Chong cooked and Reuben learned to change a diaper. Verdita left Hildy's room only long enough to make chicken soup or to smash garlic in hot milk.

In a town of only a few hundred settlers, word of her illness spread fast. One afternoon Samuel knocked at the door. Reuben, who held a big wooden spoon in one hand and wore a flour sack apron, answered the door.

"Hildy's sick."

"I heard. How bad is she?"

Reuben's eyes filled with tears. "No one will tell me, not even Chong, and I'm not allowed to see her."

"I'll go up." With Reuben's eyes on him, Samuel climbed the stairs. His soft, leather-clad feet making soft, whispering sounds on the wooden floorboards. He remembered the day he'd shown them the house and the room that Hildy had claimed for her own. The door to that room stood open and he looked in. Verdita slept the sleep of exhaustion in a chair near the bed. Perhaps sensing him, Hildy turned her head and tried to smile. As he stood in the doorway, he could hear the sound of her labored breathing.

Back on the first floor, he walked toward the kitchen, saying to Reuben, "She needs sweating. Come on. I need flour sacks and lots of boiling water."

Reuben filled a pot with water and put it on the stove. He found the sacks and Samuel stitched them into a large square. Outside, he cut three stout tree limbs and attached them together loosely at the top so that he could spread them apart at the bottom. Then the two boys climbed the stairs. Reuben carried the sticks and cloth while Samuel brought a jug of hot water and a box. He put the box next to the bed and the jug of water on it. Then he showed Reuben how to spread the small teepee frame around Hildy's head and draped the flour towels over both it and the water. Within a few minutes, the makeshift tent filled with warm steamy air. Though Hildy's eyes remained closed she started to breathe easier. Verdita woke while Samuel worked and smiled at him gratefully. He nodded at her and left the room. An hour or so later, when Verdita descended to the kitchen, she found him heating something on the stove.

"It's licorice and Oregon grape," Samuel said. "My—some people say tea made from their roots is good for catarrh."

After a few minutes, the concoction began to boil. Samuel poured the peculiar-smelling beverage into a cup, wrapped a piece of cloth around it, and carried it upstairs. Reuben went downstairs to replace the hot water in the jug and Samuel lifted the edge of the makeshift tent. Under it, Hildy's face glistened with sweat. He carefully removed the cloth, tipped her head and held the cup to her lips. "Drink it all."

Hildy's stomach and chest ached from coughing but, at the sight of Samuel's face so close to hers and his gray eyes staring so intently, her heart also felt strange. She did as she was told, pausing to rest occasionally, her eyes never leaving his. When she was done, she leaned into his hand. "Thank you," she said, before falling back onto the pillows.

Verdita, who had followed him, dipped a cloth into a basin of warm water and wiped Hildy's face before Samuel replaced the tent. The queer feeling in her own chest was very different from Hildy's. *She's only barely thirteen and she's setting her heart on this strange boy.* However, Verdita was too tired to argue when Samuel sat in the chair, crossed his arms, and said, "I'll stay."

Day turned to night and then returned. Verdita, Reuben, and Ira ate in the kitchen and Samuel disappeared for an hour or two to his own home. Verdita spent some time with Dovie. Chong and Reuben ran the house as best they could. Ira went to work and, when he returned, sat with Samuel so his wife could sleep. A mouse scurried on the windowsill outside. It disappeared when an owl hooted. Suddenly, Hildy began coughing violently and she sat up. This time, she was able to bring up some of the choking phlegm. Ira helped her out of the bed and onto a chair so he could change the wet bedding, and Samuel went downstairs. He returned with more hot water and another cup of the root tea. As dark gave way to light, they kept Hildy sweating and drinking, and the coughing began to clear her chest. When dawn broke and Verdita returned to her vigil, Hildy was resting peacefully. Ira stood up and put his arms around Verdita and she started to cry. While they held on to each other, Samuel disappeared.

Two weeks passed before Hildy was able to leave her room. During her convalescence, spring gave way to early summer. The first morning she came downstairs, Jenny Lind sang rapturously, responding to the wild birds' chatter, and the back door stood open, allowing fresh air to sweep the house clean of its stale smells. In the yard, Verdita hung laundry on a line Chong had strung. Chong fussed over the vegetable garden, and Dovie walked a few steps, fell on her chubby bottom, and pulled herself up again. Every time she fell, she laughed and clapped her hands.

Hildy sat on the step in the sun and Reuben saw her first. "Hildy," he shouted. "You didn't get a ride on my swing." He dropped a load of stove wood and ran to where she sat. "Come on, I'll push you."

Verdita draped the shirt she'd picked up over the line and crossed the yard. "Daughter, do you think you should be up?"

"Oh, Mama, yes. I'm tired of bed and it feels so good out here." Hildy closed her eyes and, as was her habit, lifted her face to the sun.

Verdita sat next to Hildy and stroked her hair. It hung in lackluster strands and she'd lost weight. She watched as her daughter put her arms behind her and supported herself on the palms of her hands. Hildy leaned back, extended her legs out into the warmth, and took a deep breath. The color will return to her face, Verdita thought, but Hildy's birthday had come and gone and, somehow, it seemed as if the illness had stolen Hildy's youth and replaced it with the beginnings of a young woman. *Ah, well.* Verdita watched Dovie toddle toward them. *Dovie is a baby still and maybe there'll be more.*

While thoughts of another child went through Verdita's head, Reuben came and sat on Hildy's other side. The step was barely long enough for the three of them and he pushed and pushed until Hildy started laughing and pushed back. She laughed harder when Chong joined them.

"When you teesh English?"

"Mama?"

Verdita looked at Chong's eager face. "How about every morning for half an hour right after the breakfast dishes are done? You can use your slate and I'll have Papa get some chalk." She started to say more but a man came around the corner of the house.

"Mr. Peak." Hildy stood up. "I'm so sorry that I haven't been able to bake any bread but I will be starting to bake again tomorrow."

"Well, now, Miss Hildy, you don't make no never mind about that. I heerd that you was poorly and I brung you a little present."

Mr. Peak brought out something he had under his coat. He held both hands out and put a small yellow chick in Hildy's. She took the bird carefully and held it loosely so that it could wiggle. Then she put it to her cheek to feel the soft baby feathers.

Verdita also stood up and Mr. Peak took off his hat and revealed a fringe of gray hair on an otherwise bald head.

"This is awfully kind of you." Verdita smiled and Mr. Peak's dentures gleamed when he smiled back.

"He's lovely, Mr. Peak," Hildy continued. "Does he have a name?"

"No, Miss Hildy. I figure you can do that, and if it's a gal chick, well, you'll have some eggs for that cookin' of yours."

"And your pie, I haven't forgotten about that. Give me a couple days and I'll have the pie ready for you."

"Yes, ma'am. I will. You take care now."

"I've never had a chicken before. Thank you, Mr. Peak."

Mr. Peak left and Hildy asked Chong if he could make a box for it to live in until it was big enough to go outside. Verdita returned to her laundry and Reuben filled the woodboxes. Hildy put the chick on the ground and was watching it explore when Nell appeared.

"Gosh, I'm glad to see you." Nell took over Reuben's spot on the step. "It's been really dull since school got out and Mama kept me home because she's been under the weather and Pa's stayed out late and that makes her cry. I tell you, if my man stayed out late, I wouldn't cry, I'd just lock the door on him. Of course, Mama cries most all the time anyway, especially when another baby is about to show up. I hope one isn't. We don't need any more. Wash and cook, wash and cook, that's all I do. When I get old enough, I'll do all I can not to ever have one."

Hildy laughed. "Not all babies are as sweet as Dovie is, I guess."

"Oh, Dovie's all right but think how much more you could have without her. Why everything I get has been worn by my two sisters before me. At least she's younger than you."

Verdita crossed the yard carrying her empty laundry basket. "Hildy, Nell dropped by almost every day to see how you were doing. You'll stay for dinner, won't you, Nell?"

"Can Hildy and I go for a walk, too?"

"Hildy can walk to Fife's Store and see if there's any mail, but she'll have to rest after dinner."

"In that case, yes. Mama's having fatback and greens, and for dessert a slice for each of us of fruit cake. We've had that old thing since Christmas and it tastes like it, too, but Mama shares it out so it'll last until next Christmas. When I get rich, I'm never going to eat fruit cake."

The girls hopped up and left, and Verdita continued on inside, wondering if Nell was a good companion for Hildy. *If she just weren't so outspoken.* It was obvious that her mother either didn't know how to or had no time to teach the girl how to behave in polite society. But Hildy liked her and Hildy was stubborn, and like a prickly pear when it came to making friends. She either liked people or she didn't. If she did, she was loyal to the nth degree and if she didn't, she couldn't be bothered to pretend. "I'd rather be alone than with people I don't like," she explained once. "It seems like such a waste of time." Oh, well, Verdita thought, at least Glady doesn't have to meet Nell. The idea made her laugh, then shudder.

Nell, in the meantime, felt like she'd done something wrong but wasn't sure what. "I'm going to ask your mother to teach me how to be a lady," she said abruptly as the pair passed an empty lot belonging to Mr. and Mrs. Blackwell.

"What?"

"Well Ma can't teach me."

Hildy stopped abruptly and two Chinese men carrying slop buckets veered abruptly to the side to avoid a collision. "My Aunt Glady is a lady and she's as dull as dishwater, and poor Cousin Elsie doesn't have a bit of fun the whole day long."

"I don't care. I want a pretty house and pretty clothes and a maid so I'll never have to do a lick of work. And I can't get them going on the way I am." Nell's eyes narrowed and her expression grew fierce. "New Tacoma's okay for now but I'm not always going to live here."

Hildy clapped her hands together. "You can be like Miss Caroline Richings. She came here once; Mrs. Blackwell told me all about her. She sings opera. Can you sing?"

"I can whistle." Nell demonstrated and a horse tied to a nearby hitching rail pulled at his reins and whinnied.

Both girls laughed and Nell linked her arm through Hildy's. "We best be getting along or we won't get back for dinner. And I don't want to miss it."

"Lesson number one." Hildy pulled her arm loose and turned to face her friend. "Never talk about food like that and don't say bad things about your family. It isn't done. Find everything good to say and never speak of the hurtful things."

"Not even to you?"

"You can talk to me because we're intimate best friends, but no one else. Always hold your head up and if anyone says something you don't like, you look down your nose at them and say, 'do tell.' "

Nell giggled. "I can do that easily enough. You just watch me."

As they continued walking Nell gestured toward one of New Tacoma's better homes. "Look, there's the roof of the Wilkesons' house. It's the absolute social center of New Tacoma. Your mama knows Mrs. Wilkeson, doesn't she? Do you know they fill twelve tubs of water every morning and water their plants every evening? Imagine having the time to do that for a bunch of flowers. Last year their garden was a regular bower."

"Why don't they irrigate like the Chinese do?"

"I think most people around here would as soon cut off an arm as copy the Chinese. Did you know that Mr. Cogswell once paid a Chinaman to get him to move off a lot next to where the Cogswells wanted to build?" She stopped and caught Hildy's hand. "Hildy! Look."

They had reached Fife's Store and a piece of paper was tacked onto a wall.

An invitation is extended to you and yours to repair on July 10th, at 8:00 to the Reynolds and Howell Hall on the second floor, above their livery stable to see Mr. James H. Guild demonstrate that crown jewel of modern inventions,

The Phonograph.

Donations taken at the door.

"Miss Sparkle mentioned phonographs, once, remember?" Nell reread the sign. "She has a sister who lives in Michigan and the sister wrote her it was a new machine that plays sounds. Imagine someone bringing one clear out here."

"I simply have to see it." Hildy could hardly take her eyes off the flyer. "Aunt Glady thinks we live in teepees and that the Indians might scalp us. She doesn't think we have the least bit of culture. If I write and tell her that we sat in a hall and listened to a phonograph, she'll be absolutely green with envy."

The door to Mr. Fife's store opened and a man stopped to avoid a collision with them.

"Hello Mr. Cosper. How's your new wife?" Nell smiled at him.

"Fine and dandy, thank you for asking."

"Did Mr. Fife order anything exciting for the store?"

"You'll have to wait and see, miss." He tipped his hat and hopped into a buggy.

"He's a traveling salesman," Nell explained as she and Hildy went inside and waited for their eyes to adjust to the dimness, "and he just got married. Miss Sparkle told Mama that his new bride is ever so pretty and that he worships the ground she walks on. Hello, Mr. Fife."

"Good morning ladies. Hildy, are you here for the mail?"

"Yes, sir."

Hildy and Nell followed Mr. Fife through a maze of molasses barrels, kegs of nails, and crocks of sauerkraut whose pungent odor permeated the store, to a counter where he sorted the envelopes. He handed Hildy several.

"Here you are."

"Thank you."

"Did you see the flyer about the phonograph? Should be something—to hear actual recorded voices. Just think, the president can talk into it and his voice will be recorded for all posterity, for anyone anyplace, to hear. Why, it'll keep him alive even if he's dead. That'll sure be something."

"It certainly will, Mr. Fife," Nell said, "and when I'm famous, I'm going to have my voice put on a recorder so people can hear me forever."

Mr. Fife scowled, leaned on the store counter, and looked at Nell over his glasses. "You mocking me, young'un?"

"No, Mr. Fife. I'm just telling it true."

"Don't sound to me that way."

Nell tossed her head and turned toward the door. "Do tell," she said. "Do tell."

CHAPTER 9

To Hildy's amazement, her parents had little interest in seeing and hearing the phonograph demonstration. On the day of the event her father had to go up to the Carbonado-Wilkeson coalfields in the foothills of Mount Tacoma to make a report for General Sprague, and her mother was uncomfortable going to a hall in town, at night, on her own.

"We're not going without your father."

"But, Mama," Hildy pulled out her chair and sat down to supper. "Probably everyone in town will be there and Chong can come with us. I'm sure it will be safe."

"Chong won't be allowed." Verdita started passing slices of venison.

"Why?"

"Because he's Chinese."

At her words, Reuben's eyes widened. "What difference does that make?"

"None, if it was up to us, but it isn't up to us."

Hildy and Reuben look puzzled. "Who is it up to?"

"Well, most everyone else, I guess."

"Could he go if he was a Negro?"

"Yes, probably."

"What if he was an Indian?" Hildy wanted to know.

"I think so."

Bread followed the venison, then a gravy boat, and finally something unfamiliar to everyone except Verdita.

"What's this?" Reuben looked suspiciously at the pinwheel of something green.

"Fiddlehead fern." Verdita avoided his gaze and took a bite. When even Ira's eyes widened she added, "Mrs. Wilkeson says it's very popular in Portland."

"Well," Ira winked at Hildy and Reuben, "if it's popular in Portland then we'd better give it a try."

Supper was a more informal meal than dinner. Hildy put the meat on her bread and covered it with gravy. Reuben made a sandwich, adding lots of horseradish. Verdita fed small spoonsful of food to Dovie, between her own bites.

"But that isn't fair." Hildy washed a bit of the fern down with a large gulp of milk. "Why can't the Chinese go?"

Her father put down his fork, wiped his mouth with a napkin, and sat back in his chair. "I guess it's because many people are afraid of the Chinese."

"Afraid? Jehoshaphat, why?" Reuben looked taken aback.

Both Hildy and Reuben stopped eating to stare at their father. Even Verdita waited quietly to hear how he'd answer the question.

Ira sighed. "Men aren't always rational beings," he began. "In the United States the Chinese are supposed to have all the privileges that everyone else has. We signed a treaty with their government saying that Chinese subjects here would be treated like everyone, even be free to practice their own religious faith. But then the railroads started bringing Chinese men over by the thousands to work laying tracks, and people saw how their ways were different and that they ate strange food. But worst of all, they would work for less money than a white man would. That scared folks because when times are tough and there aren't many jobs, companies naturally want to hire the cheapest labor they can. When they hire Chinese men, the white men and their families go hungry."

"Why don't they just pay everyone the same?" Reuben asked.

"Because the white men wouldn't stand for it."

"But . . ." Hildy stopped. "It's awfully complicated, isn't it?"

"Yes, little cabbage, it is. Now eat your supper and let me eat mine." Ira smiled at her in a way that said the discussion was over. However, when it came to something she really wanted, Hildy wasn't a person to give up easily, and even if her parents wouldn't go and Chong couldn't go, she was determined to see the phonograph demonstration. There has to be a way, she thought.

"Do you have to work on the Fourth of July, Papa?" Reuben asked, a few minutes later.

"Nope, and we're going on a picnic."

"Chong, too?"

"Of course, Chong if he wants to, but he might want to be with his own people."

"Down at the end of the wharf?"

"Yes, or on the beach toward Old Tacoma. A dozen or so Chinese live there, too."

"I didn't . . ." Hildy stopped. She was going to say she'd seen much of that stretch of beach there and that there was no Chinese community in sight. However, she'd told no one about watching the Indians fishing or about seeing Samuel among them and now wasn't the time.

"Didn't what?" her mother asked.

"Nothing. I guess I just didn't know some Chinese lived there, that's all."

They finished eating in silence and after she cleared the table, Hildy went to feed food scraps to her new pet, which she'd named Chicken Little after a book Cousin Elsie once loaned her. When the chicken was big enough she would be able to roam the yard during the day, scratching for worms, but until then, Chicken Little was kept in a box behind the stove, much to Chong's disgust.

Outside, the soft evening air beckoned and Hildy left the house and sat in the swing. She was very tired but hated to go to bed before dark. And she needed to think. I just have to see the phonograph, she thought. Maybe Nell will have an idea.

However, Nell sent a short note that her family was going to Olympia to visit relatives and she didn't know when they'd be back.

In the meantime, the Fourth of July arrived and Hildy put the phonograph out of her mind. Everyone was up early. Ira carried a wooden crate to the kitchen and Verdita put in chicken she'd fried. Hildy added a dried apple pie and Reuben scrubbed potatoes they would bake later in the day. By the time everyone had added something, the box was stuffed with bread and jam, pickles, and a fat watermelon Ira had ordered from Portland. Chong, who wanted to go with them, was taking his own food. Verdita was surprised that Chong didn't want to go to the Chinese community for the rare day off. Then she remembered Alice Blackwell's words during their brief stay at the Blackwell Hotel: "he's very young and he loved taking care of Dovie." Why, thought Verdita, we've become his family. She looked at where Chong was getting a small rice pot ready and smiled.

When the food box was full, they set off. Most of the mud in the roads had dried leaving a rough, uneven terrain. The little group passed Frank Cook's house and Verdita glanced at it with envy. It wasn't just the beautiful flower garden she admired; she also envied the ingenious arrangement of pipes connected to a spring up on the hill that brought water into both the kitchen and the bathroom Mrs. Clark had held a musical at-home recently at which nearly all the ladies in town attended, and she used the occasion to proudly show off her barrels on stilts that provided water for a sink and a galvanized tub. Not even

General and Mrs. Sprague, who lived near the Clarks, had such an innovation. Hildy forgot her envy, however, when a shabby middle-aged man left Spooner's Tin Shop and walked toward them.

"Hey, it's Potato Brooks," Reuben said and shouted, "hello, Potato."

"Don't shout like that Reuben," Verdita said, "What will people think?" She nodded at Potato and would have kept walking had not Ira stopped. He handed the picnic box to Reuben and shook the man's hand.

"How are you, Potato? I heard you nearly got killed."

Potato wheezed a laugh. "The billiard table took the hit, bullet skimmed acrost it and sliced the cloth the whole way. Liked to have a fire though, when the fellow I was playing with smashed a lamp over Mr. Miller's head. Mr. Miller was the fellow what took a shot at me. I Dad, but it was some night. Courst I won't be playing at Louis's for a while. He's a mite vexed he is, blames me for the whole thing . . ." Potato looked like he was settling in for a long chat about the unfairness of barkeepers when Ira took Verdita's arm.

"Well, I'm glad to see you're okay. New Tacoma can't afford to lose her upstanding citizens. You take care of yourself now."

Potato wheezed out another laugh. "Well, sir, if I don't, who will?" He doffed his dirty, battered bowler hat, adding, "Mrs. Bacom, you're a vision of loveliness," and continued down the road whistling.

Hildy giggled and Reuben said, "Frank Clark says Potato dived right under the billiard table when the gun went off. That's what saved him." He handed the box of food back to his father.

"Mr. Clark should be more careful about what he says when children are present. I don't want you hanging around the newspaper office anymore." Verdita shook her head. "But you shouldn't repeat gossip, Reuben."

"What's the difference between repeating gossip and writing it up in the newspaper?"

"Precious little, I'm afraid. Now come along children." Ira picked up his pace and effectively put an end to the conversation.

They continued down A Street and cut over to Pacific Avenue, heading for the wharf road. While they walked Hildy looked enviously at Reuben.

"How do you know these people?"

Reuben grinned. "It's because I'm a boy." He jingled some coins in his pocket. "I run errands for people and meet all sorts. You can't 'cause you're a girl. Say, Hildy, if you was—were a boy, we could have all kinds of adventures."

"I know." Hildy agreed, and the phonograph demonstration popped back in her mind. If the rest of the family wouldn't go, she'd go alone and seeing it would be her own adventure. An idea began forming.

They passed a few men headed uptown. Hildy knew the Blackwell Hotel had a two-drink maximum and the railroad men had to go to town for more. As if echoing her thoughts, Verdita looked at them in disapproval. "I suppose they'll drink all their wages."

She and Hildy took turns carrying Dovie and once Hildy saw the eyes of feral cats watching her from under a boardwalk. A group of young men and women rode south on Pacific toward where the road ended and where people regularly gathered for picnics. Hildy wondered if she'd ever have a pretty riding costume and horse to ride.

Another ten minutes of walking down the wharf road and five minutes beyond that brought Hildy and her family to a spot where the low tide left a small rocky beach exposed. In front of them, three- and four-masted schooners, tugs and steamers bobbed in the bay. Sails snapped and seagulls swooped, hoping for handouts. Hildy loved seeing the different kinds of boats but thought the sailing ships were the prettiest. As she stared, their size overshadowed a man rowing a group of people toward Old Tacoma.

"Look, Verdita." Ira also caught sight of the rower. "There's the man I was telling you about. The next time you want to go to Old Tacoma, get John Wren to row you. He makes four trips a day."

"But I like the walk." Verdita gestured toward a spot near the high tide line. "Now, here's a good place to enjoy the day."

Ira put down the box of food with relief and helped Reuben spread out an old blanket. Verdita set Dovie on it and she, Chong, and Hildy started gathering firewood. Hildy watched as Chong made his own small fire pit, surrounding it with large rocks and covering it with a piece of metal. When both fires were burning, Ira put potatoes deep in the ashes of one and Chong set his little pot on the metal so it rested directly over the flames. He put in water and when it started to boil added the rice. Then he began examining some of the uncovered rocks.

"What are you doing?" asked Hildy who accompanied him.

"Fine food." Chong pulled a narrow blue shell about two inches long off a barnacle-covered boulder. "Mussel." He opened it with a small knife, scooped out the insides, and dropped it into a tightly woven Indian basket. When the bottom of the basket was covered with mussels, he picked up a stick and dug in the beach, uncovering some small clams. With a quick movement of his knife, Chong opened their shells and pried out the meat. He did this several times and when his basket was half full washed the basket's contents in the salt water. At the same time, he picked up some of the paper-thin, green seaweed that drifted near the tide line. Back at his fire, he cut the shellfish into small pieces and added it and the seaweed to the rice. Hildy gulped and averted her eyes.

"I brought the slate, Chong, do you want to practice?"

Hildy chose a spot upwind from the rice pot, and while they sat on a log and worked, Dovie picked up and discarded shells, and Reuben and Ira walked far enough away to where they could take their clothes off out of sight, and swim. John Wren came rowing by from the other direction with several women in his boat. Hildy saw them point and gasp before they tipped their parasols to block the sight of the naked swimmers.

"Mr. Wren had better row fast, the water is freezing." She giggled when, as soon as the rowboat was at a safe distance, Ira and Reuben dashed from the water and ran for their clothes. Then Ira threw himself on the blanket, put his hat over his eyes, and dozed off while Reuben joined Hildy and Chong.

"Chong," Reuben said, "where is your home?"

Chong looked puzzled. "This home."

"No, I mean in China, where is your home?"

Chong said something that, by careful repeating, Hildy and Reuben figured out was a place called Canton.

"How did you get here?"

"Umm," he paused to search for the words. "Govenment have company men, men bling Chinee to wok in United State. I come with oncle. Chinee govenment get pay, men get pay, Chinee get pay least."

"Does your uncle live in New Tacoma?"

"Oncle die."

"Why do you have a pigtail?" Chong looked puzzled and Reuben touched the braid that hung down the Chinese boy's back.

"Haff to haff when go back to China."

Reuben started to ask another question but Hildy saw sadness in Chong's face and interrupted. "You said those words really well, Chong. All except the R. Watch me."

Hildy opened her mouth and showed him how her tongue was positioned. "R," she said.

Chong's effort was closer to an L but she clapped her hands together and exclaimed, "Much better."

He repeated it several times, stopping when Verdita called that dinner was ready. They sat on the blanket. Verdita handed around plates and forks and Ira gave everyone but Chong a potato. Chong filled his own plate with the rice and shellfish and ate it with chopsticks. The presence of food attracted the gulls. They fought viciously over every scrap tossed their way. Verdita saw Chong eying the watermelon and decided to cut it and save Hildy's pie for later. Soon Hildy, Reuben, and Chong sat on a log competing for who could spit the seeds the farthest.

When everyone had eaten their fill, Hildy rinsed the dishes in the bay and packed them away. The temperature had climbed and Ira pulled their blanket under the shade of the trees jutting out from the wooded bank at a near right angle. He opened a book he'd brought; Verdita and Dovie fell asleep, and Chong and Reuben waded out to a submerged rock and climbed on it to fish. Left to her own devices, Hildy found a downed log big enough to stretch out on. She lay on her stomach and thought about the phonograph.

"If neither Mama nor Papa will go then I'll have to go alone, unless Nell gets back in town," she said to herself. "That means I'll have to sneak out of the house." Hildy didn't like the idea of such deception; sometimes, however, it was necessary. "But if I do, someone will see me so I'll need a disguise plus a lantern for when it gets dark."

The lantern was easily resolved. One of the first things the whole Bacom family learned in New Tacoma was how to break off the bottom of a bottle and shove a candle stub down the neck. Everyone had discarded bottle lanterns around. A proper disguise was the real issue and would take some thought.

While Hildy mused, a gentle north breeze began cooling the air. That's another thing I've learned, she thought. A north wind means more good weather.

The tide turned and started back in; Reuben and Chong climbed off their rock. A blue heron flew low on the horizon and coots bobbed along on barely perceptible waves, intent on their own business. When a piece of bull kelp surfaced, Reuben grabbed the large bulbous end and swung its long fronds around his head. "Yippee!" He ran toward Hildy, who rolled off her log and took refuge behind her mother, laughing.

"Who wants pie?" Verdita asked and everyone but Chong was ready for a slice. While they ate, and Verdita complimented Hildy on the flaky crust, Chong finished the watermelon.

In addition to his book, Ira brought a board game called "Mansion of Happiness" that Hildy and Reuben hated. "Reading all those virtues on the board is like going to church," Reuben said.

"But it has a teetotem instead of dice," Hildy said and they fell on each other laughing.

Neither of their parents knew what was so funny and Verdita agreed that it was a tedious game. However, Glady had sent it and Ira defended his sister's choice of an appropriate gift for Hildy and Reuben. They played until the temperature dropped. Then everyone pitched in and packed up so they could start home.

If possible the streets in town were even more crowded. The picnic group was headed back. Some of the men belonged to the newly organized Tacoma Invincibles and had a baseball game scheduled for later in the evening. The door to Louis Levin's saloon flew open and two men came out fighting. They were followed by a crowd hooting them on.

"New Tacoma needs its own policeman here, or at least a man closer than Sheriff Davisson over at Steilacoom," Verdita said to Ira as they hurried by.

"From what I hear, he spends most of his time arresting men in Old Tacoma. The real problem is that the jail is in Steilacoom," Ira replied.

By the time they were home, everyone was tired and feeling the effects of their sunburns.

"Hildy, can you please bring in those clothes from the line?" Verdita asked, indicating Aunt Glady's latest gift of trousers and jackets that her son had worn almost to threads.

"What a motley collection," Hildy muttered and she gathered them into a pile. But then her lips parted in a smile. *The perfect disguise. With my hair under an old hat and some coal dust on my face, no one will know me. And no one will pay any attention to a boy with a dirty face who can't cut a swell. Good Old Aunt Glady. For once she sent something useful.*

CHAPTER 10

Hildy's father was scheduled to leave for his trip to the coalfields in the foothills of Mount Tahoma on the same day as the phonograph demonstration. The family was up early and walked him to the wharf to catch the early morning train. Hildy was glad for the activity; it kept her thoughts diverted. A mismatched set of clothes from Aunt Glady was hidden in her room along with an old hat, and she'd even tested the stairs until she knew where the squeaky spots to avoid were. *Nothing to do now but wait.* For that reason, she offered to take a pair of boots down to Mr. Doherty's shoemaking and shoe repair shop to have the sole stitched.

After the Fourth of July, summer had settled in and Hildy enjoyed the walk. Stores bulged with merchandise, and the streets were crowded with people, horses, and roaming livestock. *No need now to struggle in finding dry places to cross from one side to the other.*

The cobbler's shop was one of the oldest establishments in New Tacoma, and one of the oddest places Hildy had ever seen. The shoe man had put a roof over a three-foot-wide space between two buildings, closed in the back, installed a door in front, and opened for business. If it hadn't been for the tap tap tap sound of hammering, she would have walked on past it. Fortunately, the day was warm and Mr. Doherty had his door opened. He sat on a cobbler's stool just inside with a mouth full of nails and a shoe on a cast-iron cobbler's form between his legs. While Hildy waited for him to finish, she examined the little space with interest. In the far back was a small Sibley stove and near it, a cot. The wall on one side of the narrow space had shelves that held his equipment. It's a good thing Mr. Doherty is thin; otherwise he wouldn't fit in his own shop, Hildy thought. The top shelf was piled with pieces of leather. The lowest shelf held several sizes of hammers, leather punches, a chisel, a number of differently shaped awls, and an assortment of knives. The one in the middle had an assortment of cast-iron forms in various sizes from a child's foot to a man's. Mr. Doherty had them lined up from smallest to largest.

When the cobbler's mouth was empty of nails, he looked up. "State your business, young woman."

"Someday I want a little shop just like yours." Hildy surprised even herself with the words. "It's so tidy, and everything is in reach."

"Gonna be a cobbler, are you?"

"No. It'll be a bakery."

"Hmmm. Good money in stomachs. They gotta be fed regular, three times a day. Now, state your business."

"Can you mend these boots?"

" 'Course I can. Be ready tomorrow."

Mr. Doherty took them and set them inside the door. Then he picked up another boot, put more nails in his mouth, and went back to work.

"My Uncle Edgar, Mama's oldest brother, told me that his first pair of shoes had identical shapes for the right and left foot."

This time, Mr. Doherty removed the nails and responded. "Started making a different shape for the left just before the war." He squinted at Hildy. "Your uncle in the war?"

"Yes, Papa couldn't go but Uncle Edgar enlisted in the Union Cavalry."

"Lived to tell about it?"

"Yes, but he lost an arm at the Battle of Dry Wood Creek."

Mr. Doherty nodded. "Fought for General Lee, myself. Lots of us soldiers came West after the war. Likely you'll meet some men who knew your uncle." He put the nails back and returned to the shoe. Since it was obvious the conversation was over, Hildy started home.

Thanks to the heat, the low tide, and the proliferation of roaming animals, Pacific Avenue smelled more than usual. During her various excursions to town, Hildy had seen roaming cows, a rooster charge a stray dog, and lots of chickens. Recently the newspaper contained a series of editorials protesting the antics of Mr. and Mrs. Graham's pig. Her father read the articles at supper and Hildy tried not to laugh at hearing that the swine charged ladies carrying baskets of groceries. And now, she spotted the fawn that belonged to the Lister foundry, adding its own droppings to all the rest.

The fawn was used to people, and while Hildy rubbed its ears, she watched people coming and going. Dr. and Mrs. Bostwick had been gone while she was ill, but here was Mrs. Bostwick walking down the street, attracting attention with her new hat. Hildy memorized the size and shape of the black frame. *It's draped with tulle, and has an entire white bird attached to the front. Gracious.*

Knowing her mother would be interested, she joined two other women in time to hear Mrs. Bostwick explain that the bird was mounted on wires so it could move in a lifelike way as she walked.

"All the chickens roaming around had better watch their selves," Hildy said, and received a dirty look from the women.

A little farther on, she saw F.H. Lamb, who ran the Western Union office, talking to Mr. Lister, who owned the foundry. Papa had told Hildy and her family New Tacoma was getting telephone service, and that Western Union, the Foundry, and the *Tacoma Herald* all wanted the first one.

"I can't see what difference having the first telephone will be," Hildy had pointed out. "Until a second person has one, there's no one to call."

Her father allowed that Hildy was right but later commented to Verdita that her daughter was getting a little above herself when it came to men and business, and expressing her opinions. Reuben heard him and passed the information on. Seeing the two men brought back the remark and the hurt Hildy felt. *Why shouldn't I have opinions?* Without stopping to eavesdrop on their conversation, she hurried home. To her surprise, Kezzie was in the kitchen drinking a glass of milk and talking to Verdita.

"Hello, Kezzie, what are you doing here?" Hildy said, adding, "Mama, the boots will be ready tomorrow."

Kezzie put her empty glass on the table. "I heard you were sick and dropped by to visit."

If Hildy was surprised, she didn't show it, After all, she told herself, a lady always rises to the occasion.

"I haven't seen you since school got out. How have you been?"

"I'm well. Mama had another baby and we've all been kept real busy. Dr. Bostwick said she had to stay in bed for a full month."

"He wasn't in town when I was sick." Hildy poured herself a glass of milk and sat down at the table. "But I saw Mrs. Bostwick near the cobbler's shop just now. She has a new hat. You should see it. It's two feet across and has a dead bird on it."

"Surely not." Kezzie's eyes opened wide.

"I heard her say so. Can we go outside and play Authors, Mama?"

"For a while, then I need you in the kitchen. Papa brought home a crate of strawberries before he left and I want you to help me make jam."

Hildy and Kezzie sat under a tree and Hildy dealt the cards. "What have you been doing since school ended?" she asked.

"I learned to turn a heel. Can you do it? It's terribly difficult. Do you have a Walt Whitman?"

"No," Hildy said. She focused, for a minute, on putting her cards in groups.

"What?"

"No, I don't have a Walt Whitman and, no, I can't turn a heel. When I get that far, Mama turns it for me." Hildy laughed. "A two-for-one answer. Anyway, I don't like knitting. I like to bake."

Nell would have gotten the little joke right away, she knew, but Kezzie looked puzzled for a moment. "You mean bread?"

"Yes, and I make pies, too, and sell them. Someday I'm going to have a bakery of my own. Do you have a Nathaniel Hawthorne?"

They played in silence for a while, and then Kezzie said, "Did you know Ellen has designs on William Fife?"

"William Fife? Why, he's one step away from the eternity box."

Kezzie giggled. "Young William Fife. Ellen's fourteen and William is twenty and she says that when she's eighteen they'll be the perfect ages to get married."

"Does William know?"

Before Kezzie could answer, Verdita appeared in the doorway. "Sorry to interrupt you girls, but I need Hildy now."

"That's all right, Mrs. Bacom. I expect by now Mama needs me, too. Goodbye Hildy. Next time why don't you come to my house to visit?"

"Goodbye. Maybe when Nell gets back we can come together. You say hello to Ellen for me, hear."

Kezzie left, passing and ignoring Chong on her way. *Hump.*

He might as well have been invisible. Hildy gathered up the cards. *Nell always speaks to Chong. That's one of the things I like about her. She's nice to everyone.*

In the kitchen, while Hildy washed bottles, her mother heated and mashed the berries, slowly adding sugar. "Kezzie is a lovely girl." She tasted the fruity mash with a wooden spoon.

Hildy rinsed the first batch of bottles and put them in boiling water.

"Very ladylike." When Hildy didn't comment Verdita said. "Hildy, I'm talking to you."

Hildy glanced up from putting the sterilized bottles on the counter. "I like Nell better."

"I can see why you would." Verdita paused and chose her words carefully, "only, she's . . ."

Hildy knew what her mother was going to say and struggled to keep her temper. "Nell knows she isn't as much a lady as she wants to be." She removed the first batch of sterilized bottles and added more. "Nell told me she's going to ask you how to improve herself."

Hildy continued washing bottles and jars, and Verdita added more berries into the pot on the stove. To lighten the mood she asked Hildy more about Mrs. Bostwick's hat and the tension eased.

"Ladies are serious about their hats, aren't they?" Hildy said.

"Yes, but the hat sounds wonderful." Verdita looked wistful.

"You're much prettier than Mrs. Bostwick and maybe Papa can buy you a new hat."

Verdita laughed. "I have about as much chance of Papa's buying me a fancy hat as I do getting one from Aunt Glady." She turned back to the stove.

When the fruit reached a full boil, Verdita ladled it into the jars and Hildy covered the tops with wax. They left the jam to cool and went outside to work in the vegetable garden.

"At least we don't have to can most of this." Hildy worked carefully among the carrots. "Thank goodness for root cellars."

"There will still be plenty of other vegetables to can, though—tomatoes, string beans, beets, and we'll have to make pickles and put down a crock of sauerkraut."

"Gracious, and it will have to be done during the hottest time of the year."

Verdita sat back on her heels and looked at Hildy critically. "If you keep on growing the way you are, next year you'll be in stays. When that happens you'll see what real suffering in the heat is." She laughed and then sighed.

"If they're so uncomfortable, why do women wear them?"

"Because they help remind us to be gentle and womanly." Verdita tossed a weed on to a growing pile. "I got mine when I was fourteen, but I think you will have to have yours earlier." She wiped her forehead. "Since you were sick it doesn't seem like you're my little girl anymore."

"Reuben says if I were a boy we could have lots of fun together."

"I think," Verdita said slowly, "in a few years you'll find being a girl isn't so bad."

"I'm not sure being gentle and womanly will help me be a good business woman, though."

"Business woman?"

"Yes, I've decided on my life's work."

"Oh, have you?"

Hildy missed the tone in her mother's voice. "I'm going to have a bakery all my own. I thought about it today. Aunt Glady can tell me the newest things back east and I'll make them and be the first to sell them in New Tacoma."

"You seem to have this all thought out."

Hildy moved further down the garden. "Washington Territory isn't like back east. Here a person has to be independent and get on with life their selves. I don't want to teach school and I can't sew like you do but I've got my flour thumb." She waved the appendage at her mother. The flour thumb was an old joke between them.

"Your husband might not want you to work."

"Then I won't have one. I'll just have lots of beaux instead."

Hildy gathered up her weeds and those of her mother and went to throw them over the bluff at the edge of their yard. Dovie, who had been napping on a blanket under a tree while they weeded, woke up and Verdita took her to the necessary.

After the heat outside, Hildy found relief in the cool kitchen. Chong had gotten the dishes off the shelf and was slicing bread. Reuben set the table and Hildy washed her hands.

"Say, Hildy. Do you think Papa would buy me a rifle?"

Before Hildy could answer, Chong said, "What you want gun fo?"

"To kill rats. I can get a job down at the wheat sheds killing rats—a cent for every ten. Gosh, I'd be rich in no time."

"Maybe Papa will." Hildy looked thoughtful. "Or maybe you can write Uncle Edgar and ask him if he has an old one lying around."

"Has what lying around?" asked Verdita, as she came in with Dovie.

"A rifle so I can shoot rats." Reuben's eyes widened with excitement.

"You most certainly may not ask Uncle Edgar for a gun. You don't ask people for things. And you're too young, anyway. Did you wash your hands?"

"But Uncle Edgar can't shoot anymore," Reuben protested as he put the silverware down and went to the washbasin. "How's he gunna shoot with only one arm?"

"You heard me." When Reuben looked as if he was going to protest, Verdita gave him a steely eyed look.

After they ate, Reuben went to work on the wood pile, Verdita sat down with her sewing, and Hildy got out a cookbook. She had a bad minute as her mother pawed through a selection of Aunt Glady's old clothes, but eventually Verdita settled down with a woman's dress and Hildy breathed a sigh of relief.

"What are you looking for?" Verdita asked after a few minutes.

"Things to make in my bakery."

"You know you will have to finish school, don't you?"

"Yes, but I can practice on things now so I'll be all ready." Hildy waved a fly away and turned another page.

"Why don't you try cinnamon buns? You have everything you need except cinnamon and brown sugar and I will give you some of them."

"That's a wonderful idea, and it's so warm the dough will rise in the sun."

Hildy got busy in the kitchen measuring flour and breaking eggs. While the dough rose she washed the dishes, and wandered around picking up and putting things down.

"You're awfully fidgety, Hildy," Verdita said, finally. "If you don't have something to do perhaps you can stack wood for Reuben."

And so the afternoon passed. Reuben pitched a piece of wood to Hildy, who passed it on to Chong. Chong had a knack for piling wood so that the logs didn't roll off. When the dough had doubled in size, Hildy punched it down and set it to rise again. The buns were finished in time for supper and everyone pronounced them a success. After the kitchen was cleaned up, Hildy walked over to Nell's house to see if her friend had returned home and hadn't had time to visit. However, the Tanquist house was still closed up. She continued walking to a spot that overlooked the bay and sat on a log. *Oh, I wish Nell was here. Maybe I shouldn't go, but if I don't, what will Nell say, and everyone else will be there.* Hildy leaned back and lifted her face to the sun. *I need a sign, something to tell me what to do.* Nothing happened, though, and after a while she stood up, brushed her skirt off, and started home. I can only go if Mama is in bed and I can sneak out, she thought. That will be my sign. It all rests on Mama.

CHAPTER 11

When Hildy returned from her walk, Dovie had her nightie on and Verdita was checking a protesting Reuben's neck and behind his ears.

"It's too early to go to bed."

"Yes, it is," his mother agreed, "but maybe this will teach you a lesson about not coming home when you're told to." She handed him a towel and carried the washbasin of dirty water out to pour on the vegetable garden.

"Jehoshaphat." Reuben rubbed his face with the towel. "I've got soap in my eyes."

"I'll take Dovie up. Tell Mama." Hildy picked up the little girl and started out of the room.

"Horsie," Dovie cried and wiggled until she rode piggyback.

"Half a league, half a league, half a league onward," Hildy cried, bouncing her sister as she climbed the stairs.

Dovie laughed and Reuben followed them shouting, "Forward the Light Brigade, charge for the guns."

In the kitchen washing her own hands and face, Verdita heard them and sighed. Here was Reuben running all over town as soon as his chores were done, meeting who knows what kind of people, and getting into what kinds of scraps, and her daughter wanting to be a business woman instead of a young lady. How long would either of her children remember their Tennyson? And would Dovie ever have poetry books to read or time to read them? They'd had to leave so many of their books behind when they moved from Johnstown. She sat down on one of the hard, wooden kitchen chairs and looked out the window. It was the first glass window Ira had bought for the house because they spent most of their time in the kitchen.

I have no right to complain, she reminded herself. Except for Hildy's illness, the climate seems to agree with us, even Ira. I have a house and Mrs. Cook has invited Ira and me to join the new literary society, and, and . . . Verdita leaned her head on her hand. *I'm just tired. Think of those men you can hear outside still working. In New Tacoma, men cut wood and hammer and saw as long as there's daylight to see by.* She stood up and grinned. *I should be thankful I can go to bed, but before I do, I'm going to do something Ira need never know about. I'm going to have a wee bit of Tullamore Dew. It'll help me sleep. Not real Irish whiskey, of course, but the bottle of Old Overholt is for Ira's cough. Lord help me, though, if anyone ever finds out, especially Glady.*

Verdita found the bottle, poured some into a glass, and tried to sip. *How do men do this?* She coughed and her eyes watered. Screwing up her courage, she swallowed the rest and put the glass on the dry sink. After a moment, during which she struggled to catch her breath, lovely warmth flowed through her body like a soft wind on the prairie grass. She walked upstairs feeling more relaxed and heard Hildy's voice coming from Dovie's room.

"And, then, just as the sweet pea petal fell off the stem, but before it hit ground, it turned into a lovely blue butterfly and floated across the garden carried by the breeze that birds' wings made. Pretty soon a pink petal turned into another butterfly and then a yellow one until the garden was full of butterflies all fluttering to the music of the bluebells." Hildy stopped when her mother reached the bedroom door.

"That's lovely. You know, you've been telling stories to Reuben and Dovie even before they could understand the words.

You should write your stories down. I liked the one where fairies rode the fireflies."

"I like the gingerbread story best," Reuben shouted from his room. "Remember, Hildy?"

"Yes, I do. It was Christmas Eve and at the stroke of midnight a strange whirlwind blew off a giant grandfather fir tree and right down the chimney in the cottage where a little girl named Beth lived. Riding on the wind was a mischievous piskie named Lutey. Lutey saw the gingerbread men Beth and her mother had made and hung on the Christmas tree and wanted to play with them. So he stood on his head, spun around three times, and started to chant, 'Mist from the hill, Brings water for the mill; Mist from the sea, Means you have to play with me.' And all the gingerbread started to dance. They danced so hard the Christmas tree almost toppled over and then one gingerbread man fell and broke off a leg. When Lutey saw the broken leg, the naughty piskie was very sorry. At the next gust of wind in the chimney, he hopped aboard and disappeared. The next morning Little Beth came downstairs and saw the gingerbread man with the broken leg. 'Tsk, tsk,' she said. 'I guess I'd better eat this cookie right now, that way no one will know I didn't do a good job tying him to the tree.' So Little Beth ate the cookie before anyone saw it and . . ."

"Got a belly ache!" Reuben shouted.

"Which is why we don't eat cookies for breakfast," Verdita finished. "Come on, Dovie, let me tuck you in." She snuggled Dovie down and kissed her goodnight.

Hildy went to her room while her mother crossed the hall to check on Reuben. Hildy was sitting on her bed when Verdita came in and joined her. "Do you remember a book Aunt Glady had called *Flower Fables*?" When Hildy nodded she said, "Well, the author, the lady who wrote that book, was Miss Louisa May Alcott and she wrote all the stories for a little girl named Ellen.

I think that you could do the same thing with your stories."

"You mean write a book?"

"You could write your stories down until you have enough to make a book and maybe your friend, Mrs. Money, can help you bind it. It's a very ladylike thing to do."

"Gracious."

Hildy looked at her mother and, as she did, Verdita realized Hildy was tall enough to meet her gaze squarely on. She thought, again, how pretty her oldest daughter was and remembered the look Hildy and Samuel had exchanged. *I will have to tread carefully with Hildy's future.*

"I'll have to study terribly hard at school now, won't I," Hildy was saying, "if I want to write stories and bake bread? Wait until I tell Nell."

Verdita hugged Hildy and stood up. "Goodnight, dear."

Her footfalls faded away down the hall until Hildy heard her enter her own room. Then Hildy's thoughts immediately turned to the night to come. *Imagine the wonderful story I'll have to write down if I see the phonograph. I mean after I see it.*

She got up slowly and went to stand by the opened door. Reuben whistled through his nose as he slept, but other than that, the house was quiet. She fished the boy's clothes from under her pillow and changed. Then she plumped up the covers on her bed to look like someone was sleeping in it and left the room.

Has the floor always squeaked this much? A wagon rattled down the road outside and made enough noise for Hildy to get to the top of the staircase. The stair steps seemed even squeakier than the floor. Hildy pressed her back to the wall where the joists were firmer, and went down one step at a time. When she reached the bottom, she sat down to catch her breath.

More noises came from outside. Hildy guessed that everyone in town was headed to the demonstration. She tiptoed to the fireplace and rubbed soot on her hands, and then on her face and neck. After that she pushed her hair under a cap, pulled it low on her forehead, and left the house.

A Street was empty and Hildy started running. *Oh, I can't be late.* However, when she turned off A and started up Eighth Street, people still crowded the dusty road. With a quick glance she found a group of boys pushing and shoving each other, and straggled behind them.

The demonstration would take place at Howell's livery stable. A year or so before the Bacoms arrived in New Tacoma Mr. Howell built a livery stable with a meeting hall on the second floor. An outside staircase ended on a small landing where a door opened into a large room. Hildy joined the excited crowd, which pushed her up the steps. Staying away from the wobbly hand rail took all her concentration. Once inside she saw several rows of mismatched chairs, mostly occupied, facing a makeshift stage. Women sat on most of the seats. Men stood along the walls. Mrs. Bostwick's hat with the bobbing bird was conspicuous among the old-fashioned bonnets. A man she didn't recognize stood on the stage with Dr. Bostwick, saloon owner Louis Levin, and several men Hildy had seen about town but didn't know by name.

As she looked around, Hildy saw Miss Rose, Miss Lily, and Miss Violet, who had places in the middle. Each wore dresses and hats appropriate to her name and had matching fans of ostrich plumes. The colors stood out against the black, brown, and navy blue most of the other women wore. Hildy noticed that her friends had painted their lips and cheeks bright red and the other women had not. Her gaze traveled back and forth between the two groups. Though the three ladies looked altogether brighter and more cheerful, something about them bothered her. While she tried to puzzle it out, two men carried out a large object covered with cloth and put it on the stage.

"Ladies and gentlemen," Dr. Bostwick shouted.

Only a few people quieted down so he clapped his hands. When that didn't work, Louis Levin put his thumb and forefinger to his lips and gave a shrill whistle. One of the men in the crowd shouted, "Atta boy, Levin."

The room became quiet and Francis Cook, editor of the *Tacoma Herald*, stepped forward. "Ladies and gents," he began. "Just a few years ago, only the Indians and the Northern Pacific Railroad knew anything about the magnificent Puget Sound. However, where a railroad goes, man must surely follow. Where once there was little on the wharf but the Blackwell's hotel, now businesses operate day and night and more people are coming to our fair city each and every day. Where once Commencement Bay was empty of all except a few dugout canoes, now steamships, schooners, and sailing ships fill the harbor. Where once trees crowded the banks clear down to the shore, now houses proliferate. For New Tacoma, these are just some of many auspicious events that have taken place in our fair city."

At this point Hildy quit listening. Several latecomers entered the room and one was Samuel. She just caught a glimpse of his profile before the man next to him shifted and blocked her view. The thick crowd of people prevented her from edging closer to him. For a moment, in spite of the room's heat, she felt a chill.

On the stage, Dr. Bostwick replaced Francis Cook and told people about his recent trip to Portland, comparing that city to New Tacoma. In the audience, men lit cigarettes and cigars, and a haze of smoke filled the room. Ladies either waved their fans vigorously or pressed handkerchiefs saturated with scent to their noses. For a minute, Hildy wished she'd remembered to bring a scented hanky, but then she thought about how it would look with her boy's clothes, and giggled.

As the room grew darker, Mr. Howell lit lanterns hanging on

the walls. When Dr. Bostwick ended his speech with something about New Tacoma's harbor being the best in the Pacific Northwest, bar none, the crowd laughed, recognizing his swipe at the troublesome Columbia River that bar ships had to cross before making port in Portland. However, when B.A. Chilberg replaced the doctor on stage, the audience showed signs of impatience. He was smart enough to keep his comments about the city's newly formed literary society to a minimum. By the time the room had grown so warm Hildy thought she'd faint, James Guild took the stage.

"Good people of New Tacoma," he began, "I welcome you to a demonstration of the most amazing invention of the decade, direct from the laboratory of French inventor Édouard-Léon Scott de Martinville.

"Immediately after its arrival from Paris, France, a mere nine months ago, the phonograph quickly became the marvel of the entire Eastern seaboard. And the way it works is this." Mr. Guild gestured with a long pointer. "In this device, a diaphragm which engages a ratchet-wheel and provides continuous rotation to a pulley. This pulley is connected by a cord to a little paper toy representing a man sawing wood. Hence, if one shouted 'Hip, hip hooray,' the paper man would start sawing wood. Using a cylinder with a grooved surface over which is placed tinfoil, which easily receives and records the movements of the diaphragm, a recording is made. But enough ado about the mechanics, what you have come to see and hear are the first sounds ever recorded for the posterity of all mankind. Ladies and gentlemen," Mr. Guild stopped speaking long enough to half-bow to various corners of the room, "without further ado, I give you the first ever recording played and heard in the good town of New Tacoma."

He fiddled with his machine until the scratchy sounds of barnyard animals filled the room. After a moment's stunned silence, people leaned forward, stared at the phonograph, and then exchanged glances.

Pigs and chickens? Hildy thought. Gracious, I can hear them any old place. Others may have had the same idea because some started laughing.

Realizing he was losing his audience, Mr. Guild changed something on the machine and music poured forth. Hildy smiled with surprise and pleasure, and she automatically glanced toward where Samuel had been standing. He had stepped away from the man who'd blocked him and was looking in her direction. Hildy's eyes widened and then she smiled. After a startled look, Samuel grinned back, the dimple in his cheek plainly visible. Then the crowd of people shifted and he was lost to view. The music ended and Mr. Guild played a third recording. After that, he invited people to come forward, one at a time, if they wished a closer look. Clearly, the show was over. Hildy pushed her way through the throngs of people toward the door.

The night air was warm and fresh. For a few moments, she sat on a step to think. *How wonderful to have music or any sounds, for that matter, recorded and to be able to listen any time. Wait until I tell Nell. She didn't think I would have the nerve to sneak out.* As Hildy hugged her knees anticipating Nell's surprise, a man ran toward the hall crying, "Fire!" He raced up the steps, burst into the hall, and shouted over the noise. Hildy barely had time to get off the stairs before men burst out of the door and ran past her. In for a penny, in for a pound, she thought, and followed the mob.

Earlier in the year, in preparation for the dry season, various merchants on Pacific Avenue donated oil cans, and a tinsmith named Quade turned them into buckets and painted and lettered them in readiness. Hildy ducked into the shadows and watched the men fill the buckets from William Fife's water system and toss the water on the flames.

"You, boy!" one of the men shouted. It took Hildy a minute to realize he was talking to her. "Get over here and hep with these here buckets."

Hildy pushed her way into the line, took the pail handed to her, and passed it on. In a matter of minutes she felt blisters from the wire handles forming on her hands. Men tossed some of the water on the fire and some on to the buildings nearby. Pitch from green wood snapped and sparks flew up. Several men wetted blankets that they snapped against the flames. In truth, it wasn't much of a fire, just one old shed. And it's a good thing, Hildy thought, because it wasn't much of a water system, either. Her father called it nothing but a bunch of puny little arteries.

Foul-smelling black smoke hovered over the area. Hildy's eyes burned and watered. Then the shed's roof collapsed, sending up a hail of new sparks and a final cloud of smoke before the fire was out. The men dropped their buckets and slapped each other on the back. "It was Louis Levin's shed," one of them shouted, "drinks are on him."

Hildy was caught up in the crowd and swept inside Levin's saloon.

"How old are you, boy?" one of the men asked Hildy.

"Thirteen."

"Well, you fought like a man so I figure you can drink like one, too." He put his arm around Hildy's shoulder and hustled her to the bar. "A beer for my young friend here and one for me."

Beer! Hildy looked frantically for a way to escape, but the room was packed with men who milled about waving glasses.

"What's your name, young'un?" The man handed Hildy a glass.

"Uh, Hill."

"Well, here's to you, Hill, down the hatch."

Hildy took a sip and grimaced. Her friend saw and laughed. "Drink up, Hill," he said and slapped her on the back. Hildy's head snapped back, her cap fell off, and her hair fell around her shoulders. While the man choked on his beer at the sight, she scrambled on the floor for the cap, pushed through the crowd, and took off.

Oh, what if someone recognized me? What if they tell Mama and Papa? Why did I go tonight?

Well away from the salon, Hildy stopped running and leaned against a building to catch her breath. Her hands hurt and her face felt burned. She sniffed at a strand of hair and grimaced at the smoke smell. After a minute she slid down the wall and rested her head on her knees. *If someone says they saw me tonight I'll have to lie.* A phrase she'd once heard Aunt Glady say popped into her head. *Oh, it is a tangled web we weave when first we practice to deceive.*

She slowly stood up, shoved her hands in her pockets, and strolled down the street wishing she knew how to whistle.

For the most part, the roads were empty. A small dog came around a corner but seeing Hildy turned back the way it'd come. Even though most of the mucky skunk cabbage patches were dried up, they'd stayed wet long enough for mosquitos to breed. They buzzed around and Hildy swatted at them and walked faster. Within minutes she reached her home. The lights were out. *That's a good sign, I hope.* She made her way around back. Unfortunately, she wasn't alone. A figure stood near the edge of the embankment, his shape and the piece of wood he held clearly outlined in the moonlight. Hildy froze.

"Hi, hi!" he said.

Hildy recognized Chong's voice. "Chong, it's me, Hildy," she whispered.

Chong started forward, still holding the wood. "You boy."

"No, really, it's me, look." Hildy pulled off her hat and her long hair fell about her shoulders. "See."

Chong was clearly displeased. "Why you dess like boy?"

"I had to go out and didn't want anyone to see me."

"Where you go?"

"To see the phonograph."

"Aiyaa! Shame, you bad. I tell Mama."

"You better not or I won't teach you English anymore."

"You do that to Chong?"

"I will if you tell."

"That bad. You bad." Chong shook his head.

"I won't do it again, Chong, honest, at least," Hildy hesitated, "probably not, but I had to see it and Mama wouldn't go. You know what it played Chong?" Hildy stopped and giggled, "crowing roosters and oinking pigs."

Chong ignored the description. "Where you clothes?"

"Chong! You said an R. That was very good."

"Hump." He wouldn't be appeased. "You wash face, change clothes."

"And you won't tell on me?"

"Maybe yes, maybe no." He turned and started back the way he'd come.

"I trust you, Chong," Hildy called after him, "because we're friends and friends don't tell."

"Aiyaa, aiyaa." He shook his head and continued muttering as he walked.

The water barrel was half full. Her hands and face stung. Hildy dipped out a bucket of water, washed off the soot, and poured water over her head, hoping to get rid of the smoke smell. Once Chong was out of sight, she took off the heavy jacket and washed her arms and chest. "Why, I'm getting bosoms," she whispered, noticing for the first time that her chest was no longer flat. She took off the heavy wool trousers and saw other signs of her changing body. Suddenly, she realized she was standing in the backyard wearing nothing but her chemise and drawers.

The door squeaked as she walked inside carrying her disguise. The kitchen was cool and the wood floor felt good under her feet. Hildy put the clothes back where she'd originally found them and started up the stairs.

"Who's that?" her mother called in a sleepy voice.

"It's me, Mama," Hildy said, using the opportunity to scurry up and down the hall. "It's so hot; I wanted some fresh water from the barrel." She grabbed her cotton shift and pulled it on. At least that's not a lie, she added to herself.

"Well, go to sleep, dear." Verdita's voice faded and Hildy knelt in front of her window, which overlooked the backyard, and stared across the embankment. The moon hung above the water making silver zigzag lines on the bay, and a shooting star cut across the sky. Quick, make a wish she thought, but the only thing that came to her mind before it disappeared was the name Samuel. He didn't seem at all shocked to see me, she realized. *Gracious, maybe he thinks I'm a fallen woman.* But somehow, she didn't think so.

I wish Nell could have been with me. Nell is the only person who understands things. Hildy sat quietly and saw a barn owl sweep by, silencing a chorus of frogs. She pulled her hair up, found a piece of string, and tied it into a knot. Sounds carried easily in the still, breathless air. She heard a dog bark, men's voices, and someone singing. Then she heard someone close by whistling. The song was low and plaintive. It sounded something like the sunset cry of a loon. *But I haven't seen any loons in New Tacoma.* She leaned out the window but there wasn't enough moonlight to see anything beyond shadows. The music went on for a few seconds more and then stopped.

"Hello," she whispered into the night. "That was lovely.

Thank you."

Nothing stirred and the frogs began their courtship chorus again. Then she saw the bushes move as someone walked away.

Chapter 12

In spite of her late night, Hildy slept poorly and woke with sore shoulders and aching hands. She got up and dressed but when she smoothed the bed covers down, blisters on her palms reminded her of the bucket handles from the fire brigade. Oh dear, she thought, I'll have to hide my hands until they heal. Down in the kitchen, she braided her hair and tied it with a piece of yarn before punching down the day's bread and setting it near a window to rise under the heat of the early morning sun. Chong had started the stove and put on a pot of coffee, and Hildy poured a cup, adding plenty of milk. After that, she sat at the kitchen table with her slate and tried to think of how to ask Aunt Glady for some new recipes. She was tapping the chalk against the table when Verdita came into the room.

"Good morning, Hildy." She poured water into a basin and washed her face, and Hildy realized that she'd forgotten to do the same.

"Morning, Mama." She began to yawn and hastily swallowed some coffee.

"What are you doing?"

"I'm trying to figure out what to say in a letter to Aunt Glady because I want some new recipes. Maybe I can start my bakery and get rich right away." Hildy stopped the tapping and put the chalk down. "If I tell her I want to make something besides bread to sell she'll just answer back with a lecture about ladies and needlework." She sighed and Verdita laughed.

"Well." She poured her own cup of coffee and sat down at the table across from Hildy. "I have an idea. Why don't you tell her about the literary society Papa and I are joining and ask her for any new recipes she's gotten that I can make."

"Oh, what a good idea. Are you and Papa joining a literary society? You never said before."

"I don't know for sure. We've been asked but your father isn't very enthusiastic. He hates that sort of thing."

"But if you don't, my letter will be a lie."

"Whether we join or not, asking won't hurt Aunt Glady."

"Does that mean it's all right to lie sometimes, if you want something and the lie doesn't hurt anyone?"

Verdita looked at Hildy closely. "Why the sudden interest in fibs? Have you been telling them?"

"No, Mama, but what if I have to someday?"

Verdita thought for a moment, trying to find the right way to answer. "I think," she said slowly, "if the lie will save someone from pain and there is no other way, then it might be permissible. The problem is, sometimes, when you don't lie—when you tell the truth, well, you might feel better but you shift the burden to the other person."

She gave Hildy's hands a little squeeze and was startled to see her flinch. "Oh, Hildy, you have blisters from all the weeding." She looked at the raw palms. "You work so much harder than Reuben, leave the garden to him; it's his job, after all. Let me get some ointment."

Verdita left the room and for a moment, Hildy was overcome with remorse. *Reuben is always sneaking off to visit the Scott boys and he should work harder in the garden but I hurt Mama, and I sort of lied.* However, remembering the excitement of the phonograph and the fire, and how horrible it was in the saloon, she perked up. *Oh, it was fun, and I saw Samuel and gave him the surprise of his life.* She was smiling when Verdita returned with a pot of Poor Man's Friend.

"What about your stories?" her mother asked. "I thought you were going to write them down."

"I am but that won't take much time. I can do that while the bread rises. Of course," Hildy added, working the salve into her hands, "cookies and such take lots of concentration."

At that moment Chong came in. "I pick." He held out a bowl of small balls of fruit, some orange and some deep purple.

"Huckleberries. Oh wonderful," Verdita beamed. She and Chong loved produce of any kind and she took his knowledge of what was edible seriously. "We'll have some for breakfast and make jelly with the rest. We have plenty of sugar."

Behind her back, Chong glared at Hildy and for a moment, she held her breath. When he turned away and began fussing with pots and pans, she sighed. *Now I've sort of made Chong lie, too. And more jam. I think Chong did it on purpose. Well, I just won't think about it anymore.*

"Mama, do we really need more jam?"

Before Verdita could respond, Reuben came running into the kitchen, his socks slipping and sliding on the worn wooden floor. "Reuben!" She snapped. "How many times have I told you not to do that?" Hildy missed the rest of her words when she went out to visit the necessary.

Over the next few weeks, it seemed as if all the fruit to be canned ripened at once. When Reuben wasn't bringing in firewood, he was brushing the cinders and ashes out of the grate and into the pan to empty, or weeding under Chong's watchful eye, or scouring the streets for old bottles. Verdita wrapped the bottles with string she soaked in kerosene and then lit on fire. When the string burned at its hottest, she plunged the bottle in cold water and snapped it in half. Then Chong smoothed off the edges and Hildy scrubbed and boiled them.

The bottom portions were perfect for jellies, jams, and preserves, which Hildy and Verdita protected with a thick layer of wax.

"More jam?" Hildy protested one day in late July when Chong and Reuben came in with a box of salal berries.

"You've be glad for it next winter," Verdita said. "Don't you remember how much you liked the jam at the Blackwell Hotel when we first came to town?"

"I do," shouted Reuben, "and we're going to pick lots more berries, aren't we, Chong? Chong knows all the best places."

"There's no need to shout, Reuben. Anyway, Papa and I thought that at the end of the month we'd have a picnic and you can invite your friends."

"Jehoshaphat!" Reuben's hazel eyes lit up and almost disappeared when his face crinkled into a big smile. "Can I go to the Scotts' house right now and tell them?"

"Have you done your weeding?"

"Yes, I have, haven't I, Chong?"

"What about chopping wood?"

"I'll do it right after dinner when it's cooler. Please, Mama. Mr. Scott made a swimming hole out of a spring and I can take a bath in it and get all clean. I bet if I swim in my clothes, they'll be all clean, too. Please, Mama, it's so hot."

It was hot and Reuben's face was red and sweaty. Verdita gave in and Hildy scowled. "Can't I go, too? I'm just as hot as Reuben is."

"Hildy, really. You should know better than to even ask. Of course you can't go swimming with your brother and his friends. Please start washing these berries." Verdita went to get the sugar, thinking, my goodness, what next?

They were done by late afternoon; Hildy washed and pegged out the towels they'd used, then took a pencil and clean paper and went to sit on a secluded spot overlooking the bluff to copy

131

her letter to Aunt Glady. She was sealing the envelope when Samuel came up from behind and sat down. Hildy looked at him from under her eyelashes. "Hello," she said shyly.

Samuel tipped his head slightly and said, "I think I like your other clothes better." He grinned, his dimple coming and going.

Hildy's eyes widened and then she laughed. "Ssh, it's a secret. You are the only person who knows, except for Chong. He saw me when I got home but I told him I wouldn't teach him English anymore if he told."

"I heard men down on the dock wondering who the girl was."

"Gracious." Hildy's eyes widened in alarm.

"It's all right. They don't know."

"I'd for sure and certain be in a pickle if anyone found out."

On the wharf below where they sat, a mill's saw started up and a tugboat's shrill whistle scared the hovering cormorants. They flew up angrily, protesting in their deep, guttural grunts. She relaxed again and took a deep breath. "Mama doesn't think it proper for me to go down to the wharf unless I have a reason, and don't dawdle, but there's always something happening and I love the air close to the bay. It smells like salt water and fresh-cut wood. If that one tree was shorter," Hildy pointed toward a hemlock growing out of the bank, "I could watch everything from here."

"They kill the forests, though."

"What? Who?"

"All the loggers and mill owners. If you go to where they're cutting the trees, there's nothing but dirt and stumps left. A forest is better."

"But there's lots of trees and they'll just grow back, won't they?"

"Not for years and years."

"I guess I don't know anything about that but Papa read an editorial asking people living uptown to plant trees. Pacific

Avenue would be really pretty if it was lined with maples."

In spite of her mother's constant warnings that a lady prized her pale complexion, Hildy lifted her face to the sun. For a moment they were quiet. A bee buzzed by and Hildy watched it hover on a nearby bush.

"Aren't you afraid of bees?" Samuel asked.

"Not really, my Cousin Elsie is. She runs around flapping her hands, making a fuss and sometimes goes into a swoon, or pretends to. No wonder bees don't like her."

Samuel laughed. "Don't you ever go into a swoon? I thought all girls did."

Hildy gave a deep sigh. "I tried, once, but I felt so silly, I never did it again. It's like telling fibs, isn't it? And Mama says we should never do that."

"But you didn't tell her that you went to see the phonograph."

"No, but now I have a dilemma because I had to sneak out and not tell anyone, and it weighs on my conscience." Hildy put a hand over her heart and lifted her eyes to his. "And then Mama saw the blisters on my hands," she showed Samuel her palms, "and assumed I got them from working in the garden, so she's making Reuben do more work there. Chong saw me sneaking home and he really wants to learn English so by not telling anyone he's sort of lying, too. It's all very difficult."

Samuel looked at her, his body still but his gray eyes searching her face as if committing it to memory. "I'm going away."

Hildy's hand dropped to her lap. "What?"

"I'm going away for a while—with my father. We're going to Oregon."

"Why?"

He shifted slightly until he was in the shade and his face was partially obscured. "My—my parents aren't like yours. They don't always see eye to eye about things. I had a brother, once, and when he died, they—after he died they never seemed to get

133

along amymore. Ma has a job and Pa doesn't approve." He pressed his lips together and Hildy saw his Adam's apple jerk. "So, Pa and I are going to a place called Wallowa in eastern Oregon."

"For how long?"

"All winter, at least."

"Oh." Hildy turned away. The happiness of her afternoon disappearing.

"When are you going?"

"Soon. I'm not sure. As soon as Pa gets our gear together."

"I can write you if you give me your address. I write my cousin all the time."

Samuel got to his feet without responding, picking up something as he did. "Anyway, will you tell Reuben for me?"

Hildy stood up and faced him. "Yes." Her voice was so low he had to lean down to hear her. The proximity made him blush and he hurriedly straightened up.

"I have something for you."

"What?"

Samuel handed her a package clumsily wrapped in brown paper. "I'll send a card if I can," he said. Then he turned and walked away.

As always, Samuel moved quickly and silently. Hildy looked at the gift and when she looked up, he was gone. She sat slowly down again and was so still, a robin hopped on the ground near her feet and a small mouse came out of the underbrush to investigate. When her mother called, she wiped her cheeks, put Samuel's gift in her pocket, and stood up. Holding her arm close by her side, she returned to the house.

"Did you finish your letter?" Verdita asked as Hildy approached the porch.

"Yes and I'm going to find an envelope. I'll be back in a minute." She hurried inside, ran upstairs, and hid the package under her pillow. Her father was coming in the door when she ran back down and she hugged him.

"How's my little cabbage?" He returned the hug.

"I'm really tired of making jelly and jam."

Ira laughed. "Well, Mrs. Money came by the office today to drop off some papers and said you hadn't been in to see her lately."

Verdita, who was working at the stove, heard him. "Why don't you walk down to visit her after supper and take her a jar of jam?"

"All right, Mama." Hildy put as much enthusiasm into her voice as she could and began setting the table.

Reuben rushed in the door and began washing his hands without being asked and Dovie waddled by dragging a towel that had blown off the line. Hildy picked her up and buried her face in the baby's neck. Even the thought of seeing Mrs. Money wasn't enough to cheer her up.

While they ate, Reuben's chatter and Ira's news from the waterfront covered her silence. The Scotts were excited about the picnic and Mrs. Scott said she'd send a cake and some fried chicken. As usual, though, their father had the most important news. A man named Henderson had tried to rob Father Hylebos.

"Goodness me, what happened? Is he all right?" Verdita asked.

"General Sprague heard the story from Colonel Ferry and the Colonel got the information when he was over in Steilacoom filing some papers. Seems Henderson hired a man named Joseph Jacobs to help him dig up some money an old miner had buried. They set off and along the way, en Henderson told Jacobs that what he was really going to do was rob the Father."

"I didn't think priests had much money."

"Somehow, Henderson heard that he had $1,500 hidden in his house down on the Cowlitz Prairie. Who knows where it came from?"

"Maybe he got it from Father Blanchet," Reuben said.

Both Verdita and Ira looked at him, startled. "Who?"

"Father Blanchet. Remember, Hildy?" Reuben shoveled a mound of meat and potatoes in his mouth and had to work hard to chew and swallow.

"Miss Sparkle told us," Hildy explained. "It was in a history class. Father Blanchet came here with a great big church bell that he hung in a blessed tree. What's a blessed tree?"

"Uh, Miss Sparkle probably meant a tree that had been blessed," Verdita said. "St. Peter's down in Old Tacoma has a bell in a tree, too."

"And we're way off the subject," said Ira, who didn't approve of what he called popery. "Jacobs said he hadn't hired on to murder a priest and he and Henderson got in a big fight. Henderson tried to kill Jacobs but Jacobs shot him instead."

During the ensuing babble of questions and comments, Chicken Little wandered in and Hildy scooped the little hen up into her lap.

"Well, my heavens," Verdita said, as the noise quieted down. She didn't share her husband's religious prejudices and had a sneaking admiration for the hard-working nuns she occasionally saw. Until she spotted Chicken Little, she seemed at a loss for additional words.

"Hildy, take that hen outside immediately. The very idea of having a chicken at the table. And you," she turned to where Reuben had stuffed his cheeks full of more potatoes and was pumping them in and out. "Stop that at once."

They finished eating in silence; Ira decided to lie down for a while and Verdita took Dovie for a short walk. Reuben went out to chop more firewood and Hildy did the dishes. When she was done, she washed her face and tucked her hair under a sunbonnet, found a jar of mixed huckleberry and salal berry jam, and started for the wharf.

Pacific Avenue was full of railroad men who lodged at the American Hotel coming home from work. Hildy was careful to keep her face turned away from them. She was glad to reach the trail down the hill, which, in spite of weeks of hot weather, still had plenty of wet places where the planks didn't quite meet. The air was full of mosquitoes and she hurried to get away from them

At the bottom of the hill, an old man driving an empty wagon was coming in her direction. He tipped his hat and rattled on by. Up ahead, a young man tied his horse to a hitching rail and hurried inside the telegraph office. Hildy paused outside to listen to the clicking sounds that meant messages were coming and going. *Imagine how surprised Cousin Elsie would be if I went inside and sent her a message. I could tell her everything that happened this morning and she'd know right away instead of having to wait for a letter.* For a moment her dull spirits lifted. *Maybe I can learn to send messages and have a telegraph at the bakery.*

Hildy was smiling when she pushed open the door to Mrs. Money's store.

CHAPTER 13

One hot morning in early September, while Hildy sat at the table slicing apples to dry, Ellen appeared at the door.

"The Saratoga Trail out to Wapato Lake is finally graded and I've come to invite you to a berry picking picnic party tomorrow," she said.

Hildy put her knife down and giggled. " 'Picking picnic party.' Sounds like Peter Piper."

"Pardon me?"

"Never mind," Hildy said, thinking that Nell would understand. "But why do they call it the Saratoga Trail when it's just an extension of Pacific Avenue?"

"I don't know, anyway what does it matter?"

"Oh, it doesn't. I just wondered, that's all. But isn't Wapato Lake a long ways to go for berries?"

"We won't have to go that far. There's lots of berries on the hill above Gallagher Gulch where the burn is. We can easily walk there."

"It sounds wonderful. I've hardly left the house since school got out."

"Picking wild blackberries is hardly a wonderful experience; it's just plain a lot of work, and making jam with them is hard work too."

Hildy looked puzzled. "If you don't like to do it, why don't you just buy some? The Indian ladies have been selling berries uptown."

"Mama doesn't like to buy from them. She says if they have money they'll just use it for whiskey. And, really, Hildy, they aren't ladies, you know."

Hildy stiffened. "Mrs. Blackwell has several Indian women as friends and she's about the most important lady in town."

"Well, Mama says Mrs. Bostwick is more of one. Anyway," Ellen tossed her head. "Do you want to come or not?"

"Of course," said Hildy. "I had wild blackberry jam when I was getting over being sick and it was delicious. Who else are you asking?"

"Well, Kezzie, of course, and we have two new neighbors with girls our age and, I suppose, Nell since she's back home."

"What's the matter with Nell?" Hildy was beginning to wonder if she wanted to go after all.

"She's awfully rough around the edges, don't you think? Mama says that Nell's mother was a nice person until she married such a hard-case man and now she's practically been knocked into a cocked hat."

Hildy's eyes blazed. She was about to remind Ellen that a lady didn't use slang or talk about her friends that way when Verdita appeared and put her hands on Hildy's shoulder's. "A berry picking excursion? How nice. Hildy could use a break, couldn't you, Hildy?" Without waiting for an answer she added, "We have some lard pails with handles that will be just the thing to put the berries in."

Verdita kept her hands on Hildy until Ellen left, after saying she and the other girls would stop by at ten o'clock the next morning. When she was gone, Hildy pulled away.

"She's just hateful, Mama. I don't know if I want to go tomorrow or not."

"Oh, I think you should. Ellen's just repeating what she hears at home. She hasn't learned, yet, to think for herself."

"Why not, for goodness sakes? I always think for myself."

"I won't argue with that," Verdita said, wryly, "but you need to have more friends than Mrs. Money and Nell."

And Samuel. Hildy hadn't seen him since he told her he was going away. She put the thought aside.

"Why? I like them and they like me and why do I have to fill my life up with people I don't really like at all? They'll just waste my time."

Verdita sat down and pulled Hildy on to a chair next to her. "You don't have to 'fill your life' with them, Hildy, but as you meet more and more people, you will have to learn to at least get along with them. They don't have to become your intimates."

Hildy scowled. "All right, but if Ellen isn't nice to Nell, tomorrow, I won't stay."

Verdita sighed. "I trust you to do what's right."

Hildy was alone in the kitchen the next morning when she heard several voices outside singing.

> *Five currant buns in a baker's shop,*
> *Round and fat with a cherry on the top,*
> *Along came Hildy with a penny one day*
> *Bought a currant bun and took it away.*

In spite of herself, she giggled and ran to join the others, her lard pails clanging together and her sunbonnet sliding off her head. "Bye, Mama," she shouted.

As they started toward Pacific Avenue, Hildy turned to one of the new girls and smiled. "I'm Hildy," she said.

"I'm Fern."

"Did you hear her accent?" Ellen asked. She was carrying a flour sack containing their lunch, and a large pail. "Fern is from Virginia."

"And this is Sarah," said Nell, who had been walking next to the other girl. "She's from New York."

Hildy turned toward her with pleasure. "I'm from Pennsylvania so that practically makes us neighbors."

"Sarah's family is related to Abe Gross."

Fern gave the girl an odd look. "Then you must be a Hebrew. I never met one before."

Sarah's olive skin flushed. "There's lots of Jews in New York."

"Will your pa work for Mr. Gross?" Kezzie asked.

"Father is a tailor so, maybe, if Uncle Abe needs him. Otherwise he'll have his own shop."

By this time they reached Pacific Avenue, and turned south. The street seemed even more congested and smelly than usual. It appeared to Hildy as if a pall of smoke from men's cigars covered the town.

"Our thoroughfares in Virginia are brick." Fern looked at the pitted road where horses' hooves kicked up dust and wagons bounced in and out of ruts.

"Well, ours will be, too, one day," Nell said. "But right now we're a new town and we can make it anyway we want. Besides, we have a mountain. Does Virginia?"

"No, although I'm not sure how important a mountain is."

"We have the Catskill Mountains," Sarah said, "but Mount Tacoma is much prettier."

They fell silent after that. Hildy was glad when they reached the end of town at Thirteenth Street where Pacific Avenue dwindled down into little more than a path.

The sun beat down and occasional little eddies of wind made whirlpools out of dead leaves. At a half-a-mile marker, they reached the Saratoga Trail's official start and began a gradual southwest climb.

"The horses will have a tough time on these rocks," Ellen said after she nearly lost her footing.

"Not to mention a wagon." Nell laughed. "It's so rough; milk in a wagon will practically be churned to butter."

A quarter of a mile more took them to the hill's crest where they left the trail. Gallagher Gulch was a deep ravine with a creek that ran west to east and ended in a wide mouth at the edge of Commencement. On one side was the burn where Hildy and her friends were headed. Its mangle of brush and berry vines was lined with trees. The girls collapsed gratefully in their shade. From where they sat they saw that the Saratoga Trail crossed the burn and small wooden bridge over the gulch, before continuing south to Wapato Lake.

"Gracious. I'm hot." Hildy took her sunbonnet off and used it as a fan.

"I can hear the creek even from here," Nell said, "and look, there's a deer's path down the bank. Maybe we can climb down to it."

"Goodness." Fern gazed at her surroundings. "It's very— harsh looking, isn't it?"

The acre or so of cleared land was the result of men's felling trees to feed the Gallagher Gulch mill, and burning the stumps that remained. Nature had already gone to work weaving wild blackberry vines and other vegetation amongst the leftover debris. Remembering Samuel's words about forests, Hildy looked at it with new eyes.

"I think it's nice even if it is hot." Sarah closed her eyes and added, "I like the noisy silence."

Ellen looked puzzled and stood up, "Well, I'm going to start picking before it gets hotter."

"Me, too," said Hildy. "The quicker we pick, the quicker lunch will come."

Nell laughed as she hopped up. "That doesn't make sense at all."

The berries were abundant but hard to get at. After climbing in and out of thickets and getting numerous scratches, Hildy found a long stick with a bend on the end and used it to pull the vines out of the underbrush. Nell, Kezzie, and Sarah soon did the same. Their pails were over half full when Ellen walked over to compare the amount of berries in her bucket with theirs. Her bucket was only a third of the way full and she watched Hildy pull a vine away from a stump.

"That's a good idea." she said, looking for her own stick and one for Fern.

All six of them were sticky with berry juice and scratched from the vines by the time Ellen decided they should eat.

"Ugh." Nell looked at her hands "I can't eat like this. I'm going to climb down to the creek and wash off."

"Isn't that awfully dangerous?" Fern asked, but Nell had already started down the embankment with Hildy, Kezzie, and Sarah right behind her.

The dirt path Nell followed was six inches wide and had been created by deer's hooves gouging out the thick moss that covered the hillside. It zigzagged between downed limbs, sword and maidenhair ferns, cedar trees, and large rocks. The trees, many of them draped with lichen, met overhead, creating a green tunnel of soft filtered light that was scented with the smells of vegetation and rich organic soil. Their feet dislodged bits of scree that rolled down and disappeared in the leafy compost.

"Wow! That was farther than I thought," Nell said when she reached a small sandbar that jutted into the water at the gulch's bottom. The creek rushed by, leaping around partially submerged logs, creating little waterfalls over rocks, and dividing and coming together again when something blocked its path. Except for the sandbar on which they stood, the water was overhung with foliage.

"It's so pretty, isn't it? Just the way a cathedral must look," Sarah said.

In front of them was a deep pool created where a pile of fallen trees created a dam, and Nell looked at it with a dangerous glint in her eyes.

"I'm hot and that pool looks just the thing." With that, she walked in until her dress floated around her waist and sat down. "Woo, it's cold." She jumped up.

Hildy, who had been trying to scrub the stains off her hands, laughed. "I'm smarter than you." She hurriedly took off her dress, draped it over a bush, and waded in beside Nell. They laughed and splashed each other and then Sarah, who had tucked her skirt into her knickers and was splashing them, while Ellen and Fern looked on with disapproval and Kezzie had a laughing fit.

"You'll be a mess by the time we get back up to the top." Ellen frowned with disapproval.

"I don't care," Nell called back. "It was a raggedy old dress anyway and I'll dry off way before we get back to town."

"Well, Fern and Kezzie and I are hungry and we're going to go eat."

They started up the hill and Hildy put on her dress and helped Nell wring hers out. The three of them quickly caught up with the others and back at the burn, Ellen unpacked their lunch: thick venison sandwiches, apples, and sugar cookies.

"Golly, this is good," Nell said. "I was just about ready to eat my berries, I was so hungry."

Ellen smiled and basked in the compliment and Hildy decided she might let bygones be bygones. They were finishing when Sarah lifted her head and looked around. "Do you smell fish?"

"Fish? Up here?" Ellen said.

Nell looked around and sniffed. "I sort of think I do."

In the quiet that followed, branches snapped as something approached the clearing. After a minute, it stopped but the fishy smell grew stronger. Then the snapping started again. Something grunted softly and huffed the air. The sounds of breaking branches came closer. Nell stood up, moving slowly.

"I think it's . . ." she started to say when a large brown bear ambled into the clearing.

Hildy froze as the animal stopped and raised its head. It looked round, snorting softly, and sniffed the air again. When Fern gagged at his rancid odor, he looked at the girls. The bear's close-together eyes fastened on them and it grunted and swung its head back and forth.

"It's been eating salmon, that's why it smells," Nell said softly.

"What'll we do?" whispered Kezzie.

"Well, we can't stay here, we'll have to go back down the bank and get in the water," Nell said.

At her words, the bear popped his jaw and pawed at the ground.

"Move slowly," Hildy said as they began to stand up.

When they were all standing, they began backing carefully away. "I sure hate to leave my berries," Ellen said. She reached for her pail and as she did the bear charged partway across the burn.

Helter-skelter the girls rushed down the embankment. The narrow deer trail was only wide enough for one at a time. As they pushed and shoved, branches caught their clothing, making them trip. Their skirts tore when they yanked them free. At the bottom, they jumped in the pool and crowded together.

"It didn't follow us, at least," Kezzie said, "It must have smelled our food."

"All those berries, he'll have a fine feast for sure." Hildy giggled and Ellen gave her a dirty look.

"Well, now what?" she asked. "We can't stay here; the water is freezing."

Hildy looked at Nell. "How far do you think it is to the mill?"

"At least a mile. It's upstream a little ways from the bay."

"Do you think we can walk down the creek?" Sarah also whispered.

"No, it'd take hours with all the rocks and fallen trees," Hildy said.

"Do you want to go back up the bank and see if it's safe?" Nell looked at the others. "How long will it take the bear to eat our berries, do you think?"

"Hump. Not long, I should say." Ellen scowled, totally disgusted with the afternoon's turn of events. "All he had to do was knock over the pails and eat."

"Well, I'm going to get out of the water, it's too cold to stay in." Hildy waded out and sat on a log. "Gracious, that hot sun would feel good now, wouldn't it?"

Nell and Sarah joined her but the others stayed put. "Let's wait fifteen minutes and then sneak back up," Nell said.

The cold eventually forced the others out of the stream and they huddled together, shivering. They were so quiet birds lit on the rocks near them and picked off bugs that fluttered over the water.

"Look at the flowers on the other side," Sarah said suddenly. "Aren't they pretty?"

"Where?"

She picked up a small rock and pitched it in the plant's general direction.

"I know what those are," Nell said. "They're called stream orchids. Ike, that's my brother, gave some to Frieda Faye once but she said she didn't want flowers out of the woods. She wanted him to buy them at a store. Ike felt awful bad about that."

"I should think he would." Hildy looked at the plant and wondered that Sarah had spotted it, so well did the yellow-green petals blend in with their background. "That's mean."

"We have a lot of wildflowers in Virginia," Fern said, "like

146

cowslips and lady slippers."

"We'll have to hope that you'll get to go back there soon, won't we?" Hildy smiled sweetly.

Nell hid a giggle in a cough and stood up. "I'm going to crawl back up and see if it's safe."

She started back up the embankment with Hildy close on her heels. Near the top, they dropped to their knees and crawled. Just below the ridge they slowly peeked over, sniffed for the fishy smell, and looked around. Ellen's flour sack was ground into the dirt near a place where the bear had rolled. He had eaten all their berries and stepped on several of the pails. His tracks in the dirt disappeared near the wooden bridge. The only thing remaining to show that they'd had a visitor was several piles of blackish-red scat.

Hildy waved to the others and they climbed up the embankment, picked up their things, and started running back toward town.

"That was exciting," Nell said.

Hildy agreed, adding that her mother would be disappointed about there being no berries for jam. "Maybe we can come back," she said as she looked at Sarah, "and if we do, I'll try and find you a stream orchid."

Sarah smiled at her, and Fern heaved a sigh. "We have bears in Virginia but they're black not brown. Black is much scarier and the Virginia bears are much bigger."

Chapter 14

To Hildy it seemed as if the late August triggered more chores than two people could do. After the incident with the bear, several men combed the land around the burn. They saw where he had been, but they never found the old fellow himself. Though it was the end of blackberry season, when the area was declared safe, Verdita decided berry picking would be a nice family outing. With four-and-a-half grownups picking—Hildy said that Reuben didn't count as a full adult—they picked more than a gallon of berries to be made into jam.

Wild huckleberries followed and, when she and Verdita weren't putting up jams, they were putting up preserves, or slicing fruit that Chong spread on the roof to dry, or making pickles. In the middle of canning season, cabbages from Puyallup Valley appeared in the markets and Verdita bought two large crocks in which to make sauerkraut. Hildy thought her arm would drop off from all the grating she did.

"At least the hazelnuts don't need something done to them," she grumbled.

And then there was the soap. One of Reuben's jobs was to clean the ashes out of the stove and put them into the ash hopper. At regular intervals, Verdita poured water over the ashes and lye came out the bottom and into a barrel. Hildy was afraid of the lye because of the way it burned things, and the process of rendering fats made her nauseous.

"I never thought I'd look forward to school," she said to Reuben.

"Me, either, chop wood, weed the garden, and haul water, that's all I do anymore."

"That's not all you do," said Verdita, who overheard their complaints. "You eat everything we put up." But she was tired, too, and declared an afternoon off for all of them.

"I'm going to put on my best bib and tuck and go to town. We're all going to have a day of rest."

"Except me," Ira said, "what about poor Papa?" Then he pulled Verdita on his lap, kissed her, and fished a coin out of his vest pocket. "Buy yourself a new hat," he said. "And if Mrs. Bostwick's hat has a big black bird on it, well then, you buy one with an eagle."

"Ira, really." Verdita turned red and tried to wiggle away but her husband held on.

"And why not? I have the prettiest wife in town and a pretty wife deserves a pretty hat."

Hildy giggled. "You're much prettier than Mrs. Blackwell and much thinner, too."

However, Ira wasn't done. "And we've been invited to a dance."

Verdita managed to extricate herself and stood up to straighten her skirts.

"A dance?"

"Yes, ma'am. Rob Scott has been enlarging his scow so he can haul hay on it and he's having an inauguration dance. We've been invited and you'll need a new hat."

"When is it?"

"Tomorrow afternoon."

"Tomorrow! Ira Bacom! Couldn't you have given me a little more notice?"

Ira laughed and swatted her on her behind. "I guess this

afternoon will be your day of rest."

After that, he returned to work and the others scurried about straightening up the kitchen, putting the uneaten dinner food away, and washing the dishes. Verdita put Dovie down for her nap, pinned her old hat on her hair, and left for town. Reuben took off for the Scotts' house and Hildy found herself alone with Dovie and Chong. "You go, too, Miss Hildy, I stay," Chong said.

"Really? Oh, thank you, Chong."

"Where you go?"

"I don't know yet." Hildy grabbed her bonnet. "Maybe an adventure will find me."

She ran out the door and around the house, stopping on A Street to consider the options. Then it occurred to her that she'd yet to see where the coal bunkers were being built north of the Blackwell Hotel.

After a quick stop in Fife's Store to buy a few peppermints, she continued down Pacific Avenue to the road to the wharf. Halfway down that road, she turned left onto a narrow path cut into the side of the hill. The coal bunkers started at less than a quarter of a mile along the trail, and almost directly underneath Mrs. Ward's Cliff Hotel. They extended north as far as she could see. Her father had told them a system of gravity feeding would be used to fill the ships. *How will anyone sleep at the hotel with all the noise underneath them?*

Like so much of the area, men had slashed back or burned the existing terrain in order to make roads to new buildings. Gracious, this is ugly, she thought, looking at the nearly barren hill and piles of pipes and staves. The existing railroad lines were being extended on trestles three stories above ground and built over the water. There was a railroad siding underneath, and two wagon roads. Men were everywhere, sawing, hammering, and shouting. Beyond the bunkers, but out of sight, was the place she'd seen Samuel with the Indians and beyond that was one of New Tacoma's two Chinese communities. Deciding she'd seen all she wanted to, Hildy retraced her steps to the main trail and walked down to the wharf where she caught sight of the Chinese fishing boat Chong told them had just been launched.

A couple of men stood near the wharf's edge looking at the unusual craft. "It looks like it backed into a bunch of chicken coops," one of them said.

His companion agreed, adding, "or some pairs of stairs and all of them stuck."

While they watched, the ship's crew brought up a number of fish. "Look at that, bottom fish every one of 'em."

"I had me some flounder onct, gived to me by Indian Mosses. Twern't so bad."

"Twern't so good, either."

They continued watching the craft and Hildy moved on. She kept to the back of the buildings near the corrals along the bottom of the bank. Some Nisqually Indians had a string of horses in a small enclosure. Hildy watched as General Sprague run his hand down the flank of a dusty little pony and then pull its lips up. "A little long in the tooth." He slapped the animal's flank and it ran to the back of the holding pen.

In spite of the smell, Hildy stayed near the pens. Several were empty but one was full of sheep. As she approached and reached to scratch their heads, they crowded the fence looking for food.

"Hildy."

Hildy looked up and saw General Sprague. "Hello." A fat black ewe tried to nibble her fingers and she ran her hand through its wool, feeling the lanolin underneath. "I wonder where these sheep are going."

"Hildy—you shouldn't be here on the wharf."

"Why?"

The General took off his hat and turned it in his hand. "It's not a good place for a young girl such as yourself to be."

"But I love the wharf. There's always something new to see—it's exciting and the salt water smells good."

General Sprague gave a quick look at the group of men gathered around the Indian's ponies. "I don't want to see anything happen to you, Hildy. You go on along home, now, and we'll just keep this between you and me. Go on, now."

Hildy scowled as she turned away from the bleating sheep. "Well, I never," she muttered. "How can I visit Mrs. Money if I don't come down on the wharf? And really, what business is it of his, anyway?"

The General watched her until she'd started up the wharf trail to town, and Hildy grumbled all the way up to Pacific Avenue. At Fifth Street she decided to cut over to A Street and see if there was anything new on it. Peter Irving, Otis Sprague, and General Sprague had houses there, near each other. The General's was the nicest, but Hildy gave it a dirty look. She kicked a rock and followed its zigzag route down the road, kicking it every time it stopped. As she reached David Lister's place on Eleventh Street, she had an idea. *I'll walk to the other end of A Street and see if there's a path down the bank. I bet there is. Then no one will see me if I want to go to the wharf, and I can come and go as I please.*

The last house on A Street belonged to Christopher McMillan and she was happy to see that there was no one but a small dog sleeping under a maple tree to ask her where she was going. "And you can't ask me, can you?" she said as the dog jumped up and ran to join her. Hildy patted its head. "Well, come along, if you must."

Just as she hoped, beyond the McMillan place, A Street narrowed down into a footpath that hugged the bank. And the bank still had plenty of trees to block the August sun—tall firs, cottonwood trees, short vine maples, and alders everywhere there was a spring. Hildy was particularly fond of the vine maples, which had chubby little round leaves. *In July, when summer is really starting, the vine maples' leaves begin to turn red. They make the woods look pretty. And this is a much nicer way to the waterfront than the wharf road is. Oh, I hope it goes all the way to the water. If it does, I won't tell anyone but Nell.*

She walked quietly. Once or twice rocks scooted under her feet and the movement kicked up dirt. Occasional breaks in the foliage gave a view of the water much as it must have looked before the railroad came. Birds chattered; when they landed on a bush the speckled pattern of sunlight changed. She stopped to look at a garter snake sunning itself on a rock. As she did, a long-horned beetle scooted across the path. Then from a place only they knew about, a number of blue tail butterflies flew up to keep her company. Hildy forgot her anger at General Sprague and was enjoying the solitude when she saw an obstruction on the path. Even as her first thought was "a bear," she knew it wasn't. She found a piece of wood and approached cautiously. She was within a few feet when the shape moved and a face looked at her.

"Why, it's a child. A little Chinese child."

She dropped the wood and squatted down. The toddler had straight black hair combed forward, and wore a jacket and pants, and a small straw hat. "Since you have pants on, I'm guessing you're a little boy." Hildy assumed she wouldn't get a response and was surprised when he handed her a small rock.

"Thank you very much." She put the pebble in her pocket. "You know, I have a little sister named Dovie who I'll bet is just about your age." He looked at her solemnly for a minute and then smiled, revealing a couple of baby teeth.

Hildy pulled out one of the peppermints she'd bought. "Would you like this?"

When the child continued smiling, she unwrapped the sweet

153

and popped it in his mouth. His eyes widened for a minute over the unfamiliar taste and then he broke into a grin. Hildy put a peppermint in her own mouth and stood up. "You must have come up the trail because I didn't see you going down." In the silence, as they looked at each other, a squirrel ran up a nearby tree and scolded them. Hildy laughed and after a moment the child did, too.

"I guess I'll take you down to the wharf and see if I can find your family."

She held out her arms and picked him up, thinking how much lighter he was than Dovie. At first, he looked surprised but he didn't cry and Hildy started down the path. After a few hundred yards, the trail widened and turned left toward the bay. At the bottom, the dog disappeared on business of his own. Hildy heard voices before she saw anything, but as she rounded the bend, New Tacoma's Chinese settlement on the wharf came into view.

It was larger than she expected. Shacks built out of miscellaneous pieces of discarded wood were strung along the wharf. Close behind them were the railroad tracks and on the other side of the tracks she saw several pens where fat lazy pigs snoozed in what shade they could find. Someone had tapped into a spring in the hill and water flowed nonstop out of a wooden pipe. Ropes extended from the houses to tall poles and were draped with laundry. Fish hung from the crossbars on fences to dry in the sun. It was the gardens in front of the houses, though, that caught her attention. Rather than planting their produce in boxes such as Mrs. Blackwell did, the Chinese had planted directly on the wharf. *It's as if the wharf itself is sending up the shoots.* She shifted the toddler to her other hip and walked closer. The people had laid layers of moss on the wooden planks, and covered it with a mixture of soil and mulch. The four or so inches were enough for things to take root. The gardens were crowded with plants that thrived in the sun and enjoyed moisture off the bay. Large baskets lush with what looked like lettuce hung over the edge of the wharf, suspended by rope.

"Gracious," Hildy whispered.

At first glance, the little community seemed deserted, but that didn't seem logical. *Someone has to be here.* Hildy started walking. The first building she passed was a store. She stopped and looked inside through the open doors. At eye level on the left she saw shelves loaded with cigarettes, cigars, and bags of loose tobacco. Just below them were matches, firecrackers, beer, incense, and gambling supplies. On the other side of the shop, shelves strained under the weight of bags of rice, sugar, flour, and folded piles of cotton fabric. There were first-aid items above the staples, and soap, coffee, tea, candles, lard, and canned goods below. Hildy recognized some of the boxes from items Chong bought. Opposite the door she saw a counter with a scale and a bamboo counting device with little round beads on wires. Behind the counter were sandalwood fans, ginseng, candy, and strange dried roots. The room had an unfamiliar smell. An old man slept in a tattered horsehair chair and Hildy stepped back hoping he wouldn't wake up.

Outside the store and set back under a tree was a flat piece of wood with small polished rocks on it and a statue in the middle. Around the wood were little dishes of sand with slender pieces of wood sticking out. Hildy was looking at it all when she heard a high-pitched voice and the little boy wiggled to be put down. Turning she saw someone running toward them.

The child waddled toward the woman, who grabbed him up, alternating between laughing, crying, and scolding. She wore a quilted coat that ended at her knees and pants with legs like stovepipes. Her hair was parted down the middle and pulled back into a knot. She ran her hands all over the boy, checking that he wasn't hurt, and then stared at Hildy with wide eyes. She doesn't look much older than me, Hildy thought.

The woman said something and Hildy shook her head, thinking that maybe Chong could teach her Chinese.

After a moment, she picked up the child and turned away. With regret, Hildy turned away too.

When she reached home, Dovie was in the yard with Chong, who was cleaning clams, and Hildy checked the noon-mark to see if it was time to start supper. Thinking chowder sounded good, she began chopping onions and melting butter. As she did, she decided not to tell anyone about her afternoon. *Why chance Mama telling me never to go back there again?*

And at supper, everyone was so full of their afternoons, Hildy found it easy to keep quiet. Verdita modeled her hat, which had huge plumes of feathers. Ira said the Hanson Ackerson Mill was getting a three-foot-high sign so the ships could easily see it when they reached the harbor, and Reuben talked about the bunting Mr. Scott was draping all over his scow. Since Chong had been home all afternoon, Verdita sent him off to enjoy himself while she and Hildy washed the dishes. It was near dusk when Chong returned and handed Hildy a package.

"What's this?" She looked at the Chinese writing on the paper.

"You find boy, family make gift."

"I don't need a gift. I liked it there and I liked the girl I met." Hildy looked at Chong. "Could you teach me some Chinese so I can talk to her?"

"Better Chinee learn English," he said in the tone Hildy recognized as the subject is closed. He pointed at the parcel. "You open."

Hildy unwrapped it, being careful not to tear the paper, and removed a large shell with small brass bells hanging off it on long pieces of red ribbon. She held it up and the tiny clappers chimed merrily.

"Wind chime," Chong said. "Hang in tree. Evil spirits go away."

"It's lovely, but I didn't need a present."

"Woman give to save face."

"What does that mean?"

"Terrible thing to lose child. You help woman save face."

"Can I go visit her sometime?"

"No. Husband bad man."

"Bad how?"

"Just bad." Chong scowled and Hildy knew she'd get no more information about that, either.

She took the wind chime around the house and climbed a tree outside her bedroom. All day long people have been telling me what to do, she thought. Someday I'm going to do anything I want to.

She lingered among the branches until mosquitoes became too much. After that, she climbed down the tree, leaving the wind chime to make music in the breeze.

Chapter 15

Summer's hot, dry weather slowly melted into crisp September days and one morning Hildy woke up unexpectedly cold. She dressed hurriedly and ran down the stairs to make sure her bread dough hadn't been damaged. Chong was already in the kitchen.

"Good morning, Chong." She punched down the dough. "It almost feels like winter."

"Yes, Miss Hildy."

"I'm so glad you started the stove, I'm sure you saved my bread."

"Frost make ground hard to dig."

Hildy knew he was referring to the root cellar he and Reuben had been working on but that wasn't what caught her attention. She stopped shaping her loaves and looked up. "I think you say your Rs better than any Chinese man in town, Chong."

A smile broke out on the boy's face. "I tink so, too."

Hildy giggled and set her pans on the back of the stove. School was starting in a few days and she cherished these quiet hours before everyone else was up. Sometimes Chong told her stories about his home in China but more and more lately he talked about the land he was going to buy when he'd saved enough money.

"When your ship comes in?" Hildy asked him once.

"Ship. What ship? No more ship. I stay on land," he said, and scowled when she laughed.

158

"It's an expression. It means, ummm, when everything is in your favor."

Since then, he hadn't talked about his plans and Hildy hoped she hadn't insulted him. Being Chinese and a boy, and not much older than she, it was sometimes hard to know.

Now that September had arrived, the stove's damper took time to set. When Chong decided it was right, he started grinding coffee beans and Hildy poured herself a glass of milk. She checked the oatmeal Verdita had put to soak the previous night, and began slicing meat off the smoked ham Ira brought home from his recent trip. The floor overhead squeaked under footsteps, Verdita's light ones, going to get Dovie, and Reuben's pounding ones. Since Ira's return from the coalfields and the long days combing the foothills both on foot and in the saddle, he was often the last one up.

Verdita came into the kitchen as the coffee began to perk. "Good morning, Chong." She tied on an apron, took the turning fork from Hildy, and gave her daughter a hug. "Thank you, Hildy."

"Where's Dovie?" Hildy poured her mother a cup of coffee and added some to what was left of her milk.

"With Reuben." Verdita turned the meat and the smell of frying pork filled the air.

"Not too much for me, Verdy," Ira said as he entered the room with Reuben and Dovie on his heels. "I'm not all that hungry."

"Seems like you haven't been hungry at all since you got back."

"I'm feeling a little tired, that's all."

Hildy poured him coffee while Reuben filled the washbasin with water from the pot on the stove and splashed his face. Verdita put the meat on a platter and Hildy served the oatmeal. While they sat down at the table Chong retired to a corner to eat his own food. Not even Reuben talked much at breakfast. He needed the morning to wind up.

When they were done, Ira left for work, Reuben and Chong went out back to continue working on the root cellar, and Verdita took Dovie upstairs while she cleaned. Hildy had a fourth customer now for her bread and she hurried to get the pans in the oven. After that, she washed the dishes, and the dishes and the bread were both done when Mr. Peak turned up.

"Good morning, Mr. Peak." She opened the door.

"Good morning, Miss." Mr. Peak tugged at his hat brim. "Feels like Indian summer has set in for sure. Been teasing at it for a week."

"We had Indian summers in Pennsylvania." Hildy took his bag and turned to get his bread. "First there'd be a spell of hot days and then a heavy frost and then more hot days. The frost turned the leaves and maked them all red-like. It was ever so pretty."

"Yes, Miss, it sure is."

"Why do they call it Indian Summer?"

"Well, I don't rightly know, Miss."

Hildy tucked the edges of the bag carefully round the loaf but before she handed it to Mr. Peak she said, "Mr. Peak, do you know where I can get a rutabaga?"

"A rutabaga?"

"Yes, you know, some people call it a yellow turnip."

"I knows a turnip when I sees it but I don't know anyone around New Tacoma as grows them. Maybe yonder in Puyallup someone does."

"Mama's going to teach me to make Cornish pasties; they're meat pies. They're awfully good. Back home the miners' wives make them in the morning for their husbands to take to work for their noon meal and they're still warm from the oven. Mr. Peak, if you can find me one, I'll make you a pastie to say thanks, and you can see how good they are."

"I'll do that, Miss. I surely could use somethun warm at dinner."

It took Mr. Peak a week to find the rutabaga. He presented it with a flourish, his false teeth slipping and clicking.

"What a lovely specimen," said Verdita, who had come out the door behind Hildy.

"Yes, ma'am." Mr. Peak immediately doffed his hat.

Hildy took his sack and hurried to get his bread.

"We have onions and potatoes in our garden and I'll have Mr. Bacom pick up some beef on his way home, tonight. You come by tomorrow morning and your pastie will be ready."

"Yes, ma'am. Thank you, ma'am." Mr. Peak took his bread from Hildy and tripped as he turned around.

"I think you make him nervous, Mama," Hildy said after he'd disappeared.

"I don't suppose he's met many ladies. Well, now, we'll get started right after supper."

Hildy spent the rest of the morning churning butter, which she and Verdita washed until the water ran clear. They poured the buttermilk into bottles, wrapped the butter in greased paper, and put them both in a cool spot under the house. Ira had sent word that he wouldn't be home for dinner and after the others ate, Chong and Reuben returned to the root cellar, which they were lining with wood and stones. Verdita went into the parlor where it was cool and where she often sewed, and Hildy pushed Dovie on the swing. She was surprised when her father appeared.

"Papa, what are you doing home?" She ran to take the meat he carried. "I thought you were staying at the office."

Before he could answer, Ira gave a deep, bronchial cough. He wiped his forehead and mouth.

"Things were quiet so I thought I'd leave a little early.

Where's your mother?"

"In the parlor, sewing. Can I get you something, Papa?"

"Not right now, little cabbage, I think I'll just rest a bit."

Ira went in and Hildy joined Chong and Reuben. The entry to the root cellar was a five-foot-long trap door that lifted to reveal a space under the house. It wasn't deep enough for a person to stand up in, but nevertheless would provide a cool place for potatoes, carrots, cabbages, and other produce to winter over.

"What a good job you've done." Hildy jumped down into the hole and peeked inside.

"We can hide here if the Indians attack," Reuben said.

"They don't do that anymore."

"I heard Mr. James Buchanan Beck say that Indian Mosses has been getting ammunition from that old Mr. John Shoudy. I bet if he gets enough he'll come and shoot everyone and scalp us, too."

Reuben crawled out of the hole and began dancing around the yard, patting his mouth to make sounds.

"Maybe we could throw potatoes at them," Hildy said.

"And carrots."

"And cabbages. Let's throw them first."

"Jehoshaphat. We'd better start right now getting ready."

Ever since he and Chong began the root cellar, Reuben had been saving the wooden boxes he found. Now he hurried to start bringing them over. Hildy put the buttermilk and butter in one and covered it carefully to keep bugs out. For the rest of the afternoon, they dug the last of the potatoes and carrots and filled the boxes, discussing what should go where. They were finishing up when Verdita called them for supper.

"Where's Papa?" Reuben scrubbed the dirt off his hands, admiring the grime accumulating in the washbasin.

"He's not feeling well so I'm going to take his supper

upstairs." Verdita poured hot gravy on mashed potatoes and picked up the tray. "I have it all ready."

Hildy washed herself and Dovie, and had just sat down when Verdita returned.

"What's this?" Reuben looked suspiciously at a platter of meat his mother put on the table.

"Grouse. Some hunters brought them to Mr. Fife's store."

"What's it taste like?"

"Try it and see." She started cutting potatoes and carrots into small bites that Dovie stuffed in her mouth with her fingers. Reuben decided he liked the bird and loaded his plate. Hildy decided she didn't and followed her usual pattern of washing bites down with milk. They ate silently and when they were finished and while Hildy cleared the table, Verdita went to get Ira's tray. She returned with it mostly untouched.

Reuben was allowed to go out and join his friends; Chong washed the dishes, and Verdita and Hildy started making pasties. Together, they washed, peeled, and sliced potatoes, onions, and part of the rutabaga, stepping around Dovie, who played on the floor with some blocks of wood. Then, while Verdita chopped pork and beef, Hildy put flour, salt, and kidney suet on the table and started making the dough. She was using a bottle to roll pie-shell-sized circles when Nell appeared at the door.

"What are you doing?" Nell came in and sat down across the table from where Hildy was working.

"Mama's teaching me to make Cornish pasties." She put the bottle down. "Now what, Mama?"

Verdita showed her how much of the meat and vegetables to put on the dough, ending with thin slices of the rutabaga. Then she added salt and pepper and folded the pastry over into a half-moon. She slid the finished meat pie onto a cooking sheet and Hildy started the next one.

"Did you hear about the deep-sea wedding?" Nell slid a little tin of Y&S licorice out of her pocket and popped a piece in her mouth.

"Who was it?" asked Hildy.

"No one from around here." When Verdita turned her back for a moment, Nell put a piece of the candy in Hildy's mouth and they both chewed vigorously. Simultaneously, they grinned at each other, revealing teeth covered with the black confection, and giggled. After Nell swallowed, she continued. "They rowed down from Steilacoom and woke Justice Carr up."

Hildy's eyes lit up. "I bet he was mad. He's awful old and cranky."

"Not since he got another wife. He got her through the mail."

"Goodness gracious." Hildy finished a second pastie and started on a third. "Why did they have to have a deep-sea wedding?"

"Because they were too young to get a marriage license and their folks didn't want them to. Justice Carr hustled them onto a steamer in the harbor and joined 'em up as quick as a flash and then they rowed back to Steilacoom."

Verdita slid the second pastie on to the cooking sheet and sighed. *Deep-sea weddings, mail-order brides, what next?*

"Have you seen Kezzie lately, Nell?" she asked.

Nell gave her a puzzled look.

"Kezzie came over one day to visit," Hildy explained. "We played Authors."

"Oh." Nell crossed her eyes and wagged her head back and forth. Hildy snickered and Verdita sighed again.

They continued talking while outside, the sun worked its way toward the horizon. At dusk, Reuben came home and Nell left. Verdita fixed a hot toddy for Ira and Hildy cleaned the kitchen and got Dovie washed and ready for bed. As she carried the toddler upstairs, she heard Ira's deep cough.

Much to her chagrin, Aunt Glady's letter answering Hildy's query about new baking ideas arrived the day before school started. She sat on the steps while her mother shelled peas and read it aloud.

Dear Niece:

How difficult it must be for you, living in such an uncivilized place, to stay au courant on styles. Apees are very fashionable now but your cousin, Elsie, says you probably don't have rose-water, caraway seeds, and mace out there in Indian Country so I will tell you about Number Cakes. They are very small and individually sized, and are served at every afternoon tea these days. They are called that because of the amounts of ingredients. The big change is that the flour, sugar, and other components are measured by cup rather than weighed: one cup of butter and milk, and one spoonful of baking soda, two cups sugar, three cups flour, and four eggs. Since I'm sure you are still weighing yours, I converted the recipe for you: four ounces of flour, seven ounces of sugar, eight ounces each butter and milk and baking soda. I suggest you break an egg and cover the bottom of one half of the shell to about a quarter of an inch for the soda. A ramekin makes a good baking dish. . . .

There was more but Hildy stopped there. "Why does Aunt Glady always do that?" she asked.

"Do what?"

"She could have just answered my question without talking about New Tacoma being uncivilized, and saying we don't have things like they do. She's mean even when she's nice."

"That's how she makes herself feel important." Verdita popped a couple of peas in her mouth, swallowed, and continued. "When your father and I started keeping company, she made remarks about everything I said or did or even wore, but always cloaked them with something sweet. I particularly remember one comment about a dress I'd just made. 'What a lovely dress,' she said, 'aren't you fortunate to be able to sew and not have to spend the exorbitant amounts of money on clothes that the rest of us do.' She hadn't really said it looked homemade, just implied. After a while I figured out that that's how Aunt Glady adds value to herself in her own eyes. If she can find a way to criticize a person then she feels that she's better than that person. It's really very sad."

"Well, I think someone should tell her that they know what she's doing."

"It wouldn't work." Verdita picked a few bad peas out of the bowl and tossed them to Chicken Little. "If I had ever said something she would have gone into a high dudgeon and swanned around as being terribly wounded. Eventually, I would have felt called upon to apologize just to make peace. She would have been sweetly gracious and we'd both have been right back where we started."

"Gracious. Ellen at school used to do that sometimes but Nell never did. But Nell's so pretty she doesn't have to make people feel bad about their selves."

"She's no prettier than you."

"Oh, Mama, I'm not pretty, I'm plain."

Verdita dropped her peapod and took Hildy's chin in her hand, turning it so she looked directly at her daughter. "You most assuredly are not, daughter. You have hair that shines like a chestnut and eyes that fairly spark when you're excited. Your skin is fair if a little bit too brown from the sun." Verdita dropped her hand and laughed. "Now that sounded just like Aunt Glady, didn't it? But never you worry, you're going to be a beautiful woman." She snapped the last peapod and stood up. "And now

I have to check on your father."

After super, Hildy and Reuben took Dovie for a short walk. A few late Canada goldenrods bloomed here and there near paper birch. Vine maple crowded western red cedar, their leaves flaming, and snowberries interrupted the colors with their thick white balls. In some places fir needles crunched underfoot, releasing a rich piney scent. A grasshopper that had survived the frost jumped ahead of them, chased by roaming chickens.

"I worry about Chicken Little all the time and look at those stray hens running around," Hildy said in disgust.

Dovie dropped their hands to run after a chick following its mother and Reuben said, "Do you think Papa is very sick?"

"I've been trying not to think about it."

"I think he must be because we didn't get our picnic."

"I know." Hildy hurried after Dovie.

They continued walking, mostly talking about going back to school, and letting Dovie carry the chick she caught. Later in the evening, they didn't know their mother left them long enough to run to Dr. Bostwick's house.

CHAPTER 16

The morning school started, Hildy slumped at the table looking morose. "I wish we were going back to Miss Sparkle's school."

Verdita sat down and guided Dovie's spoon in the direction of her mouth. "You knew that school with Miss Sparkle was temporary, until the North School building was finished."

"But it felt like home, and North School is so big. It's two stories."

"The second floor belongs to the Golden Rule Lodge." Ira, who had already eaten and was scanning through the *Herald*, looked up. "And Nell is going to North School, so you won't be alone."

Hildy heaved a sigh, leaned on her hand, and stirred her oatmeal. Out of the corner of her eye she looked at a bottle of medicine on the table. Papa is putting a good face on things, she decided, but he coughed a lot last night.

"North School has lots of games." Reuben interrupted her thoughts and spoke with a mouth full of oatmeal. "They play baseball."

Ira rustled the paper. "How many times has your mother told you not to talk with your mouth full, Reuben?"

Chong, who had been pouring water from a bucket into the kettle on the stove, glanced up.

"Girl stay home and work. Boy go to school. Important boy learn."

Verdita and Ira exchanged smiles while Hildy gave Chong a

dirty look. She filled her spoon with cereal and let it drop back in the bowl until Ira told her to quit dawdling and eat.

After they left the house, Hildy grinned. "Ha! At least Chong has to do the dishes."

"And fill the woodbox and haul the water." Reuben kicked at a pile of gravel several Chinese men were shoveling into the road's wagon groves.

He and Hildy carried their midday meal in syrup buckets and each had their copybooks, slates, and sponges.

"This old sponge is so dry it probably won't even clean my slate." Hildy seemed determined to stay crabby.

"It'll be fine when it's wet."

On Ninth Street Reuben stopped and sniffed the air. "Mr. Orchard's burning stumps again. It helps cover the smell of Mr. Graham's pigs."

At that moment, they saw Nell running toward them. Her dandelion hair bounced around her face, and her unbuttoned coat showed she was wearing last year's school dress. She was laughing when she reached them. "Did you see Mr. Fife's cow?" She laughed so hard she could hardly continue. "It got knocked into the bay by a train and the train broke off one of her horns. Mr. Fife had to rescue her from the water and lead her home and he even rescued the horn."

Hildy and Reuben laughed with her, and Hildy wondered how Nell could always be so happy. Hildy linked their arms, matched their steps, and chanted:

Gaine's Ghost sat on a Post;
His Feet were full of Blisters.
He made three grabs at Mary Tabbs
And the Wind blew through his Whiskers.

Disgusted, Reuben saw the Scott boys coming down C Street and joined them. They ran on ahead, pushing and shoving each other.

"Isn't it pretty out today?" Nell looked around. "I love the trees in September. I bet Sarah could draw pictures of the trees and paint them."

"Can Sarah draw?"

"Yes, I saw some of her pictures one day uptown after the picnic. Mr. Leve, her father, was getting his tailor's shop ready and Sarah had some of her pictures on the wall. She's really good. Ellen puts on airs about her knitting; I hope we have classes where Sarah can draw something. It'll cook Ellen's goose."

Nell giggled but Hildy sighed. "Nell." She paused and looked sad. "Aren't you ever jealous?"

"What do you mean?"

"Oh, I don't know. It's just that sometimes I think that other people can play musical instruments or sing or paint, or they're beautiful, like you, and I'm nothing but a house wren, plain looking and not very interesting."

"Oh, Hildy, you're being silly." Nell squeezed her arm. "You're more like a seagull, strong and proud and hovering all over the place, trying to keep an eye on everything, and absolutely the best friend I could ever have."

Hildy squeezed Nell's arm back and wondered why she felt so weepy.

North School sat at the top of a hill and faced the bay. It had a large porch where the students could sit if it rained, and a roughly cleared space for games. The building wasn't as big as Hildy feared. She and Nell hurried to join Kezzie, Ellen, Fern, and Sarah, who stood near the steps. Some older girls had gathered to watch the boys playing catch with a beat-up ball.

"I'm sorry I couldn't get you that flower from Gallagher

Gulch," Hildy said to Sarah.

"Oh, that's all right." Sarah smiled and looked around. "There are lots of things to draw and paint here."

Before she could say anything else, a lady came out and looked at a small watch pinned to her bodice. Then she rang a handbell, and they filed inside.

"Coats on the hooks at the back of the room, please." The bell ringer picked up a piece of paper. "And remain standing until I call your name and show you where you will be sitting."

The school room was large, with a big teacher's desk on a platform in front. On one side of the desk was a flag and on the other, about halfway up the aisle, a stove. Behind the desk was a cracked blackboard on which was written "Mrs. Stair." The students had backless benches to sit on and long planks supported by legs on which to put their slates. Hildy giggled because some of the smallest children would have to half-stand in order to write while the tallest would be humped over. An aisle down the middle of the room separated boys from girls. Large windows and a few kerosene lamps provided the light. As Mrs. Stair read names off a list and everyone took their seats, Hildy admired the work Mrs. Stair had put in for the seating arrangement. The youngest were in front, girls next to girls and boys next to boys, alphabetically by last name. Hildy found herself halfway up the room near a window but very close to the stove. Nell, whose last name was Tanquist, was in the back. Her nearest seatmate was Kezzie. Hildy's was Ellen.

When everyone was seated, Mrs. Stair stood at her desk and stared at them until the giggles and whispers stopped.

"Please bow your heads for the Lord's prayer."

After that, she had everyone stand to sing the first verse of the "Battle Hymn of the Republic." Hildy peeked at Fern and saw that her lips barely moved. And when she looked at Mrs. Stair, Hildy saw the teacher watching Fern with a puzzled look.

After that, Mrs. Stair had them sit down after which she began a speech welcoming them to the school.

"First, I want to introduce Mr. Stair. Mr. Stair and I will both be giving lessons."

Her husband smiled and nodded.

"In the morning I will teach spelling, reading, grammar, and arithmetic on your slates. In the afternoon, Mr. Stair will carry on with lessons in geography, penmanship, and history. On Fridays we will practice penmanship using ink and quill pens, have spelling bees, and do recitations. I expect the more advanced students to help the younger ones."

Gracious, thought Hildy, and she turned to roll her eyes at Nell.

"Hildy Bacom." Mrs. Stair interrupted her speech. "Do you have something to say to Nell Tanquist?"

"Uh, no ma'am."

"Then please look at me when I am speaking. Now, let us begin."

Mrs. Stair whisked them through lessons with the efficiency of a field marshal, and Hildy was more than ready when classes stopped at noon. She joined her friends under a large maple tree.

"Where's Lucy?" Hildy sat down and took a sandwich out of her bucket.

"She started school over in Sumner. Mira Kincaid got diphtheria and died. Lucy's family and the Kincaids are kin and her folks are there and thinking of moving." Ellen took a bite of her apple and Kezzie asked Fern why she wouldn't sing the "Battle Hymn of the Republic."

"Why, that's a Yankee song. Mama'd tan my hide, for sure, if she caught me singing it."

"But this is the West," Nell pointed out. "No one cares about that old war anymore."

"They do in Virginia."

Hildy looked at Nell, crossed her eyes, and got up to go to the necessary. The Lodge built two at the back of the property with a modest distance between boys and girls. When Hildy opened the door to the girls, a little boy turned around and shouted, "Hey!"

"Oh!" Hildy gasped. She slammed the door in embarrassment, double-checked the sign below a little carved half-moon, and heard a chorus of laughter. Standing far enough away so as not to appear obvious was a group of boys who slapped each other on their backs howling with delight at her discomfort. The unfortunate boy pushed his way out of the necessary and took off while Hildy glared at the culprits. "That was just—just rude!"

When word of the incident got out, Mrs. Stair checked the signs on the doors. Someone had switched them back, embarrassing Hildy even more. Five days later, at the end of the week she was still fuming.

On Friday Kezzie became the victim of a different prank. Dinner break was over and Mr. Stair rang the bell. During the pushing and shoving to get inside, someone offered her the last piece of candy in a sack. Kezzie, hurrying to get it chewed and swallowed, failed, at first, to realize it wasn't candy. Someone had frosted and sugarcoated a large piece of onion.

"Our lesson today is Great Britain as the workshop of the world." Mr. Stair turned to the blackboard. "Who can name one of the things that helped Great Britain achieve this title?"

Before anyone could answer, Kezzie stood up, grabbed her throat, and began coughing. Her face turned red and tears streamed down her cheeks.

"Argh." She leaned over and coughed up a piece of the half-chewed vegetable.

Mouths dropped open and those across the aisle from her shot off their benches and moved away. Kezzie coughed more onion up. Her lunch followed and the room broke into turmoil.

"Golly." Dan Strange was so horrified no one even noticed the swear word.

Hildy jumped up and hurried to the water bucket. She took a dipperful to Kezzie, who by that time was crying.

The door opened and Mrs. Stair rushed in. "Whatever is going on?" She stopped and took in the chaos. "What's the matter with Kezzie?"

"Uh, er . . ." Mr. Stair held a cloth over his nose. "She choked on a piece of onion."

Kezzie drank the entire dipper of water and continued to sob.

Mrs. Stair ignored the room's powerful odor and looked at the sobbing girl. "Well, that's nothing to cry about."

"I thought it was candy." Kezzie's words spewed out more onion smell.

"Candy? Why would you think that? Couldn't you tell the difference?"

"It was frosted."

Kezzie sat down and put her head on her arm. One of the boys hurried to the door and fanned it to freshen the air.

"Mr. Stair." Mr. Stair jumped and looked at his wife. "There are peppermints in the desk. Please bring one to Kezzie. And Kezzie." She put a hand on the girl's shoulder. "Stop crying and go out to the pump and wash your face. Here." She took her husband's white kerchief and handed it to the girl. "Go on, now, and suck this peppermint."

Kezzie left and Mrs. Stair walked to the front of the room. "Sit down everyone." She looked around. "Where did Kezzie get the onion?"

No one answered and in the uncomfortable silence, Kezzie returned. "Who gave you the, ah, er, candied onion?"

"I don't know."

"You don't know?"

"We were at the door and someone—handed it to me and said, 'do you want this last piece of candy?' and I don't know who it was but we never get candy at home . . ." Kezzie's voice trailed off.

Mrs. Stair looked at the room. "I think we have all learned a valuable lesson today about the danger of practical jokes and I trust there will be no more of them. Mr. Stair." Her husband snapped to attention. "Have one of the boys clean up the mess and carry on with your lessons."

Things stayed quiet over the next few weeks. Then, one day in late September, a frog jumped out of the drinking pail when Ellen removed the lid. Not long after that, Mrs. Stair found two sleeping bats hanging from a beam when she opened the classroom door. September turned into October; one day Nell was blamed for throwing spit wads because some little pieces of paper were found where she sat. Walking to the pump one day, Hildy saw Reuben running cold water on his arm.

"Your arm's all red. What happened?"

"Chinese rope burn."

"Chinese rope burn? What's that?"

Reuben shook the water off his arm and rolled his sleeve down. "Someone takes ahold of your arm with both hands and twists the skin in opposite directions."

"Well—that's just mean. Why did they do that?"

"They were making fun of the Chinese and I told them to stop."

"Who did it?"

"I can't tell you. You'll tell Mama and she'll be mad."

"I won't tell her if you don't want me to, but there's sure been a lot of stuff happening since school started."

"It's a club."

"What? What kind of club?"

Reuben massaged his arm and looked around. Satisfied that

no one was near enough to hear he said, "It's the boys who are going to graduate this year. I heard them talking. They called themselves the New Tacoma Tomfooleries and they want everyone to remember them so they keep planning all these pranks."

"I don't think this was a prank. It was a very nasty thing to do." Hildy's eyes narrowed. "What's next?"

"All I know is it's something for Halloween."

The bell rang and Hildy returned to the classroom deep in thought. After school she and Nell waited until the others left and walked slowly home. "Something has to be done to stop this. Reuben's arm really hurt." Hildy scowled.

"I purely hate to think what they have in mind for Halloween."

"We need to come up with a prank of our own."

In mid-October someone put a mouse in the desk for Mr. Stair to find. Little Manny Fox's lunchtime milk bottle was swapped for a bottle of sour milk. The dry firewood was replaced with wet wood that smoked them out of the room. Hildy and Nell racked their brains for something they could do in retaliation. One day when Mrs. Stair's back was turned, a note from Nell was passed down the aisle to Hildy. "Meet me at the necessary."

Rain fell hard. When school broke for lunch, students milled around on the porch before dividing into groups. Hildy put on her coat and slogged through the mud to meet Nell.

"Ike caught a skunk last night."

"How'd he do that?"

"He baited a little box. Mrs. Steele, who has the hotel in Old Tacoma, got him to do it because the skunk was after her chickens. Ike is smart. The box was so short when the skunk went in it couldn't lift its tail and spray but Ma said Ike smelled bad. She made him go up to Mr. Halstead's bathhouse and he has to get rid of it. I asked if he'd give the skunk to me. Ike wanted to know what for and I told him about the Tomfoolery club."

"What did he say?"

"He said he knew most of the boys and that they deserved to get their comeuppance. So he agreed to bring the skunk up tomorrow just before school gets out. Most of the boys who have been causing all the trouble have to stay after school tomorrow and study for their teaching certificates. They got behind. Can you imagine any of them as teachers?"

"I hope they get students who are just as bad as they are."

The girls giggled and Nell continued. "I figure you can get Mr. Stair outside and I'll turn the skunk loose inside. I'll get Ike to bring home a herring to coax him out of the box; they're biting real good and we'll toss it in. If the boys even start to make a move the skunk will blast them."

"Where will he put the skunk?"

"Out back behind the bushes next to the wall."

Hildy's eyes sparkled. "Nell Tanquist, that's just genius."

They hurried back to the porch and luckily no one noticed how long they'd been gone.

The next day Mrs. Stair had a cold, and filled half the blackboard with fractions for them to work out on their slates while she rested at her desk. Hildy didn't mind fractions because they related to baking ingredients. She finished quickly and fidgeted until Mrs. Stair had her help the youngest students with their addition and subtraction. Most of them had made progress but Graham Blair looked discouraged.

"I just don't understand, Hildy."

Hildy thought for a minute. "Papa said your father caught a string of fish yesterday. How many did he bring home?"

"Five but he gave one to Mrs. Fife."

"Then how many did you have?"

"Don't you know?"

"I do but do you?"

"Well 'a course. We had four and Ma fried them up with taters and onions."

"Let's draw five little fish next to the sum." Hildy drew little ovals. "Now, cross one out. How many are left?"

"Four."

"You see, that's how I do arithmetic. I think of something I know about. What about this one?"

"It's a seven."

"What if it was seven crows and one started to fly away?"

"I'd throw a rock at them and they'd all fly away. There wouldn't be any, a'tol. I hates crows."

Hildy started to laugh but caught Mrs. Stair's eye. To her surprise, the teacher smiled.

The day dragged on. Lunch came and went. Fern, Ellen, and Kezzie wanted to walk home with Nell and Hildy but Hildy made up an errand she needed to run. When the school yard was empty, she and Nell sneaked back and found a box holding the skunk and a dead fish wrapped in paper.

"I don't know how to get Mr. Stair outside."

"I'll think of something."

As it turned out, Mr. Stair left the school and went round back to the water pump. Hildy took the fish and Nell took the box, which she held at arm's length. They walked as fast and carefully as they could up the stairs. The skunk protested, making noises that sounded like a combination of a cat and a piglet.

"Open the door and throw the fish in fast and I'll tip the box over and pull the door shut."

Hildy stood at the left and inched the door just far enough to throw the fish in. Moving fast, Nell turned the box on its side and pushed it through. She yanked the door shut and dropped the bar in place. For a minute they heard nothing. Then the boys shouted and yelled.

"How'd that get in here?"

"Watch it."

"Look out."

Footsteps pounded; benches fell over. Someone tugged at the door. "It's locked."

After that, the skunk sprayed and even outside Hildy and Nell fell back to avoid the smell.

"The window. Open the window."

"It's nailed down. Aaggg."

"Break it."

Hildy and Nell were doubled up laughing when Mr. Stair appeared. "What's going on?"

"Ah. Nell and I were walking by and heard racket coming from the school. We were just about to look in and see if everything was all right."

"Oh, that's most kind but the boys are studying and it's not appropriate for you young ladies to be there. I'll just check myself. My goodness, what's that smell?"

Hildy and Nell hurried far enough away to hide and watch. Mr. Stair fumbled with the door latch. When he pushed the door open, six boys burst out gasping. Yells and bits of comments carried to where the girls were hiding.

"My lungs are ruined."

"Can't get the smell out."

"We gotta get even."

"Yeah but with who?"

Mr. Stair watched them with a little smile on his face. "Sorry boys, the latch must have fallen when I shut the door. Well, you better get on home and try to clean up. My, that is a powerful smell."

The boys scattered. Two went to the pump and doused their heads with water. Mr. Stair left the door open to air the room, clasped his hands behind his back, and strolled near where Hildy and Nell hid.

"My, my, I don't know what Mrs. Stair will have to say about this but I do know what Lord Byron wrote: 'Sweet is revenge, especially to women.' "

CHAPTER 17

Hildy wrapped herself up in a quilt and stood at the kitchen door watching fat, fluffy snowflakes fall. Reflected in the moonlight, the snow weighed fir limbs down, and branches covered with ice resembled fine lace. Small animal tracks on the white crust looked like the hieroglyphics Miss Sparkle had once shown them pictures of. Even in the stillness, though, men's distant voices reached her ears. In a few minutes it would be midnight and the drinkers were priming themselves to welcome in a new year.

When the cold on her feet became too much, she sat in front of the stove and listened to the pitch snap. From past experience, Hildy knew that sparks would pop out of the chimney and shoot toward the sky. Once, when Reuben was little and wanted to know where stars came from, she told him that they were sparks from fires all over the world. After that, and much to their parents' dismay, he continually poked sticks in their stove saying, "make stars."

Hildy smiled at the memory and wiggled to get comfortable on the hard, wooden floor. She'd brought her journal with her and had to catch up before the happenings lost their importance and memories faded. Not that the memory of her father's illness and what it meant would ever go away, but she needed to capture the details. In September she'd written, "School, Dr. Bostwick, wool," on a page of the journal, and those three words were enough to bring back the days when autumn's beauty belied her family's struggle.

Ira had never really recovered from his first bout of pneumonia. In late fall she and Reuben met Dr. Bostwick leaving their house as they came home from school, and Reuben ran up to him.

"Is Papa all right?"

"If he was I wouldn't be here, would I?"

Hildy blanched at the sharp words and the doctor, seeing it, was ashamed. "I'm sorry, child, I haven't had enough sleep. Delivered twins over near the reservation and was up pretty near all night." He shifted his medical bag from one hand to the other, and the stethoscope around his neck swayed. "Your father has pneumonia again, ordinarily not a bad case but you know the state of his lungs, and he's been working too hard."

"Yes, sir," Hildy said. "That's why we came West, so Papa would get better. He was, too, until he went on that trip up to the mountain . . ."

"Yes, right, well . . . er, well, he went and got himself all clapped out. I can hear congestion in his lungs, not a lot. I bled him and left a pneumonia jacket with your mother to keep him warm. He needs rest and quiet."

A nippy little wind swept leaves around their ankles. The doctor grabbed the lapels of his coat and held them around his neck. "Go on in now; be good and help your mother."

"We're always good," Reuben said when he was out of earshot. "I don't think I like him very much."

They ran around to the back of the house but remembered not to slam the door. "Ummm, it smells good in here." Reuben took his jacket off and hung it up.

Verdita, who was doing something at the stove, turned and smiled at him.

Hildy, however, saw the pinched look on her mother's face. "Dr. Bostwick says Papa has pneumonia." She sliced a piece of bread for Reuben, spread it thickly with butter, and waited for her mother's reaction.

Verdita saw the look of fear in Hildy's eyes.

"Papa will be fine. We're going to take care of everything so he can rest and not worry." She touched Hildy on the cheek. "Why don't you get yourself some bread and butter, supper will be a little late."

"What are you making?"

"Calfs-foot jelly in this pot and I'm rendering bone marrow in this one."

"I can make custard," Hildy said. "Aunt Glady used to say that custard is good for invalids and mentally deranged people."

Verdita sighed and took the pot off the stove. Reuben sat at the table to eat his bread and Hildy hurried to take a piece of wood from Dovie, who was banging it on the floor, and replaced it with a rag doll.

Chong came in with an armful of towels that had whipped dry outside, bringing a gust of cold air and dead leaves. Verdita started scraping the marrow from the beef bones. "Do your schoolwork, and when I'm done helping Papa eat, we'll have our supper."

Now, sitting on the kitchen floor and remembering that day and those to follow, Hildy felt as if she'd never forget the smell of marrow or the glutinous look of the jelly as her mother strained it. She shuddered slightly and looked at her journal. *Just those three words and look at how much I remember. Words are powerful things.*

As she wrote, the sounds of the pitch competed with tiny tapping noises. The snow had changed to ice pellets and the wind was pushing them against the window. Hildy put a piece of wood in the stove and held her blanket open to the heat. The Sibley stove Uncle Edgar gave them when they came West had been installed in the hallway upstairs, its pipe ventilating out a hole in the wall. When it was as cold as it currently was, though, the only really warm place in the house was the kitchen.

Maybe when I get enough money from my bread I'll buy my own stove, Hildy thought. Would that be selfish? She had a nice little pile of coins hidden in her room but so far very little at the merchandise stores had tempted her to spend them.

From outside came the slow screech and loud snap of a tree limb breaking, and Hildy gave a start, smearing ink in her journal. She blotted it with her finger and looked at the words "ugly wool dress," which stood out boldly in the paper. They brought back the sad reminder that not even her mother had been able to do much with the salmon-colored wool dress trimmed in black Aunt Glady sent, which was now her school dress. While Reuben had been comfortable in his Knickerbocker suit, she'd itched in the overheated classroom until the teacher let her share a desk closer to the door. Unfortunately, the new desk put her across the aisle from Kezzie's cousin, George Meyers, who had recently come to live with Kezzie and her family. George had red hair and freckles, and seemed to spend most of his day making eyes at Hildy.

"I simply can't stand it," Hildy complained to Nell.

"If it wasn't for the freckles, he'd be almost handsome."

"Ugh!"

"Kezzie told me he wanted to carry your books home yesterday."

"I can carry my own books."

Seeing the look on Hildy's face, Nell changed the subject.

What with George and his calf eyes and Papa's illness, the autumn months have been dreadfully wearisome.

The day after Dr. Bostwick's visit, Verdita sat Hildy and Reuben down at the table. "I need your help while Papa is sick," she said.

"Does that mean we don't have to go to school?" Reuben asked.

Under ordinary circumstances, Verdita would have laughed. Instead, she said, "You'll still go to school but I want the woodbox filled every morning and afternoon without my having to remind you. I also want you to make sure all the buckets have water. Hildy, I need you to cook breakfast and get yourself and Reuben off every morning. Come right home every day; I may need one of you to run errands. I'll start dinner but, you, Hildy, will have to finish it. We'll have to do the laundry on Saturdays and press the clothes when we can. Above all, we are not to spend any money unless we can't help it."

"If Papa can't work, how will we get any money?"

"Right now we don't need any. We have a house and plenty of food and firewood." She stroked Hildy's hair and smiled. "Now, aren't you glad we did all that canning?" Hildy nodded and started to speak but Verdita wasn't through. "One last thing, Alice Blackwell has offered to take Dovie . . ."

"What!"

"Sit down, Hildy. Just until I don't have to spend so much time with your father. It's a very kind thing for her to do."

For a minute Hildy thought she might faint. "She won't want to give her back," she said in a dull voice.

Before her mother could respond, Chong, who had been peeling potatoes, spoke unexpectedly. "I take Miss Dovie."

The room was silent as Verdita, Hildy, and Reuben looked at the boy.

"Chong," Verdita hesitated, "that's wonderfully kind of you but you already do so much. I can't ask you to take care of a three year old. She's . . ."

Before she could say more Chong put on the stubborn look they knew well. "Miss Dovie good girl. I have warm house. She sleep there, be here all day."

Verdita put her face in her hands and started to cry. Reuben was horrified but Hildy felt tears forming in her own eyes. "Oh, Mama, don't cry. Please don't cry."

Verdita fished a handkerchief out of her pocket and blew her nose. "Just a little weep," she said. "I've been so dreading Dovie's being gone; she's so joyous to have around the house. But Chong," she nodded to a chair. "Sit down, dear, and let's talk. Are you sure you want to do this? Dovie still has to get up sometimes at night and she kicks and rolls around. I sometimes have to get up three times."

Chong sat down. "Like little sister," he said.

"Did you have a sister once?" Reuben asked. He felt better now that the crying had stopped.

"Reuben, it's not our business."

"Had sister at home. Her name Mingzhu. It mean bright pearl."

"Is she still there?"

"She die. No food. Honorable parents also die. Uncle find me and bring me here. Then he die, too."

The simplicity of his words made them seem even more poignant to Hildy. She couldn't imagine not having family. "You took care of Dovie when we were looking for a house. Remember, Mama?"

"I do, and if this is something you really want to do, Chong, then I'll accept your offer with thanks."

"Gosh, Chong," Reuben stood up, "why do you want to take care of a baby, anyway?"

"Be quiet, Reuben," Verdita said.

"You bad boy, go fill woodbox," Chong added.

Reuben left without rancor. Chong often called him that but never in anger and Reuben had decided it was just his way.

And so Dovie spent nights curled up on the heated bed that he called a *kang* in Chong's little house, Hildy and Reuben got up early to do the chores, and Verdita fought for her husband's life. Mustard plasters, hot toddies, the pneumonia jacket, making him eat the calf's-foot jelly, the bone marrow, and the custard, drink water when he didn't want to, and no break until one night when she fell asleep and Hildy tiptoed into the room with a small stool and a copy of the *Tacoma Herald*.

"Papa," she said to the sleeping figure, "when you're well you're not going to know anything that's been happening so I'm going to read to you."

She lit a candle, put the stool nearby, and sat down to read. " 'Mr. Howell is enclosing his residence lots with a substantial fence and proposes planting fruit trees. He has room for a fine orchard.' Now, Papa, why would he start building a fence in autumn? Why not last summer when the weather was warm?" She rustled the paper. "Oh, listen to this. 'The work of excavating at the Wilkeson mines has progressed sufficiently to allow the introduction of mule power in the locomotion of the mine cars.' That's where you were, wasn't it? General Sprague is certainly making hay while the sun shines, isn't he? Except, of course, the sun isn't shining at all. It must be dreadfully cold up there."

She shifted the candle and continued, "Here's a joke, Papa. Mr. Cook mustn't have had enough news. Oh, dear, it is really bad. 'Why is an industrious legislator like a good business mosquito?' " She paused slightly, " 'because he is always anxious to introduce his bill.' I heard a better one at school but don't tell Mama I told you. 'The melancholy days have come, the saddest of the year; it's a little too warm for whiskey punch and a little too cold for beer.' "

While Hildy looked over the section of the paper Mr. Cook called "Local Intelligence," she heard her father give a weak laugh. "Your mother has given me enough whiskey to pickle Nelson's corpse."

His voice was weak but his eyes were opened and the flush was gone from his face. Hildy dropped the paper. "You're awake, Papa, are you feeling better?"

"If I get well will you promise never to tell me such bad jokes again?"

Hildy giggled. "I'll tell them to Reuben and he'll tell them to you. I'll make him stand in the doorway so you'll have to get out of bed to make him stop and then you can run after him down the stairs and surprise Mama."

Ira gave a long, slow breath. "Read me one more thing and then I'm going to sleep."

Hildy scanned the paper. "Here's one, Papa. 'Messrs. Blackwell and Kelly have moved their dining room and the room formerly used for that purpose is to be partitioned off for bedrooms.' Poor Mrs. Blackwell; she'll have even more work to do." She looked up expectantly but her father was asleep and didn't respond.

His recovery from then on was steady but very slow. Fall slid into winter; Dovie moved back, and one school day after another passed by. Thanksgiving came and went with little fanfare and few opportunities to go uptown. As a result of reading the "Local Intelligence" column to her father, Hildy learned the gravel that men had put on the road at the end of summer was causing horses to slip and slide in trying to get traction, and Mr. Cook wrote that Mrs. Money had a horned owl in her shop. However, one rainy day after another made it impossible for Hildy to visit her. Then the rain turned to snow. It snowed part of every day and froze at night. Runny noses and hacking coughs predominated at school.

Hildy had made notes in her journal throughout autumn. Now, on New Year's Eve, she sat on the kitchen floor, breathing warmth on her fingers as she wrote all she remembered.

One morning when Ira was feeling well enough to dress and

come downstairs, Reuben asked, "Will we have presents for Christmas, Papa?"

Hildy saw her parents' eyes meet and knew the only thing they were likely to get was a parcel from Aunt Glady. The previous week, Hildy and her mother had thought long and hard about what gifts to send back east. In the end, they packed a box with preserves, some small Indian baskets, and two otter pelts. Then Reuben found some unusual seashells one day after a storm, and they included them. "Though what your aunt will say when she gets these things, I definitely don't want to know," Verdita had said.

"You know Papa hasn't been working," Hildy reminded her brother when he had asked.

"I know; I just wondered." Reuben wandered away and Hildy decided she'd try to get him something important. Only what?

One day not long after that morning, a group of sailors from a British barque came up from the wharf and took over the Palace Saloon. They hooted and hollered until far into the night, and the next day, when Hildy walked uptown, she saw the owner outside the saloon's door loading bottles into a wagon.

"Good morning, Mr. Longpray."

"Good for some, not for others." He hefted a box over the side of the wagon bed.

"What are you doing?"

"Dang blasted Limeys, pardon me, took over my place and drank theirselves under the table. I had to draw my gun and now I'm under a bond. I'm going to move to where things is more congenial."

"What's this?" Hildy picked a strip of something out of the mud.

Mr. Longpray looked up briefly. "One of them Jack Tars was showing it around. Said he used to work for the North India Rubber Company. Must of dropped it."

Hildy examined what she'd found. "It stretches," she said, but Mr. Longpray had disappeared inside his saloon. She put the curious stretchy thing in her pocket and forgot about it until a rat ran across the road. Walking home, after her errands were done, she got the idea to make Reuben a slingshot for Christmas.

It was Mr. Boyer, the pile driver, who helped her out. He'd brought a small pumpkin one morning when he came to pick up his bread and asked if Hildy could make a pie.

"Why I surely can, Mr. Boyer. This pumpkin is plenty big enough for two pies."

"Well, one is all I need; you keep the rest for yourselves."

Hildy put the vegetable on the table and returned to the door with his bread. "Mr. Boyer, can I ask your advice about something?"

"What be that, Miss Hildy?"

"I have a piece of something stretchy and I want to make Reuben a slingshot for Christmas. Exactly how should I go about doing that?"

"Well now, that's easy. I expect you have some rubber. You find yourself a strong piece of forked wood and nail the ends of that there rubber to the ends of the fork. You find yourself a piece of madrona if you can because that's the strongest wood there is."

"Thank you, Mr. Boyer, that's just what I'll do."

With her father on the mend, Hildy was able to dawdle on the way home from school. Dodging George, who didn't want to be dodged, she and Nell explored until they found a broken limb, and Chong helped them attach the rubber.

"What are you getting your Mama and Papa?" Nell asked one afternoon as they sat in the kitchen talking and doing their schoolwork.

"I found the perfect thing for Papa." Hildy put her chalk down and went to see that he wasn't anywhere near. "Mama sent me up to Nolan and King's Grocery and Hardware and I found a copy of *American Agriculturist.* It's not a new copy but I ironed every page and Chong made adhesive out of plant resin and helped mend the pages that had tears."

"Chong knows a lot of strange stuff, doesn't he?"

"He is very smart. Sometimes he reads my school books."

"Ugh."

"Papa loves to read and there are all kinds of ideas in it for making things; we could even make an icebox if New Tacoma ever gets ice." She stopped and looked at Nell. "We had lots of ice in Johnstown."

"Mr. Ryan wants to build a flume from Mount Tacoma to town so we'll have ice all year."

"Gracious me, imagine that." Hildy's eyes sparkled. "Why, when it's finished, a person could take the train up to the mountain, hop aboard a block of ice, and slide all the way down."

She stopped talking when they heard Verdita and Chong outside.

"I think I have this sum figured out," Nell was saying as the two came in. She looked up and smiled. "Hello Mrs. Bacom, hello Chong."

"Hello, girls," Verdita stooped and kissed Hildy's cheek. "Almost done?"

"I have two more sums and I'm going to read the history lesson aloud to Dovie tonight," Hildy said.

Nell laughed. "Doesn't it put her to sleep?"

"Yes, that's why I do it."

Nell stood up and bundled her things together. "Mrs. Bacom, can Hildy please walk with me halfway home?"

Chong started putting their purchases away while Verdita found her apron. "You can walk as far as Pacific Avenue but then you have to come straight back. I don't like for you girls to be out when it's getting dark."

They hurried into their coats and Nell grabbed her slate and books. Outside, she returned to the topic of Christmas. "What did you get your mother?"

"A flower."

"A flower?"

"Yes, I went down to see Mrs. Blackwell and she sold me a pink violet. She wanted to give it to me but I couldn't do that. It wouldn't be my gift, you see."

"That was very brave of you."

"I was scared; she's terribly . . ." Hildy paused, looking for the right word.

"Exactly," said Nell. She shifted her books and slate from one arm to the other.

"But really, she was awfully nice and you should see where they live."

"Don't they live at the hotel?"

"Yes, on the second floor and their rooms look right out at Mount Tacoma, and they have the most beautiful furniture. It's all mahogany and Mrs. Blackwell paints watercolors and she has them hung on the walls. She trades shells, too. She collects shells here and trades them with people all over who send her other kinds."

They were reaching Pacific Avenue and Hildy slowed her steps. "Guess where the furniture came from?"

"Portland, no wait, Chicago?"

"Sort of, almost, anyway. They bought it from Mr. Jay Cooke."

"Who?"

"You know, the man who was selling railroad bonds and then went bankrupt. Remember, Miss Sparkle told us all about it."

Nell heaved a sigh. "I miss Miss Sparkle, don't you?"

"I surely do. When Mr. Stair bends down to help me with geography, he smells like Bay Rum."

They started laughing and Nell shifted her books once again, and shivered. Her coat was inadequate and she had circles under her eyes and a chilblain on one hand. Hildy knew her friend was often up at night taking care of her mother's latest baby and that their house was cold and drafty. Surprising even herself, Hildy wrapped her arms around Nell and gave her a hug. "I do value you so, Nell."

Nell was quiet for a long moment and when she pulled away Hildy saw tears in her eyes. "I'll see you tomorrow." She gave a shaky laugh and turned away. Hildy was sure Nell's family wouldn't have Christmas presents.

Now, shivering in the kitchen and thinking it was time to go back to bed, Hildy remembered the day she'd given Nell her gift. School was out and though snow lay heavily on the ground, the sun showed its best against a cerulean blue sky. She and Reuben had set off early on Christmas Eve morning to find a tree.

"Not too big," said Ira, who sat at one end of the table working on a pile of papers General Sprague had dropped by the previous day. At the other end, Verdita was measuring flour into a big bowl. Chong sat on the floor poking holes in acorns and inserting bits of yarn. Dovie sat near him, pulling the string on an old jumping jack of Reuben's. The cozy scene was lost on Reuben but not on Hildy, who was putting on a pair of Reuben's shoes that he'd outgrown.

"Come on, Hildy," Reuben shouted. "Don't be such a sluga-bed."

"I'm coming." Hildy gave the room a look of regret and slammed the door behind her.

In spite of the muddy roads and steaming piles of horse manure, the filthy wooden sidewalks where men freely spat, and the ever-present roaming pigs, the little downtown was filled with excitement. Frank Ross, a newcomer to town who was setting young female hearts aflutter, was shoveling gravel into potholes. Shopkeepers swept debris out into the street. Women, their skirts pinned up slightly to keep the hems clean, bustled in and out of stores, filling baskets they carried and stopping to talk. Some men shouted and waved papers, and as far south on Pacific Avenue as they could see, other men were hammering and sawing on the new buildings going up. It occurred to Hildy that it had been a very long time since she'd stalled around in town, eavesdropping on conversations.

She and Reuben planned to climb the hill on the west of town, to E Street above the Chinese gardens to where the Land Company had logged the largest trees, leaving stumps and saplings. There, much of the snow had been stomped into the dirt. They tramped through mud thick enough to tug on their boots, stepped over debris, and jumped across springs. The skunk cabbages were gone and the smells of dead foliage and downed fir filled the cold air. The bushes were full of birds looking for seeds; chipmunks ran up tree trunks and a pileated woodpecker pounded on a snag. Hildy knocked snow off a small pile of boughs to hang in the parlor, and then they turned to the task of finding the perfect tree.

"I can't find a good one," Reuben complained. He picked up a leaf and blew his nose.

"That's because there's so many of them." Hildy laughed. "Look here's a good one."

They ran from one sapling to another, laughing and arguing until the realization of water seeping into their boots forced them to make a choice. Reuben cut it down and Hildy piled on the boughs she'd collected and wound a rope around it all. Then they each took an end and started home. Somewhere a band was practicing; somewhere else sleigh bells sounded.

"That's Mr. Scott," Reuben said. "He got bells for his milk wagon." He started singing "Goober Peas," Hildy joined in, and they marched off the hill, the tree swaying between them. Just as they reached Alley Street, they met Kezzie, George, and Nell.

"A Christmas tree!" Kezzie's face lit up in a smile. "Ma won't let us have one; she says they're heathen."

"Pagan," George corrected her.

"Why?" Nell asked.

"Something about the Prophet Jeremiah," Kezzie replied.

George, relieving Hildy of her hold on the tree and addressing her, said, "Jeremiah was a very smart man. I can tell you all about him if you want."

"Maybe you could teach Sunday school instead," Hildy replied sweetly. She hurried to catch up with Nell.

"We've never had a tree," Nell said. "But last year there was a party at the Odd Fellow's lodge. There was a big tree and everyone got bags of candy and hot cider."

"Well you can help us decorate ours." Hildy looked at Kezzie and George. "You, too, if you want."

While Hildy and Reuben had looked for a tree, Verdita had made gingerbread men. When everyone burst through the door, the kitchen smelled like spices. If she was surprised at seeing so many people, she didn't show it.

"They're going to help us with our tree because they don't get to have one," Reuben shouted.

"Well, I was going to string snowberries and many hands will make light work." Verdita looked at the woodbox. "Reuben, you forgot to fill the woodbox. The rest of you, hang your wraps up and sit down."

The girls started tying pieces of yarn to the cookies and stringing the berries while the boys and Chong took the tree into the parlor. Under Verdita's supervision, they shifted furniture and stood the little fir in a bucket of dirt near the fireplace. Verdita had brought a few decorations from Johnstown and by the time they were hung, the snowberry chain was ready.

The girls helped wind it among the boughs and added the gingerbread men. They decorated the fireplace's makeshift mantel, scattering Chong's acorns among the greens. Verdita returned to the kitchen and presently she called for them all to come and wash their hands so they could pull taffy. Their excitement and the kitchen's heat made Kezzie's cheeks look like polished apples, and Nell's translucent skin took on a pale pink glow. George got so red his freckles all but disappeared and, as Hildy told Nell later, she was hard-pressed to know where his face stopped and his hair started, but she guessed that wasn't a kind thing to say.

By the time the taffy was pulled, cut into pieces, and wrapped in greased paper it was time for everyone to leave. They were almost at the street when Hildy called Nell back.

"You forgot something."

While the other two waited, Nell ran back and Hildy shoved a package in her hand. "Merry Christmas, Nell."

"Oh, Hildy . . ."

"Ssh. Hide it and open it later."

Hildy had thought hard about what to get her friend, but the sight of Nell's threadbare coat gave her the idea to crochet a scarf. Verdita had some tatty sweaters from Aunt Glady's boxes and she and Hildy spent several evenings unraveling the yarn. There wasn't enough of any one color so Hildy crocheted strips of shells in different colors and bound the four sides in a single row of red. She hadn't seen Nell since Christmas. When Mr. Scott delivered milk he told her that half the family was down with ague and the other half seemed to be waiting to take their turn. That had been two days ago.

Hildy closed her journal. Her nose had started to run and she realized that her bed would be warmer than the kitchen in spite of the stove. She got up with a sigh. Hildy loved these secret times when the kitchen was a shadowy, magical place and nothing disturbed her thoughts. In her own room at night, even with the door shut, she could hear Dovie's thrashing, and the weird, adenoidal noises Reuben made. As she clutched her blanket and journal and walked through the cold rooms, Christmas smells reminded her of the holiday.

I'm so lucky, she thought, as she passed the parlor and started up the stairs to the sounds of clanging bells and men shouting and firing guns and rifles. New Year's and we're all well and happy. She put her journal under the mattress and then found the box where she kept special things. In it was the gift Samuel had left the day he and his father went to Oregon. Hildy unwrapped the paper carefully and took out a pair of deerskin gloves beautifully made with fine stitches and small scallops at the top. She slipped them on and closed her eyes but in spite of her best effort, memories of Samuel were fading.

"Please come back," she whispered as fireworks from the Chinese section of town rent the air.

Chapter 18

January dragged on much as it had started, with snow and freezing. Ira's recovery seemed to have lagged, and he rarely made it to work. Then Chong came down with a cold and gave it to Dovie and Reuben. One morning, when Hildy went to feed the chickens, she found that something had broken into the little coop they'd made and killed Dovie's chick. Its bloody, feathered remains dotted the snow. Her own hen, Chicken Little, huddled in a corner, looking morose.

"I'll bring you in tonight," she promised.

After a month of dreary days, she awoke one February morning to sounds of dripping, and looked out the window. Overnight the temperature had warmed, melting the snow and ice, and turning the landscape into a muddy quagmire.

"The Chinook's here at last," Mr. Peak said, "and it ain't any too soon."

"I love the Chinook, don't you?"

"Yes, Miss Hildy, I do, too. Lets my bones know that summer's just around the corner."

"Do you think winter is over?"

"Mebbe, mebbe not, depends."

"Depends on what?"

"Depends on what Ol' Man Winter decides to do. Just might start raining and carry on 'til summer or might just up and start snowing all over."

"I call that highly unsatisfactory," Hildy said.

"Yes, Miss Hildy, it truly is."

Mr. Peak turned to leave but Hildy called him back. "Mr. Peak, can I ask you something?"

"Why, sure."

Hildy hesitated, uncomfortable with what she was about to say. "Mr. Peak, as you might know, Papa has been sick since last fall."

"Yes, Miss Hildy, and I is hoping he'll get better right soon."

"Well, the thing is," she paused and gave a long sigh. "We need money. Mama has scrimped and saved every way she could but we're plain running out."

Mr. Peak shifted his bread and stuck a hand in his trouser pocket. "I got a couple of bits, here, I could give you . . ."

Hildy interrupted him. "Oh, I'm not asking for money—but thank you very much. I just want to know if you think any of the men on the wharf would buy some of my baked goods. I can make lots of things and we could sell them if people would buy them."

Mr. Peak took his hand out of his pocket and said quietly, "Why, Miss Hildy, you just tell me when you have something to sell and I'll rustle you up some hungry men."

"Thank you, Mr. Peak, you're a true friend."

On their walk to school, Hildy talked her idea through with Nell.

"You see," she said, "Mama doesn't know I know, but I heard her and Papa talking one night. General Sprague's been away for a long time and no one brings Papa any work. Mama wanted to write Uncle Edgar and ask him to loan us some money but Papa wouldn't hear of it."

"Well, gosh sakes, no. And if your Aunt Glady got wind of it, she would plague your mama's heart out."

Hildy laughed, and they paused to let a young man with a wheelbarrow of gravel cross in front of them. "There's Frank

Ross," she said.

"He got a job trying to fill in some of the holes."

Hildy never asked her friend how she knew so much about who people were and what was going on. What Nell, herself, didn't find out, her older brother did.

"They surely do need filling in," Hildy said. "Mr. Stone got thrown from a horse, yesterday, when it slipped in the mud on Railroad Street. Of course," she added, "there was so much mud to fall into, he wasn't at all hurt."

"Pa says the road to the wharf is almost impassable. I haven't been down to the wharf in ever so long and three steamers have come. Pa and Ike have had steady work."

"Is Ike still courting Miss Frieda Faye?"

"Sometimes, but she called him a feckless Rusty Guts, and said since he was the oldest son, he'd have to take care of our ma and pa when they got old and she was too delicate to do that."

"Delicate!" Hildy said. "That's the last thing I'd call her. Humble pie is the only thing she doesn't eat. What fimble-famble."

They stopped before crossing Eleventh Street to adjust their scarves against oncoming rain.

"So I'm thinking that I will start my bakery now," Hildy continued.

"Your bakery? You mean, quit school and just cook all the time?"

"No, Mama would never let me do that, but I can bake on the weekends and sell what I make."

They stopped again to let a wagon driven by Mike Murphy pass. He tipped his hat and called, "Good morning, ladies!"

"Good morning, Mr. Murphy. What are you hauling today?'

"Coals to Newcastle, ladies, coals to Newcastle." He snapped a whip over the heads of the horses pulling his wagon, and they picked up their gait, hooves squishing in the mud and sending it flying.

Nell looked puzzled. "What does that mean?"

"I don't know. Wasn't the wagon full of wood? The coal bunkers aren't done yet. Is there a place around here called Newcastle?"

"I never heard of one."

They crossed the road carefully and breathed sighs of relief for a few seconds on the other side.

"I wish the school wasn't so far away," Nell said.

"How come it was built six blocks up St. Helens, anyway? Why not closer to town?"

"No one ever said but school was lots more fun when it was closer to town and at Miss Sparkle's house."

"My feet are soaked, how about yours?"

"Mine too, so let's not think about them. How will you sell what you bake?"

They bent their heads against the wet and Hildy said, "I don't know, yet, but Mr. Peak said he would help me."

When they finally reached St. Helens Avenue, it was tough going, and the rain had increased so that North School was all but invisible. Nell tucked a loose end of her scarf into her coat and said, "I saw Reuben going down to the wharf."

"He has a job. He kills rats at the warehouses."

"With his slingshot?"

"Yes, aren't I lucky I found that piece of rubber?"

Before she could continue, Kezzie, George, and Ellen joined them. Hildy scooted to the edge of the walk and Nell grinned. Suddenly, they heard tree limbs snapping. An unfamiliar rumbling sound was followed by the sight of the saturated hillside in front of them sliding down, bringing trees, large rocks, and debris. Muddy rubble slid across St. Helens, its mass growing wider as it continued down to C Street. Then, as quickly as it started, it stopped. In the silence they heard nothing but pounding rain.

"Goodness me," said Kezzie. "That was really loud."

"Are you all right, Hildy?" George asked,

"Of course, why wouldn't I be? Gracious that was close."

"I've never seen anything like that before." Nell's eyes sparkled with excitement.

They stood in dumbfounded amazement until Ellen staggered slightly and grabbed George's arm. "I declare, I think I feel faint."

George immediately became concerned and Nell rolled her eyes at Hildy. "Well, we can't go to school today and it's raining harder than ever."

Hildy agreed. "I guess we should go home."

With George helping Ellen, and Kezzie carrying her books, they turned around and started back toward town.

They hadn't gone far before they saw men running up the road. "Anybody hurt?" one shouted.

"No, but we can't get to school," George said.

"How about down below?" Hildy asked.

"Mud knocked down two buildings on C and part of Fife's water system. It's a regular hog wallow down there and this here rain ain't helping."

"Want to come home with me?" Kezzie asked after the men had passed them. "Ma's having her Methodist ladies church group today and she baked cookies."

"I'll come," said Nell, but Hildy shook her head. "Reuben wears Mama to a frazzle when he has a cold. I'd feel guilty if I didn't go home."

"And Jesus loves you for that," George said.

Hildy glanced at Nell and Nell flashed her a knowing grin. "And so does Mama," Hildy said, thinking, really, he's such a bore.

Men continued running up the road. A couple of smaller mudslides followed the first one and nudged the pile in front of it. Hildy wondered how long before they could get the road cleared, but she wasn't sorry to be going home. Her feet were soaking wet, and strands of hair were plastered against her face.

They parted at the corner, and Hildy continued on, slipping and sliding until she reached Pacific Avenue. At Spooner's Tin Shop, Frank Ross stood near his empty wheelbarrow while another man waved his arms. "Sixteen dollars," the man said, "took it right out of my till last Saturday, bold as brass. I'll have to extend my hours to make it up."

"Well, hunger will make a thief of any man, that's sure and certain," Frank Ross said. "I heard that both Chilberg Brothers and Abe Gross's places were hit last week, too." The two men turned aside to avoid an onslaught of wind-driven rain and Hildy scooted by, almost glad for a reason not to stop and listen.

Once home, while she stopped outside to take off her soggy shoes, Hildy heard her mother's voice coming from the kitchen. "How could Glady ask that of us? It really is beyond nerve."

"Well, there's little Elsie . . ." Ira began.

"And what about our children? Dovie is too young to understand anything and Reuben won't notice, but what about Hildy? I put up with a great deal of condescension from Glady as it is, but Hildy is heads above Elsie."

"I won't argue with you there. Glady is turning Elsie into a mealy-mouthed little prisms-and-puss but I don't see how we can refuse. Glady is my sister. And we can use the money."

"We can find another way to make money. I won't have that girl in my house."

"Well, then we'll have to find another house where she can stay."

Hildy, hearing a chair scrape as someone apparently got up from the table, opened the door.

"Hildy," said Verdita, who was pouring herself a cup of coffee. "What are you doing home from school?"

Hanging up her wet coat, Hildy saw her father put an envelope in his pocket. "There was a mudslide on St. Helens and it blocked the road." She turned a chair to face the stove and sat close. "Gosh, this feels good. Where's Reuben?"

"Asleep," Verdita said.

"What are you and Papa doing?"

"Just talking, and now Papa's going to check on Reuben. Would you like a little coffee?"

"Oh, yes, please."

Hildy took the milky coffee her mother poured and sipped slowly. "Mama," she hesitanted, "Mr. Peak has some friends who want to buy my baked goods."

"How many friends?"

"Ummm, I'm not sure, yet. He said he'd let me know."

"I really don't want a lot of strange men coming here at all different times to buy food."

"Well, maybe I could deliver it."

"Deliver it. Deliver it where?"

"Ummm, probably down somewhere near where he works."

"The Hatch Mill?"

Hildy shifted in her chair and turned to dry the side of her dress that faced away from her mother. Verdita, however, was not about to be put off. "Hildy," she said, "look at me." Hildy looked up and sipped some more coffee. "Mr. Peak has no business asking you to bake things and take them down to the wharf to sell to a bunch of men we don't know. That's no place for a little girl. I've half a mind to stop you selling bread to him."

"No, Mama, don't. It wasn't Mr. Peak's idea, it was mine."

"Yours? Your idea to traipse down there, and how were you going to tote the food, may I ask?"

"I haven't figured that out yet."

"Well, don't give it any more thought because you aren't going to."

"But Mama, we can sell them things they don't get anywhere else and make some money."

Verdita's eyes narrowed for a moment as she looked at Hildy. "We'll eat tree bark before I let my daughter cavort around with strange men, and rough laborers at that."

"Well, maybe we can get someone else to sell it for us." When her mother remained silent, Hildy continued. "Maybe we could supply things to a store like Mr. Fife's and he could sell it."

"Sell what?" asked Reuben, who had just come downstairs after his nap. He blew his nose and added, "Say, Hildy, why aren't you in school?"

While Hildy explained about the mudslide, Reuben complained it was the only exciting thing to happen in weeks and he'd missed it.

The door opened and a gust of wind and rain came in bringing with it Chong, who carried a bundle of papers General Sprague gave him to deliver to Ira and the mail he'd picked up at Fife's Store. "Mr. McLane not lost now," he said, putting the pile on the table.

"Where'd he turn up?" asked Ira, who had returned to the kitchen with Dovie.

"Go on boat to Olympia to see old friend at logging camp."

"Well he certainly wasted the time of all those people who went looking for him," said Verdita in exasperation.

"He's a grown man, Verdy, he doesn't have to check in and out with folks." Ira put Dovie down to pick up the papers, and she rushed over to Chong.

With the topic of Mr. McLane over, Reuben returned to the previous thread of conversation. "Sell what?"

"Food to Mr. Peak's friends," Hildy said.

Ira, headed upstairs to his makeshift office in the bedroom, turned in the doorway. "What? When did this come up?"

"It's just an idea Hildy and I were talking about," Verdita said. She picked up her sewing basket and sat down. "Don't worry about it. Nothing will be done without your approval. I have a seed of an idea that has barely taken root, so I'll let it grow and then we'll talk."

As she finished speaking, a gust of wind rattled the door and everyone jumped. Chong put a stick of wood in the stove, and filled a bucket to take upstairs. Ira gave his wife a long look before leaving the room, and Hildy turned to dry the other side of her dress.

The next time Mr. Peak arrived to pick up his loaf of bread, Verdita met him at the door.

"Come in, won't you, Mr. Peak? Sit down, please, and I'll pour you a cup of coffee."

Mr. Peak snatched off his cap and rain splashed on his bald head. He ran his hand over it and took the chair nearest the door. Verdita put a cup of coffee in front of him and added a plate of cookies. She sat opposite him with her own coffee and cradled its warmth between her hands.

"Mr. Peak," she said, "please, be honest with me. Do any of the wharf workers really want our homemade goods, or was that just something nice you said to Hildy?" Mr. Peak squirmed and picked up a cookie, his false teeth slipping dangerously. Verdita pushed the plate closer to him. "Take your time, Mr. Peak, and dunk if you want to, I always do." To prove her point, Verdita dunked a cookie and took a big bite. She finished it in record time and took a second. The room was so quiet the steady thump of the pile driver at the coal bunker nearly half a mile away was audible. *How does Alice Blackwell stand that all day?* She finished the second cookie and folded her hands on the table.

"Now then, Mr. Peak, Hildy told me that she told you

something of our financial predicament. Until Mr. Bacom can resume steady work we need to earn a little money. You know the men. Would they like us to come down to the wharf and sell things or would they prefer a home-cooked meal here, perhaps dinner once or twice a week?"

Verdita's plain speaking made Mr. Peak more comfortable. "Fact is, ma'am, they're a rough-speaking bunch and eating here with you all, wouldn't be right, 'sides, they most likely wouldn't want to, if you'll forgive my plain speaking, ma'am."

"Well, what if Mr. Bacom was here and Chong served? Would they be comfortable with that?"

"Yes, ma'am, they is more used to Chinee waitin' on 'em."

"And what nights would be best? Would they want a nice big Sunday meal?"

"It's my opinion, ma'am, seein' as how you're askin', that you start with a Sunday dinner and see how it goes. I'll talk you up for sure and certain, but I can't make 'em come back a second time."

"I'm aware of that, but if good food is anything to go by then they won't be disappointed."

Mr. Peak stood up, saying that he had to skedaddle on to work, but agreed to stop by in the early evening, after he'd talked to a few people. And Verdita went upstairs to talk to her husband.

CHAPTER 19

Repeated mudslides kept St. Helens Avenue blocked and North School closed for a week. One evening, while Ira was at a meeting and Reuben and Chong were out back cutting and stacking wood, a man knocked at the Bacom's door and dropped off a letter for Hildy. Hildy, Verdita, and Dovie were in the kitchen. Verdita was writing down ideas for their new dinner venture while Hildy worked on a sampler Aunt Glady had sent for Christmas. The needle flashed in and out of the fabric and fascinated Dovie, but Hildy happily put it down and examined the piece of mail. Aunt Glady always wrote on a single sheet of paper that she folded and sealed closed with wax. This was a regular envelope. For a moment, her heart leapt, thinking that Samuel had written at last, but the envelope lacked postage, which mail from Oregon required. She sliced open three sides as her father had showed her, and laid the envelope flat to write on later. Inside was a small square of paper folded in half and then half again to make a booklet.

New Tacoma
The Wharf
Washington Territory
Dear Hildy
*   I take pen in hand and please forgive my handwriting. I sprained my wrist also Mr. Money has a toothache. Could you come down for a few hours and help me with my birds?*
*   Respectfully yours,*
*   Jane Money, (Mrs.)*

Verdita look up curiously. "Who is it from?"

"Mrs. Money." Hildy's face lit up. "She wants to know if I can come down and help with the birds for a while."

"Oh, dear. Just when we want to get the dining room ready for our dinners."

"She sprained her wrist and Mr. Money can't help because he has a toothache."

"Well, I'm not sure a toothache would affect his arms and legs," Verdita said in exasperation.

"Mrs. Money was my first friend in New Tacoma and she gives me feathers and she'll want to hear how Jenny Lind is."

Verdita laughed. "You're as transparent as glass, Hildy."

"But Mama, it would be the neighborly thing to do."

Verdita gave a small snort and said, "You can go tomorrow after breakfast; I can do some of the preliminary work by myself, but when the mill's noon whistle sounds, you start home."

"Thank you, Mama. Is there something I can take to Mr. Money to help him feel better?"

Verdita sighed and look regretful. "I'm afraid not. Not this time. We're dreadfully low on everything." She returned to her writing, thinking, *I certainly hope we can make some money soon.*

The next morning, Hildy hurried through her chores and left with a happy heart. *Things always seemed more hopeful in the daylight.* In spite of the state of the roads after all the rain, Pacific Avenue bustled with activity. A man named W.F. Robertson had opened a photography shop, and Mr. Shoudy had a display of new wallpaper in his window. Hildy stopped to peer in and saw that he also had a large supply of glass panes. *To think we had to order our first window glass from Portland.* Mr. Gardener, the new barber who was relocating from Steilacoom, was hanging a sign on his door. Continuing on, Hildy stopped outside the Tacoma Land Office building to read a notice pinned on the wall:

Parties wishing to work out their road tax can learn when and where to do so by calling upon F. Carmichael, Road Supervisor.

However, the conversation of two men coming out the office door caught her attention.

". . . every sign. Every sign, I tell you."

"I know. I saw it myself. They switched the signs on the Delmonico Restaurant and Cogswell's place. Chilberg told me he saw some men just off the *Dashing Wave* who stood at his restaurant door and laughed because his sign read 'Cogswell's Stable with oysters of every style.' "

Hildy hurried away so she could laugh. Mr. Cook had an editorial in the *Herald* that complained about some of the boys in New Tacoma who caused all kinds of mischief. Changing signs on buildings had kept them busy over several nights.

A little farther on, two men her father called, "that idiot Ingall and his dumber cousin Wallace" scratched their heads over a capsized buggy while their horse tried to shake off his broken bridle. But the most important change of all was the completed railing on the wharf trail.

The *Herald* had raved for a week about improvements on the trail that led from town to the wharf. Under the planks it was still as mucky as ever, and footprints off the planks deep in the mud showed that not everyone could keep on the straight and narrow, but Hildy grasped the rail and found the walk almost easy going. At the bottom, she took a deep breath and looked around. The first thing she saw was three boys sliding down the cliff on the heels of their shoes, whooping and hollering as they slid. Her mouth fell open and envy overwhelmed her. *Oh, what fun!* Then one of them hit a root, went head-over-heels, and landed in a puddle, but even at that, the boys laughed and ran toward the wharf in order to go up and slide down again.

Over their laughter, she heard men cranking up a hawser as a three-masted schooner left the bay. But the *Dashing Wave* and the *Dakota* were still tied up. William Blackwell stood and watched men unload cargo from the *Dakota*. He had his back toward Hildy and she hurried on.

The Moneys had a big new sandwich board outside their shop. Hildy admired it before opening the door. After the fresh air she reeled slightly from the bird cages' moist, powerful smells. The birds sang as cheerfully as always but both Mr. and Mrs. Money sat behind the counter looking glum. Mr. Money had a large rag tied around his jaw and Mrs. Money had one around her wrist. Of the two, he looked by far the most miserable.

"Dr. Spinning is coming down." Mrs. Money welcomed Hildy with a hug. "When Mr. Money heard the doctor was in town, he said it was providential."

"What about Dr. Bostwick?" Hildy took off her coat and laid it on a chair.

"Well, dearie, just between you and me, Dr. Bostwick doesn't know teeth. 'Mr. Money,' I said, 'if you have to have a toothache, it's God's own mercy that Dr. Spinning is in town. He'll fix you up in no time.' "

"Do you have a pain wafer, Mr. Money?" Hildy asked. "Mama always takes one when she has aches."

"Alverson's Pain Annihilator." He waved a bottle. "Doc Alverson's new in town but between you, me, and the canaries, he don't know nothing about pain."

Mr. Money took a long drink from the bottle and Mrs. Money led Hildy over to one of the cages. "Now, dearie, you know all about the canaries but you have to be careful when cleaning up after the owl and these here parrots. Their bite'll

211

draw blood. I have gloves you can wear."

Hildy put on the gloves and went to work. Mrs. Money's new robins had four little blue eggs, and the parents flew repeatedly at Hildy's hands and arms. "It's all right," she whispered to them. The Australian parrots were excitable as well, but when one lit on her wrist, it didn't peck and Hildy smiled in delight. It flew off with a squawk, however, when an explosion sounded from outside and the building swayed. Hildy jumped. "What was that?"

"Mrs. Money sighed. "Some of them old pilings is eaten up by teredos, nasty little things, they are, look like a cross between a worm and a snake. The men are drilling holes in the wood, filling them with powder and blowing them up."

"It's awfully noisy, isn't it?"

"Not as bad as the barrel factory."

Hildy turned back to work and Mrs. Money began filling her in on the latest waterfront news. "Did your pa tell you that the railroad had to raise its track across the bay?"

"No, why?"

"Because the high tides last week covered 'em over. I saw it for myself. Did he tell you that a Puyallup gentleman walked off the edge of the wharf but was rescued by some men rowing down from Old Town?"

"Gracious." Hildy stopped her work and looked up.

"Oh, he was fine. Someone built a cabin on a barge and had it moored near where he fell in. The fellow was hustled onboard and given a healthy drink of whiskey. My, goodness," she added, "you're getting way behind on everything, aren't you?"

Hildy's eyes sparked. "Yes," she said, "but things happen uptown, too. Did you know that the Congregationalists just fenced their property but they don't have a church yet and that the Methodists have a new church but no fence?"

Mrs. Money's eyes twinkled. "Now, dearie, do you really

think that news compares with mine?"

"Oh, but there's one more thing." Hildy finished the canaries' cage and moved over to the owl. "Charlie Newcomb broke his leg playing baseball when another boy jumped on it. Dr. Bostwick fixed it but Charlie was in fearful pain for a while."

"Is Charlie your sweetheart?" Mrs. Money asked.

"Goodness me, no." Hildy looked up, surprised.

"A pretty thing like you, I should think that more than one boy would want to carry your books."

Hildy blushed and Mrs. Money began to pounce. "Aha," she said, but she was interrupted when the store's front door opened and a short, balding man carrying a medical bag came in. Before he could say a word, Mr. Money hailed him.

"Doc, doc, you gotta do something about this here tooth. I'm in a pain that even whiskey can't cure."

"Well, that is bad, then, isn't it?" said the doctor with a twinkle in his eye. He put his medical bag on the counter, opened it, and took something out. "I'm going to get right to work and I'll have that tooth out quick as you can say John Jacob Jingleheimer Schmidt."

Mr. Money eyed the shiny object Dr. Spinning held with mistrust. "What's that, Doc?"

"It's a dental key. Now, sir, stay where you are and open wide so I can see what miscreant molar is causing you pain."

Mr. Money's eyes, wide as saucers, never left Dr. Spinning's face, and after a few muttered 'ums' and 'I sees' the doctor tapped a tooth. Mr. Money gave a howl and sat bolt upright.

"Holy crawdad, Doc, that hurt," he said and tears poured down his cheeks.

"I imagine it does. That there is as rotten a gnasher as I've ever seen. But I'll have it out lickety-split." He started rooting in the dental bag again and Mr. Money explored the offending tooth with his tongue.

"Well, now, mebbe it ain't so bad after all," he said.

"Nonsense man, the tooth's got to come out. It's probably septic already. Ah," Dr. Spinning fished out a peculiar-looking metal instrument. "Here it is."

"What's that?"

"It's called a mouth gag." Dr. Spinning turned it around in the light. "It's mostly for lockjaw patients, holds their mouths open so I can get some food down 'em, but I use it for extractions, too." He held the mouth gag where Mr. Money could see it and Hildy saw him gulp. Proud of the instrument and oblivious to Mr. Money's horror, Dr. Spinning continued. "See the thread of the screw is reversed at its center so that when I turn the fixed wing nuts, it opens or closes both handles at the same time. I'll just insert it in your mouth and you won't accidently bite me. I can tell you, this has saved my fingers more times than I can count."

He set it down and returned to his medical bag. "And this is a dental forceps." Dr. Spinning found yet another tool and squeezed and released its handle a few times. "It's old," he said, "came from Italy. See how the jaws look just like an animal's head? Quite the jokers are those Eye-ties. Now, sir, I suggest you lie down here on the floor where I can get at you. Don't worry, won't take but a minute—if we're lucky." He gave a little laugh. "Don't like to think about it if we're not."

Mr. Money continued to sit in his chair, as if frozen, and Mrs. Money hurried to his side. "Come on, now, dear." She took hold of one arm. "The doctor hasn't got all day. You'll feel much better when the tooth is out and I'll make you a nice buttery sop."

For a minute after Mr. Money lay down, it looked as if he wouldn't open his mouth. But with practiced hands, the doctor pinched the man's nose shut and grabbed his chin. Unable to breathe, Mr. Money had to open wide, whereupon Dr. Spinning shoved the mouth gag in place. Then he straddled his patient's chest and applied the forceps. "Did this very same procedure last week using a bullet mold," he said, putting pressure on the offending tooth. Mr. Money made a gargling noise and then the molar was out. The doctor grinned with pleasure. "Nasty looking thing as I've seen lately." He held the bloody tooth up for them all to see. Mrs. Money blanched and Hildy felt a little light-headed, but Mr. Money had passed out.

"Oh, dear," said Mrs. Money, "I'll just get some *sal volatile*," but the doctor stopped her.

"Best let him as is; he won't like this next part any better."

He retrieved his medical bag from the counter and took out a glass tube. Then he opened a jar and fished around in it. "You ever see one of these, young lady?" He held up something black and slimy that moved between his fingers. Before Hildy could answer, the doctor said, "It's a Dalmatian bloodsucker. Best kind there is. Now, look here, I'm going to put the little guy in this tube. Mrs. Money, you'd better get down and help me."

Mrs. Money knelt on the floor next to her husband and Dr. Spinning handed her the tube. "You just hold this right there on the gums where they're all red and nasty looking and the leech will eat all that bad tissue away."

"For how long?" Mrs. Money looked pale.

"I'd say about twenty, maybe thirty minutes. I'm going to hustle on down to Blackwell's and see if Jacob Mann will give me a drink, and then I'll be back and check up on the job."

He wiped off his tools, put them back in the bag, and pushed open the door, whistling. He stopped long enough to add, "Hold on as best you can to the tube, leeches love to make a run for it right down the throat."

"Oh." Hildy bent over to let some blood flow back into her head. "Mrs. Money," she said in a muffled voice, "I think I'll go home."

"That's fine, dearie, I'd leave, too, if I could," Mrs. Money said grimly.

Hildy grabbed her coat and didn't wait to put it on. Outside, she leaned against the side of the building and took a deep breath of air. After a few minutes she shrugged into her coat and tried to find something to take her mind off Mr. Money's tooth and the leech. *Wait until I tell Reuben.* The noon whistle sounded as she walked and the sound of metal banging filled the air. Within seconds, men ran down the wharf, shouting about the Hanson Ackerson Mill. Hildy knew the mill was over in Old Tacoma and the fact that the explosion was so plainly audible meant something terrible must have happened. By the time she reached the point where the Wharf Road started up the hill to town, a man in a rowboat had appeared to say that the mill's main saw came apart, spewing pieces in all directions. *If I don't go home, Mama won't let me come back down to see Mrs. Money any time soon,* Hildy thought, *and if I do go home, I won't know if anyone was hurt.* She hesitated for a moment, and then started up the trail.

At the top of the bluff, men who had heard the blast hurried down Pacific Avenue. Hildy had to jump out of their way and ended up ankle-deep in the mud. *What next?* She hurried on and was glad to reach home and take off her shoes.

"Did you hear the explosion?" she asked as she went in to the kitchen.

"I did," said Reuben. "What was it?"

"A saw at Hanson and Ackerson came apart." She started setting the table. "Where's Papa?"

"He went to the office. I'm surprised you didn't see him."

Ira came in not long after with the news that because the noon whistle had gone off, no one at the mill was hurt. Hildy told them about Mr. Money's tooth until Verdita made her stop, and Reuben was too hungry to talk. Hildy was clearing the table when Nell tapped on the door.

"We were going to talk about the school presentations, remember?"

"What's that all about?" Verdita asked.

"It's for the end of the winter term," Nell explained as she helped Hildy with the table. "Mrs. Stair wants each student to make something and bring it to show."

"Something like what?"

"Well, that's just it. Hildy and I, we talked and talked but we don't have any ideas. Sarah can draw and paint and Ellen knits socks; even Kezzie can do something. She presses flowers and puts them in a book. All I know is taking care of babies." Nell sighed, Hildy giggled, and Verdita shook her head. While the two girls washed and dried the dishes, she got out her sewing basket.

"How far along is your sampler, Hildy?" she asked.

"Not very far, I hate working on it and my eyes get tired."

Verdita started weaving a darn in a sock. "Maybe, Nell, it's time for me to teach you to crochet."

"Oh, Mrs. Bacom." Nell turned from the sink, "really truly?"

Verdita smiled. "Yes, really truly. I have a nice pattern for a dress collar that isn't too difficult."

"Oh, but," Nell's excitement faded. "I don't have money to pay for the thread and needle."

Hildy, who had finished the dishes and rinsed the dishrag, sat down and said, "I'll buy it for you, Nell. Cotton thread isn't so very expensive."

Nell's brown eyes filled with tears. "I can't let you do that, Hildy, though it's really generous. Pa says we must never accept charity."

Her words angered Verdita, who had heard from Ira that Nell's father never turned down charity when it came to free drinks at Longpray's Saloon. She tied off the thread on the sock in her hand and reached for one of Dovie's dresses. "How about this? Hildy can pay for the thread for two collars and you can make both of them, one for you and one for Hildy. There's no charity in being paid for your labor."

"Oh, do, please," Hildy said. "I've wanted a red collar for ever so long. Cousin Elsie won't wear red, she says it's fast."

A rare, gentle smile lit Nell's face. "All right, then. Mrs. Bacom, if I work really hard, could I finish one in time for the school show?"

"I think you could. Would your mother let you come for an hour every day after school?"

"I'll tell her I have to," Nell said, "and, besides, it's time that Josie starts taking care of the babies."

"Well, that's settled then," Hildy said, "but what about me? Should I take a loaf of bread?"

"Of course, and you can take your ledgers and explain how you keep books. And Mr. Scott sells honey, now, when he makes his milk deliveries. Take some honey and when the program is over give everyone a piece of bread and honey."

"Oh, Mama, you are smart to think of that."

Verdita smiled. "I'm glad you think so, but most likely, in a few years, you will have changed your mind." At Hildy's puzzled look, she laughed and added, "Why don't you walk up to town and look for the thread? This weather isn't likely to hold."

CHAPTER 20

Nell's crocheting lessons began the next day. North School remained closed and the paper said it would probably take three days for men to shovel away the debris the slide had brought down. Nevertheless, Verdita decided that the half hour after the children usually got home was the only time she could spare. When Nell tapped on the door at three-thirty, Hildy let her in with a big smile. She had her sampler ready to work on and Verdita had her sewing basket. A kettle of broth simmered on the stove and Chong chopped vegetables to add while Dovie played near his feet. Nell dropped onto a chair with a happy smile.

"It's always so cozy here," she said. As if to agree, Jenny Lind hopped about and burst into song.

"Let's see what you have." Verdita took the bag Nell carried and looked inside. The yarn Nell chose for the first collar was Delft blue. Verdita fingered it and nodded approvingly. "Very nice. It will make up beautifully. Now, the pattern I have in mind is called the Blue-on-Blue Warming Collar. Of course, it could just as easily be a Red-on-Red Warming Collar, or Green-on-Green, for that matter. The important thing is that it's pretty and not too hard and you'll learn the basics."

She reached in her sewing bag and brought out a hook and some wrinkly yarn. "First, we'll practice. I'll tie the yarn on and then you can do it and then I'll show you how to make a chain."

Nell watched Verdita's fingers closely and Hildy watched the two of them. She and Verdita had spent the morning moving the parlor furniture into the dining room and the dining room furniture into the parlor so when they started the dinner venture and men came, they'd walk through the front door into the eating area. Then they hung a curtain between the two rooms. "I don't want them ruining my good sofa and chairs," Verdita had said.

"Not to mention the carpet." Hildy had giggled and waved a spittoon in the air.

Now, here was her mother finding time to teach Nell. Hildy's heart swelled with love and appreciation.

After Nell had mastered the chain stitch, Verdita switched her to the blue yarn and Nell looked at the pattern. "Chain eighteen," she read. "I can do that." She attached the blue yarn to her hook and started.

"Where's Reuben?" she asked, between counting.

"Up at the spring filling the smaller water barrels."

"Mr. Hosmer is having a pipe laid to bring water right to his house just like the Clarks." Nell finished the chains and looked at the pattern again. "One double crochet in the fourth chain from the hook and in each of the next three chains."

Hildy knew that their lack of piped-in water was a sore spot with her mother, but Verdita appeared not to have heard the words. She demonstrated a double crochet and Nell started in again.

"Is Josie taking care of the babies?" Hildy wove her needle in and out of the sampler, making letters with cross-stitches.

"Yes, but she isn't very happy about it."

"Is Josie your oldest sister?" Verdita asked.

"No, Indiana is the oldest. Ma named her that to remind her of her home before she and Pa came West. When we visited Bush Prairie last summer, Indiana decided to stay." She considered the pattern. "What's a TR?"

"A treble stitch, very easy." Verdita demonstrated.

Nell fell quiet as she focused on the collar. The fire snapped and crackled and Dovie talked quietly to herself as she played with an old rag doll of Hildy's. Outside a foghorn blew long, low tones. Chong finished chopping, added the vegetables to the simmering broth, and washed the knife and cutting board. The sounds of the squeaky wheel on Reuben's cart reached them and drew closer, Hearing it, Nell wound her loose yarn up and put everything back in the sack.

"May I leave this here for now? When I know all the stitches, I'll take it home but if it's lying around, one of the babies will sure as shootin' get into it."

"Of course you can," Hildy said, "can't she, Mama?"

"Put it with your sampler, Hildy, where Dovie won't get at it." Verdita stood up and reached for her apron. "It's awfully foggy tonight; would you like Chong to walk home with you?"

Nell's face lit up as she pulled on her coat and wound her Christmas scarf around her neck. "Could he, please? I purely hate walking by the saloons at night. Some of the men try to grab me sometimes."

Hildy looked horrified and Verdita unexpectedly enclosed Nell in a warm embrace. "Carry a pin and don't be afraid to use it."

Nell flushed, embarrassed but pleased, and laughed. "I surely will, Mrs. Bacom. Now why didn't I think of that?"

Nell and Chong left as Reuben came in. Ira came down from the bedroom and Hildy started to help prepare supper.

"What are you making for the school show, Reuben?" Verdita asked after they all sat down.

"It's a secret."

"A secret?"

"Yes, Samuel showed me how to do this a long time ago, before he left. Chong's been helping me."

Hearing her brother's mention of Samuel, Hildy was happy and sad at the same time. Her memories of him were fading. At times, she could barely remember his face.

Chong looked up from his bowl of rice and nodded. "Good for boy to do."

Ira spread butter thickly on a piece of bread. "Well, I don't know about Samuel but I trust you, Chong." He took a bite and looked surprised. "What's this?"

"Honey butter." Hildy beamed. "Tabitha Tickletooth mentions it in her cookbook. I bought some honey from Mr. Scott this morning and mixed the two with cinnamon and a little sugar. I'm experimenting for the school exhibition. Do you like it?"

"Enough to have a second piece of bread. This promises to be quite a show."

North School opened in three days, as promised, and as the exhibition grew closer, the students could talk of little else. Hildy wasn't nervous about her bread, but she was about standing in front of people and talking.

"I just hate to have people staring at me," she said to Nell one day during her friend's crocheting lesson.

"I'm going to ask if I can go first," Nell said. "Then I won't have to worry and I can watch everyone else."

"That's a good idea. I'll go second. Is your Mama coming?"

"Yes, and Josie, too. Pa and Ike are usually asleep during the day because they work at night and Ma says they have to mind the babies."

"Why doesn't Josie go to school?"

"When she couldn't learn to read, she got mad and quit."

"Golly, it's awful not to be able to read. How does she write?"

"She can't hardly do that either. She gets all her letters backwards."

Hildy didn't know how to respond but Nell added, "She can

play the piano, though. We had one when we lived on the prairie and if Josie heard a song just once, she could play it. She cried when we moved here and had to leave it behind. Someday I'm going to buy her one."

"Miss Rose has one, so does Mrs. McCarver in Old Town. I heard she had it shipped around the horn."

Nell laughed. "I'd better find a way to make a lot of money." She spread her warming collar over her lap and fingered the stitches. "I'm almost done and then I can start your collar."

"I'm not in a hurry," Hildy said.

"But I am, so I can try some other patterns."

The last day of the winter term arrived, and members of the lodge that occupied the school building's second floor gave permission for the exhibition to be held up there. The afternoon before the exhibition, the students stayed late to set up makeshift tables on sawhorses. The lodge had a few chairs but most parents and guests would have to stand. Some of the students had their items ready and put them on the tables; others, such as Hildy, would bring theirs the next day.

"Where's your collar, Nell?" Hildy asked.

"In a safe place." Nell shifted a few things around to make an empty space on one of the tables and put down a neatly labeled piece of paper reading "Warming Collar, 3-ply yarn by Nell Tanquist."

"Well, gracious," Hildy said, "I should think it'd be safe here." She found a vacant spot big enough for a flour sack, which she'd replace with bread the next day, and a label reading, "Bread from homemade potato yeast and honey butter both by Mathilda Bacom."

"Aren't you glad no one calls you Matty?" Nell said.

"I would hate it. Have you seen Sarah's picture yet?"

"No."

"Me, either, she's been awfully secretive. Let's go look."

They made their way to another table where Sarah was propping a watercolor up on a tabletop easel. "Oh, my." Hildy stopped short and Nell looked over her shoulder.

Sarah had painted six girls sitting or standing around the remains of a picnic. Behind them was a wall of trees and off to the side were several buckets of berries. Though the features were indistinct, Hildy easily recognized Nell from her hair, Fern and Ellen from their clothes, and Kezzie biting into an apple. She, herself, was shown in profile, looking at Nell and laughing. The figure of Sarah stood slightly away from the group, leaning against a tree.

"Do you like it?" Sarah asked.

"Oh, yes, why I can feel the heat from the sun on my shoulders just looking at it."

Sarah laughed. "I don't usually paint people but that was the first day in New Tacoma that I had fun."

"Well," Nell said, "when you're famous, I can tell people that we were your first friends." She giggled. "I wonder if Fern will think paintings in Virginia are better. Say, did I tell you that Josie dyed my old dress? When Ma let the hem down there was a line so Josie found some dye and now it's dark blue."

"I washed my good dress yesterday," Hildy said, "and Mama promised to make some starch. Do you want to come over and iron it? Sarah, you can come, too."

Nell and Sarah had to decline and they parted company.

Over the past year, Hildy had made so much bread, she wasn't particularly worried but just in case, she used every bread pan they owned so she could choose the best loaves. Her dress was washed and starched to a fare-thee-well and she had memorized a brief talk. The morning of the exhibition she wrapped three loaves in paper and put them in a large flour sack. The honey butter was already mixed and in a lard bucket with a handle.

"It's a good thing we don't need our slates, today," she said.

"Have you seen Reuben's project yet?" Verdita asked.

"No, he took the biggest flour bag we have to carry it in. I can't imagine what it is."

Hildy was getting ready to leave when her mother called her back.

"Where's your coat?"

"Oh, Mama, a coat will wrinkle my dress. It's not that cold outside, really it isn't."

"It's still winter, Hildy, even if it doesn't seem like it. You know how quickly the weather changes."

"But, Mama . . ."

"If you don't want to wear your coat then put on your zouave jacket."

"But . . ."

"I don't know what's gotten into you lately, Hildy. Quit arguing and put it on."

Chong looked up from the breakfast dishes and grinned. When Verdita's back was turned, Hildy stuck out her tongue at him. Reuben came in the back door clutching his sack and he and Hildy set off.

"How long will school be out this time?" Reuben asked.

"Until New Tacoma finds enough money to pay Mr. and Mrs. Stair for the spring session."

"I hope they never find it, don't you?"

"It'll probably rain every day."

"Jehoshaphat, you're grumpy lately."

"I am not."

"Are too."

At that point, Reuben saw Andy Flett and Edward Rigney and ran to join them, and Hildy trudged on until she met Nell. Nell had used the remnants of her blue yarn to crochet a ribbon. With her hair under a semblance of control she looked

225

more mature.

"Nell," Hildy said hesitantly as they waited at Railroad Street for a man leading a string of mules to pass, "am I grumpy lately? Reuben says I am."

"Only sometimes, but I understand why."

"What do you mean?"

Nell stopped walking and looked at her friend. Then she leaned forward and whispered in Hildy's ear. At her words, Hildy's hand went to her throat.

"You, too?"

"Yes, awful isn't it? Why, last week I slapped Josie's hand. Of course, she cried and that made me cry. Then Ma said it wouldn't be long before I had to wear a corset and there will be the end of fun."

Hildy's pale face broke into a smile. "I thought I was the only one and it was ever so lonely."

They smiled at each other and continued walking. "I can smell your bread," Nell said.

"No one will expect the honey butter. It's a surprise. I tell you, I don't know what I'd do without Tabitha Tickletooth's cookbook."

They reached the school and climbed the stairs to the second floor. With her usual efficiency, Mrs. Stair had the tables divided by age. The littlest children had drawn pictures or brought collections of stones, shells, and pinecones. The older students were putting on a play. Ever since Mrs. Stair announced the exhibition, they had been staying after classes to work on it. However, Hildy was most interested in her class's table, especially when Nell unwrapped a Red-on-Red Warming Collar and put it down.

"My collar! How did you get it done so fast and where's yours?"

Nell grinned. "I sold it."

"What?"

"I sold it. And now I have enough money to buy the yarn for two collars. I figure if I can sell one of them, I can keep a collar for myself and then buy more yarn and make more collars and sell them, too."

"Why, Nell Tanquist. You're practically a businesswoman. Who bought it?"

"Mrs. Halstead."

"No! If she wears it at their hotel and people see it, all kinds of people will want them. In no time at all you'll be rich."

Nell laughed. "I wrote down the pattern but I need others. I'll have to use some of the money to buy them."

"That's called overhead. I'll show you my bread ledger and you can make one just like it. But I bet if you ask around some of the ladies will have patterns to lend you."

Nell was about to answer when Mrs. Stair clapped her hands for everyone to finish up and go down to the schoolroom. Hildy put her bread on the flour sack with the honey butter and a knife nearby and Nell whispered, "Save me a heel."

At the beginning of the term, Mrs. Stair assigned each older student one or more younger ones to help. Now, not one to waste an hour, she handed out the school's few books and had everyone break into their groups. Hildy opened the Cornell's Geography and her group started reading about Portugal's great explorers. Each read a paragraph and then passed the book. The third time Hildy looked at the clock, Mrs. Stair, to her amazement, smiled and looked away.

They stopped for lunch at noon and then the parents started to arrive. Nell's mother and sister were among the first arrivals. Seeing Mrs. Tanquist's thin frame and small, pale face, Hildy was glad she was early enough to get a seat. Her own mother also found a seat, but in the back row. To have enough room for everyone, Mrs. Stair had the youngest students sit under the table holding their exhibits. The oldest were downstairs taking care of last-minute problems and those in Hildy's class stood along the wall nearest the door.

At one o'clock, Mrs. Stair walked to the front of the room and the crowd immediately became quiet. "Friends and families of the students of North School, welcome," she began. After a brief talk about the school and its successes and the need for more books, she introduced her husband and the program began with the youngest first. Mr. Stair called a name and the child crawled out from under the table and said a few words. Everyone laughed when little Willie Lynch became tongue-tied and ran over to his mother.

After the youngest students finished, Mrs. Stair took her husband's place at the front of the room and introduced Nell. Hildy thought Nell was even prettier than the lady on the boxes of McRae Fine Tobacco. When Nell finished, she went to stand on the other side of the room and Mrs. Stair introduced Hildy.

"When we moved into our house," Hildy began, with a quaver in her voice, "the first thing I did was boil a medium-sized potato. When it was cooked, I took it out of the water, mashed it, and added a small amount of sugar and salt and put the mixture in a jar. I added enough of the potato water to fill the jar and then I covered it with cloth, and put it in a warm place for a few days to ferment. That's how I made my yeast."

As she looked around the room, Hildy saw some of the women smile and nod. She went on to say that she began making bread when she was ten and it was one of her regular chores. She told about selling loaves, explained how she kept her ledger, and finished by saying that the bread she brought would be served at the end of the exhibition along with the honey butter she had also made. When she was done, Nell beamed and Verdita gave her a big smile.

At his own request, Reuben was the last. His surprise was an otter pelt he had cured. "I killed this otter with my slingshot," he explained, "because it was trying to kill our chicken. My friend, Samuel, showed me how to cut it open and get out all the insides but then Samuel moved away and Chong helped me finish. We rubbed salt all through it." He finished with a brief explanation of the pickling process and then Mr. Stair introduced the graduating students. Their play was actually a shadow show. Two of the boys put blankets over the windows while the girls lit lanterns and set them at various spots on the tables. Marcella Rigney read a story they'd written together while the others used their hands to make shadows on the wall. They finished to great applause and requests to perform again. Most of the youngest children and their parents left soon after. Reuben gave the otter pelt to Verdita to make a muff and Nell tucked the red collar into Hildy's pocket. Hildy sliced the bread and people stood around enjoying it and the honey butter. To her pleasure, two women asked how she made it.

"Mr. Scott will have you to thank when he sells all his honey," Verdita said as they walked home.

Hildy giggled. "It's as good as jam and not near so much work. I wonder what else you can do with honey."

"Aunt Glady might know."

"Or Tabitha Tickletooth. I wonder if I can write her and ask for ideas."

They talked all the way home, pushing open the back door just as the sky clouded over and it began to rain. "Ira, we're home," Verdita called, since the kitchen was empty.

"In here."

While Verdita took off her coat and put her apron on, Hildy went to join her father in the parlor. As it turned out, he wasn't alone. Sitting near the fire was Cousin Elsie.

CHAPTER 21

Hildy's eyes went from her father to her cousin and immediately saw two things: Cousin Elsie looked puffy, ill, and older than her sixteen years and her father's thin face was drawn and pinched.

"Hello, Hildy." Elsie gave a weak smile.

"What are you doing here? Is Aunt Glady with you?" Hildy forgot to remove her coat and hat and sat down just as her mother appeared in the doorway. Hildy saw her father level a stern look at her mother.

After a short pause, Verdita crossed the room and gave Elsie a hug. "How are you, dear?" She sat next to Elsie on the loveseat and took the girl's hands. "Your mother wrote that you've been ill." Verdita looked at Hildy. "Aunt Glady wrote a while back and asked if Elsie could come out to visit us for a while so she could get well." She smiled, but Hildy saw the same pinched look her father had. She also remembered the letter her parents received several weeks back and her mother's words, "How dare she?" There was something peculiar about why Aunt Glady sent Elsie out here when she thought New Tacoma was a godless place and that the residents were all yokels.

Pitch in the firewood snapped in the otherwise quiet room. Elsie's hands moved purposelessly over her reticule; she flinched when Dovie, who had been napping, woke and cried.

"Where will she sleep?" Hildy asked.

"We'll move Dovie in with you and Elsie can have her room,"

Verdita said. When Hildy opened her mouth to protest, she added, "having a room of your own was a luxury, you knew that."

"It will only be for a few months, just until I—well until I feel better," Elsie said.

"How do I know it won't be forever?"

"Hildy!" Ira snapped. "That's enough of that."

But at the same time, Elsie, looking at her hands, said "I just know, that's all."

"This is a frontier town," Ira said. "It's not what you're used to. And you'll have to do your share of the chores."

"What I'm used to?" Elsie gave a harsh laugh. "It was my idea to come out here—to get away from what I'm used to. I'm just—well, I'm just glad that you will let me stay here for a few months. After that, I don't know."

"You'll go home, of course," Verdita said.

Elsie gave her a funny look and in the uncomfortable silence that followed, Reuben burst in the room. "Hey, Cousin Elsie, what are you doing here?" Before she could answer he said, "Want to see the otter hide I cured? Papa, you didn't see it, either."

He ran to get the pelt and Verdita stood up. "I expect you'll want to get settled. I'll show you where you'll be sleeping. Hildy, please check on dinner and when Reuben gets back, have him make sure the woodbox is full."

Elsie opened her small handbag. "I don't aim to be a burden on you. This is to pay for my keep." She started to hand some coins to Ira but he nodded toward his wife. Verdita took the money and put it in her pocket. Elsie followed her out of the room.

"Hildy, Reuben, you heard what your mother said, go on now."

Hildy stood up and turned slowly to leave. At the doorway,

she paused and looked back. Her father had closed his eyes and he was leaning back in the chair. "Are you all right, Papa?"

"Just tired, little cabbage. I wasn't—we weren't really expecting Elsie. Life here will be very different from what she's used to." Under his breath, he added, "It's a sorry state of affairs."

"What is?"

"Nothing, Never mind." Ira lifted his head and smiled. "Is there any of that honey butter left?"

"A little bit, I'll make you more."

Hildy hung her jacket over the stair newel and went out to the kitchen. Earlier, Verdita had put a venison roast in the Dutch oven to cook. Rich, meaty odors filled the air and Hildy's mouth watered. She went down to the root cellar for potatoes, carrots, and apples, and wished they were in better condition. The potatoes had started to rot and the carrots were shriveled. In the kitchen, she cut away the bad parts and peeled them. While they cooked, she peeled and sliced apples and put them in a pot on the stove with butter, brown sugar, cinnamon, and a pinch of nutmeg. As she worked, she mulled over Elsie's sudden arrival. *There's something very peculiar going on.*

"Those apples smell good," said Verdita, who had left Elsie upstairs to unpack. "We can have them for afters. Later you can help me move some of Dovie's things to your room."

"Ummm." Hildy stirred the fruit and Chong came in with two buckets of water. He was filling the stove's reservoir when someone knocked at the back door.

"I get," he said.

A man and a young Puyallup Indian woman not much older stood outside. She wore a rough cotton blouse and wool skirt and had dark hair parted in the middle. When Chong opened the door, she pulled a wool blanket around her shoulders and stepped back to let her man speak. He wore trousers but other than that was similarly dressed.

"Mahkook," Chong said, using Chinook jargon.

"Pish?"

"Kwit shadie, ikt tahla."

"What is it, Chong?" Verdita asked.

"Have rabbits to sell."

The man shifted his blanket and nodded to the woman. She held out two by their tails.

"How much are they asking?"

"Haf dolla."

Verdita smiled at the couple and examined the rabbits. "All right." She went to get the money and handed the coins to the man. He put them in a beaded pouch that hung from his waist and nodded to the woman to hand over the game.

During the exchange, Hildy cut and spread two slices of bread with honey butter. Now, she came over and held them out saying, *"Le pan?"* The man scowled but the woman smiled shyly. *"Totoosh lakles* and *le sook."*

The woman said something, and the man grunted, but they accepted the slices. At the unexpected sweetness, the woman smiled. Hildy smiled back and pointed at herself. "Hildy."

The woman copied the gesture. "Mary." However, at a noise coming from the kitchen her friendliness disappeared. Hildy turned around and saw Elsie standing at the back of the room, her eyes wide and her hands over her mouth. When she turned back to the door, the Indians were gone.

"Oh, my," Elsie said. "Were those Indians?"

"Yes, Puyallups." Verdita poked a fork in the vegetables to see if they were done.

"Here, you'd better sit down." Hildy pulled a chair out and gently pushed on her cousin's shoulders.

"Are they dangerous?" Elsie asked.

"No, they live on a reservation and come to town to sell things."

"What was that you were speaking?"

"White people call it Chinook jargon but the Indians call it *chinuk wawa*." Verdita moved the vegetables to the back of the stove. "Most everyone here knows some. Chong used to work at a hotel and he speaks it better than I do."

Reuben dumped his armful of wood in the woodbox and looked at the dead rabbits. "Can I skin them?"

"Can you do it without mangling the meat?" Verdita asked.

"Chong'll help me, won't you, Chong?"

Before he could answer, Elsie said, "Is he your servant?"

"He's our friend and he helps us, isn't that right, Mama?" Reuben said.

"That's exactly right. Now, I don't see any dishes on the table and we're ready to dish up. Elsie, would you please call your uncle."

The Elsie Hildy remembered picked at her food; the Elsie now at their table did not. She accepted seconds of everything and complimented Verdita over the venison's tenderness. "Mama's Irish girls can't seem to cook deer or even baby lamb so it tastes good."

"We eat a lot of fresh meat here but getting fresh fruit and vegetables is another thing. Hildy, Chong, and I dried apples all through August and September."

"On the roof," Reuben said.

"Goodness." Elsie gave Chong a sideways look. "Does, er, Chong live here?"

"He has his own little place at the edge of the property."

Elsie sighed in relief.

When they'd finished supper, she pitched in without being asked to help clear the table and scrape and stack the dishes. Then Hildy served the hot apples and, afterwards, Ira went upstairs to read the *Herald* in peace. Hildy handed the bowl of scraps to Dovie, who toddled out to throw them to the chickens.

Chicken Little had made the acquaintance of a roving rooster and had a flock of chicks. Hildy was out in the yard, later, watching them when Nell showed up.

"Look." Nell opened a bag to show the yarn she'd bought. "After the school exhibition two women asked me to make them collars."

"Goodness gracious, that was fast. No one asked me about my honey butter." Hildy heaved a pretend sigh.

"Hah! I met Mrs. Scott uptown and she said three people stopped to ask her about buying honey. So there!"

They were laughing when Verdita called. "Come see Elsie's bag, Nell. It's crocheted, too."

"Elsie?" Nell's eyes grew huge.

"I was just about to tell you." Hildy lowered her voice to a whisper. "When we got home, she was sitting in the parlor with Papa. I tell you, my eyes about popped out of my head." She started to say more but Verdita appeared in the doorway.

Elsie sat near the stove with the purse on her lap. She smiled shyly and Nell eyed her suspiciously, for a moment. Then she leaned down to look at the purse. After a few seconds, she picked it up and held it close. "I think I know most of these stitches don't I, Mrs. Bacom?"

"Yes, you do and I wish I had a pattern."

"If Elsie will let me, I bet I can figure it out. Would you, Elsie?"

"Yes, but not today because I'm too tired."

"Elsie has been ill," Hildy explained. "She's come out here to rest a bit."

Under Nell's sharp gaze, Elsie stared at her lap, clenching and unclenching her hands. "If there isn't anything you want me to do, I think I'll go up now, Aunt Verdita."

"Of course. Even if you were able to rest in Portland, we all know how long the trip from Kalama is."

Elsie left the room, her footsteps barely making a sound. "Did she come all by herself?" Nell asked.

"No, that would have been highly improper. She traveled with a missionary couple as far as Portland and came up from there with Reverend Judy."

"What's the matter with her?"

"I'm sure it's nothing that rest can't cure." Verdita's tone said the subject was closed and Nell left soon after.

Dovie was in bed asleep when Hildy went up. She dropped to her knees by the side window and listened to the frogs. *It's nearly a year since we came to New Tacoma. Now I can't imagine living anywhere else.* Somewhere nearby lived the screech owl she'd heard so often, but though she waited, he didn't appear. A grouse hooted once and then was quiet. Even the pile drivers were quiet and the peeper's chorus filled the darkness. Moonlight shone through the trees and the house creaked as it settled down for the night. Hildy stayed by the window, enjoying the peace and watching fog come in to make will-o'-the-wisps. When her eyes grew heavy, she changed into her nightgown. As she shifted Dovie from the middle of the bed, she heard a sound. It stopped but then returned and she knew it came from Elsie's room. *Oh dear.* Hildy tiptoed out of her room and stepped across the hall. The door was shut and she tapped softly. "Elsie," she whispered, "are you all right?" Elsie didn't answer and Hildy opened the door a few inches. "Are you poorly?"

"No."

"Can I come in?"

"I guess."

Hildy crossed the room and got into bed with her cousin. Elsie was curled up on her side and Hildy felt her trembling. "Are you so awfully ill, Elsie? Don't worry; we'll take care of you. I was terribly sick last year and so was Papa but we both got well." She snuggled over to Elsie's back and put her arms around her.

"It's something else, something really bad, Hildy." Elsie sobbed. "I didn't mean to but I did something terrible. Mama was livid and Papa stormed out of the house. I don't think they'll ever want me home again and then what'll I do?"

"Of course they'll want you back; parents always love their children. We'll fix you up in no time."

"Parents don't *always* love their children. I don't think Mama ever really loved me."

Hildy didn't know what to say; she leaned her cheek against Elsie's back and they matched their breathing. Outside, the wind sighed and branches lifted and fell in response. A drop of rain tapped on the windowpane and others joined it. "If my friend Samuel was here, he'd know how to make you well."

Elsie choked and started to say something.

"What is it, Elsie? What were you going to say?"

"Nothing. And I'll be gone by June and you can have your room back."

"That's not important. Not a lot of people in New Tacoma have kin and now I do, so that makes me special. I can take you to meet Mrs. Money and we can go see Miss Isabeau and her ladies and, well, there's ever so much we can do. You'll see."

"Hildy?"

"What?"

"I didn't used to like you, you know, but now I think you're awfully sweet. I'm glad you're here."

Hildy giggled. "Well, I didn't much like you, either, but now I do and we can be friends."

"I hope so but maybe, later, you won't like me so much after all."

"Did you murder someone or steal from the collection plate?"

Now it was Elsie's turn to giggle. "Of course not."

"Then I wouldn't worry; you see, the only people I don't like are those who are unkind . . ."

"You mean like Mama?"

"Uh . . ."

"Don't worry. She's often unkind and I'm not sure if she means well even if she pretends she does."

"Do you think you can sleep now?"

"Will you stay with me? I feel better when I'm not alone."

"I might snore. You should hear Reuben, he wheezes like an old bagpipe."

They giggled again and then became quiet, falling asleep to the sound of the gentle rain.

CHAPTER 22

In Hildy's opinion, the city could have run out of money for Mr. and Mrs. Stair's salaries during a better month than March. The first week school was closed, rain fell nearly every day. Anyone who left the house returned with mud on their boots. Gusts of winds blew into the stove's chimney making the fire flare at unexpected times, or blow smoke back into the kitchen. The chickens quit laying and huddled in the coop Chong and Reuben built, looking pathetic. The noisier the house became, the quieter Hildy became. *I have nowhere to go to be by myself.* As a result, she got up before the rest of the family to enjoy the quiet kitchen.

Hildy loved the early morning hours. She stoked the stove embers with kindling, punched her bread down, and formed the loaves. When the stove's surface was warm, she put the pans on the back to rise for the last time. Yeasty smells filled the room as she set the table, made coffee, and sorted laundry. When Ira came downstairs he smiled at her industry.

"Good morning, Papa. Are you going to the office today?" Hildy poured his coffee and put the sugar bowl on the table.

She didn't look at him as she spoke. *Papa's too young to look so thin and pale. He's not near as old as Mr. Blackwell and Mr. Blackwell is positively hale and hearty.* Ira also wheezed a bit when he talked, and tired easily. Hildy knew her mother had asked Mr. Scott to look for a horse they could buy so Ira could ride to work. Maybe, if the money Cousin Elsie gave them was

239

enough, they could now get it.

"I think not today. General Sprague dropped off some papers yesterday for me to look at. I'll work upstairs and go in tomorrow."

Hildy put dirty clothes into a tub of water and poked them down with a stick to soak. "Life is like a game of Jackstraws, isn't it, Papa?"

Ira blew on his coffee and smiled. "How so, little cabbage?"

"Well, just when a person has the sticks tidied up, something knocks them out of the bag and they fall all over. And just when a person thinks they have life all figured out and everything is as it should be, something happens and changes the whole lot."

"You mean like Cousin Elsie's coming?"

"Well, yes, but lots more, like moving to New Tacoma and your getting sick and, well, lots of things. Don't things ever stay the same?"

"No, they don't." Footsteps sounded upstairs as Reuben dressed and Ira smiled at Hildy. "You wouldn't want us all to stay exactly as we are now, would you? You want to grow up and have a family of your own and watch New Tacoma become a real town like Johnstown. One of the best lessons you will ever learn is to be flexible with what life gives you. You can't do anything about it and being flexible makes everything easier."

Ira opened his copy of the previous day's *Herald* and turned to "Local Intelligence." After reading a moment he chuckled. "I don't think the editor is happy about the school being closed. Listen to this: 'The Do-Nothings of the city are liable to get themselves into trouble because they have nothing else to do.' And, who's more do-nothing right now then you school children?"

"Well, not me. I do lots of somethings." Hildy hurried to set the table as the rest of the household came downstairs for breakfast.

Over the next few weeks, however, Do-Nothing boys, without school to keep them busy, used their days to prey on the Chinese. When John Collins, proprietor of Seattle's Occidental Hotel, fired his Chinese staff and replaced it with white men, some of the older boys in New Tacoma took the move as a sign and declared open season to do mischief on the Chinese population.

It started early one morning when several boys saw a group of Chinese men cutting mussels off some of the wharf's pilings.

"Look at them Celestials," one of them said. "They won't eat salmon but they'll eat mussels."

"Pa says they eat skunks, too. They drown 'em first."

Not to be outdone, the third boy added, "That ol' Wo Chong built a laundry up on Rainier Street and he cooks skunks alive and uses the ashes for medicine."

One of the boys picked up a rock and threw it. The stone hit a Chinese man on the back of the head and he turned and shouted. The boys laughed and ran away.

Not long after, three men guarding a Chinese man in jail claimed to have fallen asleep at the time their prisoner hung himself in his cell. When the *Herald* reported the birth of a Chinese baby and the kidnapping of a Chinese woman, some thought the little Chinese community was becoming way too important, and rock throwing wasn't uncommon.

One morning, when Chong failed to show up, Ira went to his little shack and found the boy trying to apply a hot compress to his badly bruised body.

"What happened?" Ira knelt down and looked at the purple-black marks on Chong's arms and back.

"Boys throw rocks."

"Why?"

"I Chinee."

The words were simply said, but Ira could hardly look at the pain on Chong's face. He thought of the not-so-distant War of Southern Secession, the war he'd been too young and too sickly to fight in, and sighed. "Only ignorant people dislike others because of the color of their skin and I'm afraid there are a lot of ignorant people in this world. But there are good men, too, such as Mr. Blackwell and Father Hylebos. You have to try and avoid the first and remember the others. Now," he took Chong's arm. "Come on; let's get you to the house."

Ira kept his arm around Chong as they walked and, in the kitchen, helped him to a chair.

Chong's bruises shocked everyone. "What happened?" Verdita asked. She diluted cider vinegar with water and using a piece of toweling applied the solution to his swollen and discolored skin.

"Someone threw rocks at him." Ira poured himself a cup of coffee.

"Oh, Chong, who would do such a thing?" Hildy cried.

"It's Delmar Manches, I bet." Reuben scowled. "He's been doing that ever since school closed."

"Reuben's right. Ever since he came to town he's been putting on like he's a dude. What he is is just a big old blowhard."

From upstairs came the sounds of Elsie vomiting. Verdita sighed and shook her head. "I thought she'd be done with that by now."

"Is she a *lunger*?"

"Of course not, Reuben. Do you think Aunt Glady would have let her come clear across the country if she had consumption?"

Ira paced the kitchen looking at Chong and then out the window. "Do you want to file charges, Chong?"

"Dema Manches go to jail?"

"Maybe. Did anyone see it happen?"

"Plenty men, white and Chinee."

"I'll ask General Sprague who to consult. New Tacoma sadly lacks much in the way of law enforcement."

Verdita made Chong rest for the day. He went into the dining room and played with Dovie. When Elsie came downstairs carrying the slop bucket, she looked pale and drawn. "My ceiling is leaking." Hildy saw Elsie rub her stomach and grimace.

"Oh, dear." Verdita found a lard pail and rushed upstairs muttering something about it doesn't rain but what it pours. Hildy giggled but Elsie closed her eyes and swallowed.

Ira returned from the office at noon; he told them that Mr. Leve, Mr. Halstead, and a traveling salesman had all seen the incident and would stand up for Chong.

"New Tacoma doesn't really have a court system," he explained, "but Captain Edwards and Misters Wood, Nolan, and Johnson will hear the case."

Elsie looked at her uncle. "If the town doesn't have a court system then how is crime handled?"

"Not very well, I'm afraid."

Before Ira could say more, Reuben piped up. "Once, someone pulled a drowned body out of the bay and put it on the wharf and it was there all day 'cause there was no one to take it away."

"Goodness," Elsie said while Verdita told Reuben such talk wasn't appropriate for the dinner table.

Three days later, Chong had his day before the makeshift judges and Hildy, wanting to hear the trial, tried to find an excuse to go uptown. *Of course, I won't be able to actually go into the room but maybe I can find a place to eavesdrop.*

Verdita, however, had other ideas. "Why don't we examine Elsie's purse and write down the stitches."

"I was going to go up to Mr. Fife's store."

"It's pouring down rain and I don't want you getting wet and catching cold. You remember the last time you were sick?"

"Samuel helped me get well." Hildy looked out the window

243

and tried to remember his face. *Samuel promised to write and he never did.* The rain turned to pea-sized hail that quickly covered the ground. Then, just as quickly, it stopped and the sun came out. No, she corrected herself, he said he would try and write. *There's a difference between saying you will and saying you will try. But, I can't hold on to your memory forever.*

Elsie watched thoughts come and go on Hildy's face and was curious. "Who's Samuel?"

"A friend." Hearing the abruptness in her words, Hildy turned from the window. "Shall I go upstairs and get your handbag?"

"Would you? I feel a little queasy."

As Hildy left the room she heard her mother asking Elsie questions about her illness.

For the balance of the afternoon, Hildy, Verdita, and Elsie sat near the stove with the purse on the table examining the stitches and drinking coffee. Hildy became so involved, she found an old piece of string and a crochet hook and worked the stitches as her mother and cousin deciphered them. Dovie played near their feet, and Jenny Lind sang. Reuben went down to the root cellar and stayed playing a game of his invention. His bumps and thumps were clearly audible. Sun and showers alternated, and the rain plop-plopped steadily in the lard pails upstairs. Two hours after Ira and Chong left, they returned.

"Reuben." Hildy opened the door and aimed a shout in the root cellar's direction. "Papa and Chong are home."

Reuben came up, Hildy draped Ira and Chong's coat over the backs of chairs to dry, and Verdita helped Ira off with his heavy boots. Elsie watched with a puzzled look on her face. "My mother wouldn't think of doing that."

Chong and Ira dried their hair with flour sacks and Hildy poured coffee for her father and made tea for Chong. She sat on the edge of the chair where Ira's coat hung and waited. Ira drank half his coffee and looked at the expectant faces.

"This was the first time any of New Tacoma's Chinese went to court, even a makeshift one. I can tell you, Smith's Hall was packed. People cared."

"You mean they cared about Chong?"

"Not exactly, maybe I should say they had a vested interest in the outcome."

Elsie pushed her cup of coffee away, picked up a cookie, and then put it down. "Why? Why would they care about a Chinese boy getting stoned?"

"Because if Chong had won, it would mean all the Chinese here had equal rights." Ira gestured for more coffee and continued. "Chong told what happened. Captain Edwards asked him to point out the rock thrower. You were right, Reuben, it was Delmar Manches. He was there with his father and several other boys." Ira took a long drink of coffee and continued. "Anyway, after Chong spoke, the traveling salesman, Mr. Halstead, and Mr. Leve said they had also seen Delmar that day. He had been with a group of boys who were taunting a Chinese laundryman before Chong came along. The laundryman and another Chinese identified Delmar. Mr. Manches had a lawyer for Delmar and the lawyer and the other boys claimed Chong started a fight with them and it was impossible to tell who threw the stone. The white men agreed with the attorney and Chong lost."

"Chong wouldn't start a fight and he wouldn't lie. Did you tell them that, Papa?"

Ira looked at Hildy and shook his head. "I didn't witness the fight so I couldn't testify."

"Well, I'm so spitting mad at that old Delmar Manches I'm going to think of something horrible to do to him."

"No you're not, Hildy and anyway, it isn't necessary."

"But it wasn't fair. Everyone knows about Delmar."

"You're right; they do, including his father." Ira smiled at Chong and Chong grinned back. "You see, after the trial, Mr. Manches took a stick of wood to his son and wailed him with it all the way home. That lawyer cost Manches plenty and Delmar's going to have to get a job on the weekends and pay his father back."

Everyone, even Elsie, laughed and Verdita stood up to start supper. Chong picked up Dovie and looked happily at Ira. "Mebbe I be attoney, fight for Chinee, fight for change. Change for Chinee be good."

Hildy caught her father's eye and smiled.

CHAPTER 23

After three weeks, the businessmen in New Tacoma finally found enough money to pay Mr. and Mrs. Stair's salaries for the rest of the year. School would begin again in late March and continue until mid-June. The Saturday morning before school was to start Hildy opened the back door and stepped outside to the sound of frogs croaking and Steller's Jays chattering. The air was soft and surprisingly warm. She crossed the yard to let the chickens out of the lean-to. They followed her to the house and she backed in, shooing them away. "Go find some worms, you greedy things. We haven't even eaten yet."

Reuben burst into the kitchen followed by Verdita, with Dovie, and Ira. Elsie came a few minutes later. It seemed to Hildy that in the weeks since Elsie's arrival, she had gotten sicker rather than better. Her initial puffiness was gone. Now her eyes had dark circles under them and her cheeks were sunken. She seemed to throw up everything she ate, often seemed in pain, and went to the necessary more than anyone Hildy knew. Once, Hildy saw Elsie standing at the top of the stairs staring down with a funny look on her face. Sometimes she heard Elsie and Verdita talking softly together when they thought she wasn't around. Hildy wondered why her mother didn't seem more concerned.

After everyone came downstairs and took turns washing up, Elsie tied on an apron to help with breakfast. Hildy looked at Elsie. *How can she throw up everything and still look like she's get-*

ting fat? They sat down to grits and pork and were dishing up when a loud prolonged rumbling sound filled the room.

"Who's dragging the dining room table?" Verdita asked. As she spoke, the house rocked back and forth.

"What . . . ?" Ira started to say when the vibrations started. Two short jerks followed and the land rolled under them. Something upstairs fell over. Pots and pans bounced off shelves and toppled to the floor. Jenny Lind, the canary, let out a shriek and Dovie watched her bowl bounce and laughed. Hams tied to the ceiling beams swayed back and forth and dishes jumped up and down on the table. Reuben dove under it but everyone else froze. The sound still echoed deep and low when the back door blew open and swung back and forth. Chong half-fell into the room.

"You feel?"

"What was it?" Verdita looked pale.

'I think we may have had an earthquake." Ira stood up and then sat down. "My goodness."

For a minute, everyone was quiet. Then Hildy saw her bread pans on the floor and jumped up.

"My bread." The metal pans were on their sides and the dough was spilling out. She picked everything up, cleaned off the tops of the loaves, and put them back to rise. "Oh dear, I don't know if this can be saved."

Reuben crawled out from under the table. Now that the danger was over his face was alight with excitement.

"Can I go uptown and see if any buildings fell down?"

"Finish your breakfast and bring in the wood first, then you can." Verdita looked at the pots and pans scattered around the kitchen and ran from the room. "Oh, no, my parlor lamps."

Elsie looked at Ira. "Does this happen often?" Her face was white and her eyes wide with fear.

"It's the first since we've been here but I've heard the old-timers talk about them." For the first time in weeks Ira seemed to have forgotten his illness. His face had color and his eyes were bright. "I think I'll go to the office, after all."

"Are you sure you're strong enough, Papa?"

"This one time I'll walk uptown and hire a horse from Cogswell's livery."

Verdita returned from the parlor with the plant Hildy had given her for Christmas and pieces of its pot. "My lamps survived but this needs a new planter and there's dirt all over the rug." She didn't seem angry, though. "Goodness gracious, wait until Aunt Glady hears about this." She looked at Elsie. "As soon as breakfast is over you'd better write and let her know that you're all right. We can all walk uptown and you can mail it."

Their breakfast was cold but no one seemed to care. Hildy's loaves rose again but the tops were lopsided. She had to wait until the bread baked before going out. Elsie offered to stay and tidy up. After everyone else left, she found a rag and wiped off the shelves. "You always had a way with yeast."

"I love to see it bubble and then grow in the pans. I'm saving my money to open a bakery."

"Won't that take a long time?"

Hildy's face lit up. "Well, you know I already have some customers for my bread. I sold a pie to Mr. Peak and some pasties, too. Today is their morning to come, that's why I couldn't leave Mama. They come every other day, but I think I will just give them these because they aren't pretty."

"Why don't you sell them some of yesterday's bread and we can make bread pudding with this?" Elsie started picking up the fallen pans.

"Why, Cousin Elsie, that's brilliant, and I'll give them some of my honey butter to make up for its not being fresh-baked this morning." Hildy beamed and Elsie smiled. "And then when we go uptown I have to visit Mr. Craig at the Standard Bakery. I heard that Mr. Craig's baker went back to San Francisco and I want to bake bread for him."

"How will you do that and still go to school?"

"I'm working on a plan."

Hildy's customers were happy to get the free honey butter, especially Mr. Peak, whose dentures slipped and clicked with pleasure. While Hildy dealt with the men, Elsie cleaned the plant's soil from the parlor's carpet, tied string around the pot to hold it together, and put the violet back. She was picking up the scattered flour sacks and the contents of Verdita's sewing basket when Hildy caught a glimpse of her clutching her stomach in pain.

"Are you all right, Cousin Elsie? Do you want to rest now?"

Elsie straightened up and tried to smile. "I'm fine and I want to see the town you're so fond of."

"Compared to Johnstown, it's not much of a town. Fern— she moved here from Virginia—she thinks it's awful."

"Well, after you show me around I'll make up my own mind about it."

"Gracious. You never used to." Hildy stopped and blushed. "I mean, I always thought Aunt Glady made up your mind for you."

"Not anymore." Elsie walked to the door and looked out through the trees. "She can run Papa's life but she can't live mine."

Hildy didn't know how to respond so she offered to run upstairs for their wraps.

When they left for town, most of the people who lived on A Street stood outside talking. As Hildy and Elsie passed them, they heard snatches of conversations: ". . . it was my grandmother's Willowware platter . . ." ". . . and the soup clean put out the fire in the stove . . ." ". . . didn't have such things in Ioway, it's a godless country, here, for sure."

"I'll tell you a secret," Hildy said, as they approached a cluster of women. "If you stand near a group of people but pretend you're interested in something else, you learn the most interesting things."

Elsie giggled. "Why, Hildy Bacom, you're just devious, that's what you are, and brilliant."

On Seventh Street, the earthquake had shaken a log pile apart. Horses picked their way over the scattered wood and wagon drivers cursed when they had to help clear the road. The earthquake had knocked down loose chimney stones and jarred windows out of their flimsy frames. Hildy and Elsie stopped in front of Spooner's Tin Shop and saw Mr. Spooner wading through piles of merchandise still covering the floor. His wife, who made and sold hats in one corner of the store, fussed about with ribbons, feathers, and straw-hat forms. At the corner of Seventh and Pacific, they turned right toward the road to the wharf. Mike Murphy came down Pacific Avenue with a string of runaway horses tied to the back of his wagon.

"Good morning, Mr. Murphy."

"Good morning, Miss Hildy. I hear your pa is looking for a horse."

"Yes, sir, he surely is."

"Well, you tell him I'll be along after dinner with a well-behaved little filly for him to look at."

"I certainly will."

Mike tugged at his hat's brim, flipped the reins, and continued on his way.

Elsie walked over to a vacant lot and bent to sniff a bush with small rose-colored flowers.

"What's this?"

"Wild currant."

"It's pretty."

"It's early for wild currant to bloom. Just wait until the rhododendrons come out."

Hildy's happiness turned to concern when she looked at her cousin. Elsie straightened up slowly, took a deep breath, and coughed. "I smell pigs."

"Mr. Graham lets his roam around and they get into everything. Mr. Cook, who owns the newspaper, has been complaining about them but it doesn't do any good. Gracious, I thought there'd be more stuff to see from the earthquake."

They continued walking until they reached Mr. Shoudy's store. Mr. Shoudy was picking up rolls of wallpaper and shaking broken glass off them. Hildy and Elsie looked in and he looked up.

"Hope your windows are intact. I lost most of my inventory." He shook his head and kicked at some of the shards. "It'll cost plenty to replace this lot."

At Nolan and King's store, a bag of sugar had fallen off a shelf and split open. The spilled sugar covered canned goods and bolts of cloth. Three women stood in front of the window, talking.

"The lady in the big hat is Mrs. Bostwick and she's talking to Mrs. Halstead and Mrs. Clark." Hildy spoke low so her words wouldn't carry. "Look, there's the tame fawn. He belongs to the foundry, only I guess he's a she and she's not much of a fawn anymore."

They stopped and looked down Pacific Avenue. In front of Frank Clark's law office, men milled about blocking the sidewalk. Hildy found a place where a series of dry planks made it possible to cross the street. "The bakery is on the other side of the road. Let's cross here."

They struggled across the planks and stopped in front of a store with a lock on the door.

"It's closed." Hildy looked at the lock and scowled. "I wonder where Mr. Craig is."

"Where does he live?" Elsie asked. "Maybe you can send him a letter."

"Maybe." Hildy sighed. "It does seem as something is always spoiling my plans. Well, what can't be cured must be endured. Do you want to walk around some more?"

"Yes, please. The fresh air feels so good."

They turned and started back toward Eleventh Street and Hildy tried to see Pacific Avenue through her cousin's eyes. "It will take a long time for the mud to dry up and when it does, all the roads will be hills and dales. Pacific Avenue gets so lumpy sometimes things bounce out of wagon beds, little kids, too." She looked at Elsie, hoping her cousin would enjoy the story. Instead, Elsie panted and broke out in sweat. Hildy took her arm. "I think we should go home."

"No, not yet. It's such a nice day and this is a very lively street." A cat ran across the sidewalk in front of her and disappeared under a building. Elsie jumped and would have fallen if Hildy hadn't grabbed her.

"We have lots of stray cats, chickens, too. The rich people, like Mr. Hosmer, put up fences. I don't think they help keep chickens and cats out of their yards, though. They do it because they have garden parties and play crochet. When I have my bakery I'm going to have a little house with fences and grow all the flowers we had back in Johnstown."

"Where do the ladies who saved your life the night of the storm live?"

"Up on D Street. Gracious, I haven't seen them in ages."

"We can go there now. School starts in two days and you'll be busy, then. The sun feels so good after all the rain, even if it's a bit smelly. What *is* that smell?"

"The low tide. After a while you get used to it. We had a picnic on the beach, once, and Papa and Reuben went swimming. Chong picked up all kinds of peculiar things to eat. That's one reason why some people don't like the Chinese—because they eat different from us. Gracious, I just thought of something, all the stump houses are gone."

"What's a stump house?"

They walked down the wooden sidewalk and Hildy explained how after men cut down the cedars they left trunks that were five and six feet tall. "Some people hollowed them out and put a roof on."

"I never heard of such a thing," Elsie said. "I can't even imagine."

"Think of how good it would smell. Sometimes, when men have been clearing lots or hauling logs to the wharf, New Tacoma smells just like Christmas trees."

By this time they had reached Ninth Street and turned to walk up the hill. At the Chinese vegetable garden, Hildy paused to let Elsie rest. "Look." Hildy pointed to some small hollowed-out logs. "Those are pipes. The Chinese put them in to carry off some of the spring water so the garden won't flood in winter and wash the soil away. Then in summer, when there isn't enough water, the pipes irrigate. Isn't that smart?"

She didn't expect an answer and started walking again. A roaming calf ambled over to join them, its feet squishing where puddles hadn't yet dried. Hildy put one arm around the little cow and rubbed its nose with her other hand. "I love cows, don't you? They have such lovely eyes. I wonder who this little thing belongs to."

"It seems awfully careless to let your animals roam around, willy-nilly." Elsie leaned against the animal and closed her eyes for a minute. "It's not good animal husbandry."

"Animal husbandry. Gracious, except for Mr. Scott, the milkman, I don't think anyone here pays much attention. How do you know about such a thing?"

"Mama took me to the old homestead where she and Uncle Ira grew up and told me how our grandfather ran the farm."

"You are lucky. Grandfather died before I could meet him."

Apparently deciding they weren't going to feed him, the calf wandered away and Hildy started walking again. "Right up there by that big rock is where we turn, and the ladies live just a little ways down the street."

They stumbled more than once on the uneven ground and by the time they reached the enormous granite boulder Elsie looked sick. "I'm not sure this was a good idea after all." She closed her eyes, leaned against the rock, and clutched her stomach. Hildy, watching in alarm, had started to say something when Elsie gave a loud moan and slid down to the ground. Hildy looked in horror as her cousin spread her drawn-up knees and leaned forward groaning. Suddenly blood flowed out in front of her. "Hildy." Elsie looked up with terror in her eyes and panted between groans. "I need help."

"I—I, I'll get someone." For a moment it seemed as if she was unable to move. "Don't worry. I'll be right back." And Hildy turned and ran.

The windows on Miss Rose's house were covered. *Let someone be home, please, please.* She pounded on the door and heard Miss Rose say, "Hold your horses out there, I'm a comin'." When she opened the door, Hildy nearly fell.

"Tarnation, Hildy Bacom. What do you mean by trying to break my door down?"

"Please, Miss Rose, it's my cousin. She collapsed down by the big rock and I think she's bleeding to death." Hildy grabbed the older woman's hand. "Please come and help her."

Miss Rose straightened up and tied the belt on her wrapper. "Isabeau," she shouted. Isabeau hurried into the room and gave a start at the sight of Hildy. "Hildy says her cousin's alayin' on the ground down the way and is bleeding. Go with her and see

255

what you can do. I'll get some soap and old rags ready in case you have to bring her here."

"Hurry, Miss Isabeau," Hildy said when the other woman continued to stand. "I don't want her to die."

"Toot sweet," Miss Rose added and Isabeau flinched at her employer's attempt to say *tout de suite*—at once.

"Mon Dieu," she muttered, but she hurried across the room and followed Hildy outside and down the road.

"There, Miss Isabeau, by the rock, oh, don't let Elsie be dead." Hildy ran ahead and was relieved to see Elsie move. Isabeau caught up with her and dropped to her knees. *"Sacré bleu."* She switched to English. "How long?"

Elsie looked and fear contorted her face.

"Four and a half months." She began to pant again.

"Hildy." Isabeau smoothed Elsie's hair away from her face. "Run back to the house and tell Miss Rose that Miss Elsie must be carried. *Dépêche-toi*—hurry up."

Hildy run back and the door opened before she could knock. "Elsie needs to be carried."

"Violet, call Dyson, tell him I need him," Miss Rose shouted. She looked at Hildy's frightened face and her voice softened. "Now, don't you worry, dearie. Dyson will have your cousin here in a few minutes and we'll fix her up."

"But there was so much blood." Tears rolled down Hildy's face. "She—she just collapsed by the rock and . . ."

Miss Rose took Hildy's chin in her hand. "Before I came West with Mr. Arneson I was a nurse in the war. If your cousin had what—that is, I think I might know what's wrong with her and more than likely I can fix her up."

"Was Mr. Arneson your husband?"

"Uh, in a manner of speaking. Now," footsteps sounded and she hugged Hildy. "Go with Dyson so Elsie will know it's safe."

Dyson was a slender man with dark hair and eyes. Hildy had

to half-run to keep up with his long-legged stride. In a manner of minutes they reached the giant boulder. He looked at Isabeau and she nodded toward Elsie. Dyson picked her up and Hildy took her hand.

"Don't worry, Elsie. Miss Rose used to be a nurse and she says she probably knows how to make you better. I'll fix you some broth and you'll be absolutely ginger-peachy in no time."

Elsie managed a weak smile and closed her eyes. Dyson carried her to the house and into a small room with a bed and table. The table had a basin of water and a rag. A makeshift curtain covered the lone window, and a lantern provided the only light. As Miss Rose gestured toward the bed, he put Elsie gently down. Hildy hurried to loosen her collar.

"Thanks, Dyson, and now I need you to go to Hildy's house and bring her mother back."

"Thank you, Mr. Dyson," Hildy said.

"It's Andrews, Dyson Andrews."

"Have we met before, Mr. Andrews?"

"No, Miss Hildy but it's a pleasure to meet you." His voice was deep and his words felt reassuring. "Now, you do what Miss Rose says to help your cousin. Miss Violet is in the kitchen and she can tell me where your family lives."

Dyson left and Hildy bathed her cousin's forehead while Miss Rose removed Elsie's outer clothing and knickers. Isabeau came in the room with a warm plate and Miss Rose laid the knickers on it. Hildy caught a brief glimpse of a tiny pink hand before Isabeau turned away. "We have no priest," Miss Rose said.

Isabeau said something in French and then made the sign of the cross over the plate. "I baptize you in the name of the Father, the Son, and the Holy Ghost." She covered the plate, set it aside, and looked at Miss Rose.

"I'm going to press and see if she dispels more; if not, I'll give her something to cramp the gut."

Miss Rose pressed firmly down on Elsie's lower abdomen and Isabeau held a basin between her legs. More discharge flowed and Elsie tried to twist away but the women were able to restrain her. Hildy sat mutely out of the way in a corner, watching, listening, and thinking. *Nell was right. Elsie was going to have a baby. That's why she came out here; that's why Mama and Papa were arguing when they got the letter from Aunt Glady, they didn't want me to know because she doesn't have a husband. Nell guessed right away, though. Oh, dear, poor Cousin Elsie.*

Time passed. The lantern light flickered. Miss Violet came and took the basin away. Elsie's groans came at regular intervals. Hildy was so caught up in trying to comfort her cousin, she didn't notice when the door opened and Verdita appeared.

"How is she?"

"She'll be fine if she doesn't take infection."

Miss Rose gave a final push and stepped away from the bed. "I think that's all." Isabeau handed her a clean rag and she wiped her hands. When she was done, Isabeau gathered up the bloody cloths and took them away, and Verdita took rags from a bag she carried and dipped one in water to begin cleaning Elsie. When she was done, she bound Elsie in rags and helped her into a clean nightgown. Isabeau returned with clean blankets and they made Elsie comfortable. There was a knock at the door and Miss Violet opened it far enough to hand in a bottle and glass. "Well," Miss Rose poured a drink. "To those who done us wrong. If God doesn't turn their hearts, may he turn their ankles." She emptied the glass with one gulp, filled it again, and forced some liquor down Elsie. To Hildy's amazement, Verdita held out her hand, accepted half an inch, and tossed it back. Her eyes watered, and her face turned red, but Miss Rose only smiled and nodded.

"Now," Miss Rose put the cap back on the bottle and

upended the glass on top. "Elsie should sleep for a while and maybe you can take her home tomorrow. She'll be fine here. Isabeau will fix her something light to eat. My goodness, I'm all played out."

"Oh, Miss Rose." Hildy wrapped her arms around the lady. "You're just grand."

"There, there, dearie. Let's not make a fuss." Miss Rose patted Hildy's back and unwound her arms. "You go along now."

"I'll see you tomorrow for sure. Goodbye, Miss Isabeau, thank you ever so much."

Hildy kissed Elsie and snuggled the covers around her neck. She opened the door leaving Elsie sleeping and her mother talking softly. Miss Violet was nowhere to be seen but a few voices came from the back of the house. *I'll just go and thank her, too.* Hildy walked across the parlor and pushed a door open. In the kitchen, Miss Violet sat at a small table drinking coffee with Dyson Andrews and Samuel.

CHAPTER 24

When Hildy walked into the kitchen, Samuel automatically stood up. His face flushed and he half-smiled. Hildy's face, however, turned white before blood rushed into her cheeks. *Samuel's back and he never let me know. That's why he didn't write after he said he'd try. He forgot all about me and couldn't be bothered.* She swallowed the lump in her throat and turned to Miss Violet.

"I came to thank you, Miss Violet, for your help. Mama said Papa will come tomorrow and take Elsie home. You all have been really kind."

"That's all right, dear. We ladies have to stick together. Now don't you worry. Miss Rose knows what she's doing."

"Yes, ma'am. She said she used to be a nurse. And when Elsie is home, Mama will know how to take care of her. But, Miss Violet," Hildy stopped and tears rolled down her face. "You ladies are always here when I need you and I think you're awfully grand. I really do."

"You have to thank Samuel, too." Miss Violet put her coffee cup down, stood up, and hugged Hildy. The familiar smell of stale perfume comforted Hildy. "The night of the storm when you showed up on our doorstep, it was Samuel who rescued you and brought you here."

Tired, confused, and before the words really registered, Verdita called her from the parlor and Hildy drew back.

"Goodbye." She left it to Samuel and Miss Violet to decide who she was speaking to.

Outside, Hildy was surprised to see there was a little daylight. It seemed hours since she and Elsie had left the house that morning. Hildy walked with Verdita toward the boulder on the corner and Hildy turned her eyes away from the blood, which had dried in the dirt. The air smelled like food cooking and the streets were full of men coming home from work. Few companies had night shifts and some of the men would eat and then be back out to drink at Longpray's Saloon. However, for now, much of the usual noise had died down.

The sun was at her back and Hildy watched her shadow lead the way home. *All winter I thought about someone who had completely forgotten about me. What a foolish person I've been. I suppose if I ever do start stepping out with someone, it will be Kezzie's cousin George and he'll bore me to death. Well, I won't, that's all. I'll just be a spinster in my bakery and I'll have a cat. Papa doesn't like them, but I do. Oh, dear. I suppose I'll have to do good deeds and mostly they're terrible dull things.*

"Mama, will Cousin Elsie recover?" she asked, in an attempt to shift her thoughts elsewhere.

"She will if she doesn't get—er—a—a septic."

"Miss Rose used to be a nurse."

"She did seem to know what she was doing."

"Well, when Cousin Elsie comes home, will she have a lying-in?"

"What?" Verdita stopped and turned Hildy toward her.

"It's all right." Hildy ducked her head. "I know she almost had a baby. I saw—um—something on her clothes."

"Oh, dear." Verdita turned red and two men walking silently up the hill gave her a curious look and dodged around her. "Don't let Papa hear you say anything about it. It was wrong of Aunt Glady to inflict her . . . that is, the situation on us."

"Why doesn't Cousin Elsie have a husband?"

261

"She would have but Aunt Glady didn't approve of Elsie's beau."

"Poor Elsie. I wonder if she wants to go home at all. Maybe her beau can come here and they could get married. That would be so romantic. A love that even an entire continent couldn't break." Hildy sighed. "A lot better than a few months in Oregon."

"Pardon?"

"Nothing. I'm hungry; aren't you? Maybe Papa started dinner."

"I doubt it, so we'll have to hurry. Come along, don't dawdle."

And as it turned out, Verdita was right. Ira hadn't started dinner for the simple reason that he wasn't home yet. She and Hildy were tying on aprons when Chong appeared at the door with a salmon.

"Mista Witt send this," he said.

"Oh, good." Verdita took the fish and started cleaning it while Hildy peeled potatoes and then sliced onions to fry.

"Who's Mr. Witt?"

"He's the man whose peg leg got piling worms. I helped him the day it shattered and he couldn't walk." Verdita might have said more but the door flew open and Reuben burst in the room dragging Dovie behind him

"Cogswell's livery is on fire!"

"Reuben, how many times have I told you not to shout? And what in the world were you doing uptown with Dovie?"

"You said I had to watch her but not that I had to stay home so I carried her."

While Reuben talked, Dovie ran to Chong and grabbed him around the knees, and Hildy remembered her father's words about getting a horse from Cogswell's. She put the onion rings in a bowl and the knife in the dishpan. "Mama, the potatoes are peeled and the onions are ready; may I walk up the road and meet Papa?"

"Set the table, first."

Hildy worked hard at not looking as if she was in a hurry. Then she washed her hands and, for good measure, the dirty knife. She put on her jacket and bonnet and left while Verdita was explaining to Reuben that if he had taken care of the wood-box earlier, he could have gone, too.

Outside, heavy smoke, pushed down by impending rain, filled the air and obscured the stars. Hildy waited until she reached the corner and then ran.

On Pacific Avenue she saw horses tied to a hitching rail well away from the livery stable and a crowd of men in the road. Some carried water from nearby horse troughs and others slapped blankets at the fire. Flames looking like orange and yellow silk climbed the walls and disappeared. Smoke obscured much of the action. As she got closer, Hildy saw most of the livery stable's roof had collapsed leaving a few blackened beams high overhead. The remaining flames refused to be defeated. The fire roared and its heat forced Hildy back. Men had kicked burning hay into the street and it sent up spirals of smoke and occasional sparks. Hildy stayed as close to the buildings as she could until she found a protected location to look for her father. After a minute she spotted him near Dyson Andrews, both of them swatting blankets at burning embers that flew too close to an adjoining building. She was glad Ira had tied a handkerchief over his nose to protect his lungs from the bitter smoke assaulting her own lungs. Seeing him put her mind at ease. Then, with Dyson there, Hildy looked for Samuel.

By the time the men had emptied the troughs along the street, the fire was nearly out. They continued snuffing sparks with blankets and each slap sent up little demons of black ashes. Eventually, she spotted Samuel standing away from the others. After a minute, he looked down and kicked some smoldering wood away from a bale of hay, disturbing a small cat that had been hiding nearby. The cat ran toward the skeletal walls just as they began to give way. Hildy saw Samuel dart in the building's remains to grab the cat and she darted across the street after him. "Samuel, watch out!" She ran through the rubble and pushed him out of the way just as the final wall crumbled. The cat took off and Samuel and Hildy fell just out of reach of the blackened planks. Soot and ashes made a giant cloud, obscuring hands that reached in to help them up.

"Hildy!" Ira grabbed her away from the others and held her close. "That was a foolish thing to do. You could have been badly hurt."

For a few seconds, Hildy clung to her father, coughing. Tears rolled down her face, making black streaks. "It was just a—just an automatic reflex. I saw the cat . . ." She started coughing again and Ira led her away from the others, toward home.

Hildy woke the next morning to a room full of sunshine and the soft sound of a mourning dove. She stretched cautiously and then more vigorously, realizing Dovie wasn't there. *Gracious, I wonder what time it is.* Her face felt burned and her hair smelled like smoke. It brought back memories of the previous day: the earthquake, Cousin Elsie's losing a baby, and the fire. Just before her father helped her up out of the burned stable, she thought she heard Samuel say her name. Tears burned her irritated eyes and she got up and put on an old robe. Downstairs, the house was silent. Chong was in the yard and she walked outside. Whatever moisture had threatened last night was gone. At the edge of their yard, trillium lifted their white, three-petal faces.

"You up." Chong stopped spading the vegetable garden and leaned on the shovel.

"Where is everyone?"

"Go to chuch."

"Church?" Then Hildy remembered that the Methodists had agreed to lend their new building to an Episcopal minister who had come to town.

"Boil wata fa bath."

"Oh, that does sound nice." Hildy looked at her blackened fingernails. She remembered falling asleep over supper before she could really clean up and her mother putting her to bed. "I hope there's lots of water. Don't let anyone come in."

She ran back upstairs and found clean undergarments, a faded blue cotton skirt, and a worn white shirtwaist. In the kitchen again, she poured hot and cold water into the hip bath someone had put out, and put a bar of soap and some flour sacks nearby. Then she checked to make sure Chong was nowhere in sight. Not until she folded herself into the tub did she realize she had cuts, bruises, and burns. The hip bath didn't allow for much moving around but with her knees bent up, Hildy was able to lean against the back and rest. After a while, the water cooled down and she wiggled around to kneel and wash her hair. When she got out and saw how grimy the bath water was, she rinsed off with the clean water that was left. Then she used a pan to empty the bath, throwing the dirty water in the yard.

"Tis my last, last potato! Yet boldy I stand," she sang, going out to fling the wet flour sacks on the line. "With the calmness of Cato. My fork in my hand. Not one in the basket? Must you also go? With sorrow I ask it: Shall I peel ye or no?"

When the kitchen was tidied, she buttered some slices of bread, found a comb, and went to sit near the edge of the bluff. *I didn't get to talk to Mr. Craig, yesterday. I know he's been taking baked bread over to Puyallup every week. I just have to ask him if he'll sell some bread for me. I can make cornbread, too. As long as I get my chores and schoolwork done, Mama shouldn't care and then in summer I can make more things.*

Hildy finished her bread and combed her hair, extending the long, dark strands into the air so the sun could dry them. Eventually, it flowed clean and shining over her shoulders and down her back. She closed her eyes and lifted her face to the warmth and felt rather than heard someone sit on the ground next to her.

"Hello, Samuel." Hildy opened her eyes and turned her head.

"Thank you for pushing me out of the way last night."

"Thank you for saving me during the storm last year."

"You didn't even know it was me."

"But I know now and that's twice you helped me. So saving you makes us even."

"Not by my reckoning." Samuel's dimple appeared briefly. "I would have thought bakers knew better math."

There was a long pause. Hildy noticed that Samuel had also scrubbed off the fire's grime. He wore leather pants and boots, and a flannel shirt. He had grown over the year. Hildy felt very young next to his maturity. *How handsome he is.*

"There was no way to write."

"Where were you?"

"In Oregon, in the Wallowa Valley with Chief Joseph. Pa is half Nez Perce and the government took away some of the reservation land and says the army will attack if the people don't move to Idaho."

Samuel crossed his legs and looked through the trees toward the bay. "We got back yesterday morning. I heard the commotion but I didn't know it was you." He paused and the dimple made a brief appearance. "Again."

"Again? What does that mean? Miss Rose and Miss Violet are my friends."

"They shouldn't be."

"Why?"

"Don't you know what they are?" When Hildy looked blank he added, "They're ladies of the night."

"You mean—they're loose women?"

He nodded and quirked an eyebrow and she blushed. A breeze drifted by and picked up her hair. Samuel took a strand that flew across his cheek and wound it through his fingers. Hildy looked at his strong, tanned hand and felt unfamiliar emotions stir.

"Well, why were you and your father there?"

"One of the ladies is my mother."

Hildy's eyes widened. "Which one?"

He held up the lock of hair and let the wind pick it up. "Guess."

"Gracious." She pursed her lips and considered the question. "Well, I think Miss Rose is a little old for your father, besides she told me she came here with her husband, that is, she said sort of a husband. And I've hardly ever talked with Miss Lily. Is it Miss Lily?"

"No."

"But that just leaves Miss Violet." Hildy paused. "I guess she could be your mother. She's ever so sweet to me, but—but that doesn't feel right."

Samuel laughed and his eyes twinkled. "Don't look so worried. It isn't Miss Violet either. It's Isabeau."

"Oh, my goodness. Why didn't she ever say?"

"That's sort of why we're back." Samuel picked up a piece of dead grass and twirled it between his fingers. "Pa doesn't approve of Ma's working for Miss Rose and Ma doesn't want to go down to Oregon."

"And what about you? What do you want?"

Samuel tossed the stem away. "I don't really know. When I'm around people too much, I want to be in the woods, but then after a while, like when we were in Oregon, I got lonely and wanted to see . . ." he looked at Hildy, stopped, and cleared his throat. "That is, I wanted to see people."

Hildy recognized the quick look for what it was and looked at him, her dark eyes luminous. "I think I know what you mean. Sometimes I just have to be by myself, especially since Cousin Elsie came."

Samuel raised his eyebrows in question and Hildy explained about her cousin's sudden arrival, how Dovie moved into Hildy's bedroom so Elsie could have a place by herself. "And now my life is so crowded with people, my mind never has time to think about things." She stopped short of talking about Elsie's almost baby and lack of husband.

Samuel listened intently and then said, "Well, I'll be here for a while, now. Since Pa doesn't want Ma working for Miss Rose, he promised to buy a plot and build Ma a boardinghouse. If I study hard enough, I can graduate next year and then I'm going to apply to the Department of Agriculture and see if I can get on with them."

"I don't understand."

"It's something I heard about in Wallowa." Samuel became animated. "Lumbermen have practically cut down all the trees in the Midwest. So many trees are being cut down all over the country, Congress is worried. They appointed a man to go around and see how much has been cut and what's left. I figure, one man can't do it all and since Pa and I have been all over, I could hire on with him. I could be in the forests sometimes and back in town at others."

"That sounds like a good idea for you." Hildy's voice sounded a little flat. "Where would you live?"

"Why, here of course. Ma will be here and everyone I care about." He looked at her so intently, Hildy dropped her gaze.

"Well, you'll have to come by my bakery every time you're in town."

"I promise I will see you before the sun sets every time I return. Now," he turned and picked up a long, slender package and handed it to Hildy.

The wrapping was soft, beige deerskin tied with buckskin laces. Hildy undid the knots and unrolled the hide. Inside was a cluster of feathers that opened into a fan. Tall pheasant tail feathers made up the back. In front of them were blue jay feathers overlaid to within an inch of their tips by soft golden grouse feathers. The colors shape-shifted in the light. Hildy opened and closed the fan, and ran a finger up the feathers.

"It's beautiful. I never thought I could have a fan so, so . . ." She held it next to her chest and ran out of words.

"I remember," Samuel's voice low and slow like his father's. "When that bull came charging down Pacific Avenue . . ."

"And you pushed me out of the way in the nick of time."

"And I said, 'what in the world were you doing, that you almost got yourself killed?' "

"There was a feather on the road and I wanted it, I said."

"I remember that too. You said you wanted a feather for a fan."

ABOUT THE AUTHOR

Karla Stover graduated from the University of Washington with history honors. Locally, her writing credits include the *Tacoma News Tribune, Tacoma Weekly, Tacoma Reporter,* and the *Puget Sound Business Journal.* Nationally, she has published in *Ruralite, Chronicle of the Old West,* and *Birds and Blooms.* Internationally, she was a regular contributor to the *European Crown* and the *Imperial Russian Journal.* She writes a monthly magazine column, "The Weekender" for *Country Pleasures.* In 2008, she won the Chistell short story contest. She hosts "Local History With Karla Stover" weekly on KLAY AM 1180. She is the author of *Let's Go Walk About in Tacoma,* which came out in August 2009; *Hidden History of Tacoma: Little-Known Stories from the City of Destiny,* which came out in March 2012; and *A Line to Murder,* which came out in summer 2013.